BITTER MEDICINE

BITTER MEDICINE

BY

MAE MCGRAW

www.penmorepress.com

Bitter Medicine by (Mae McGraw) Kim Wuescher
Copyright © 2024 Kim Wuescher

ISBN-13: 978-1-957851-44-0(Paperback)
ISBN -13:978-1-957851-43-3(e-book)

BISAC Subject Headings:
FIC033000 FICTION / Westerns
FIC014060 FICTION / Historical / Civil War Era
FIC022040 FICTION / Mystery & Detective
   / Women Sleuths

Editor: Chris Wozney

Front Cover and Back Cover Illustration by
         EMILIJA RAKIĆ

Address all correspondence to:

Penmore Press LLC
920 N Javelina Pl
Tucson AZ 85748
mjames@penmorepress.com

DEDICATION

For my husband Rick, my first reader and best cheerleader.

Acknowledgement

So many people helped to make this book possible. A big thank you to my family, critique group (Deanna, Barbara, and Ed), my book club "Reading between the Wines," my first readers outside of my family, and for the inspiration and support from my sibs in the Northeast Ohio Chapter of Sisters in Crime. Thank you, Michael James of Penmore Publishing, for believing in me.

"How very little can be done under the spirit of fear."

— *Florence Nightingale*

Prologue

Thursday, June 8, 1865, Midmorning

The sharpshooter had been waiting for Reynolds for over an hour. He shifted his stance and scanned the valley. Concealed by the hillside pines, he would see but not be seen by Reynolds when he crossed the stream. The sharpshooter took off his hat to wipe his brow with his sleeve. Sweat trickled down his back from the high humidity and temperature. The heat quickened his impatience to anger. Had his informant played him as a chump?

A man whistled a tune in the distance. The sharpshooter straightened his stance and turned his good ear to the sound. The whistler could be Reynolds. The man and his mount made their way along the curves of the path. The heavy foliage and trees of the woodlands below flashed blue as the rider's uniform came in and out of his view.

When the rider reached the stream's edge, the sharpshooter narrowed his eyes. The whistler was Reynolds. A jolt of pleasure ran through him as he readied his rifle.

Reynolds stopped whistling and dismounted. He took off his boots and rolled up his pant legs. The sharpshooter's informant had been right. The creek was shallow and wide here, the best place to cross. Reynolds guided his horse cautiously across and released the reins to let his horse drink. When he squatted on his haunches to splash his face and neck, his broad back gave the sharpshooter a perfect target.

The sharpshooter moved from beneath the trees into a clearing to take his shot. His foot slid on pine needles causing a pinecone to roll down the hill.

Reynolds stood, turned, and looked up.

The man on the ridge didn't hesitate. He fired, striking Reynolds in the chest.

Reynolds collapsed and his horse bolted.

From the ridge, the sharpshooter watched Reynolds to see if he stirred, but he lay still. The horse returned and nudged his master. No movement, a good sign he was dead.

Gray clouds had darkened the sky. The sharpshooter could smell rain. He shifted his rifle and reached for the ring in his pocket, clutching it so tightly the emerald's edge dug into the palm of his hand. The pain felt good, a reassurance of his success. The ring always brought him luck.

The wind was picking up, bringing with it the strong scent of pine. He scanned the valley for any witnesses, but the valley was quiet with only the sounds of thunder in the distance. He moved quickly toward Reynolds and approached the stilled body. The horse backed away, a fine horse. He would take the horse and the soldier's boots. That's what a bummer would do.

The horse's ears were turned back. He was on high alert, fearful, but a war horse that would probably soon recover his fear from the smell of blood. Reynolds' blood pooled and made its way to the stream, giving the water a pink cast. With his pointed boot, the man gave Reynolds two hard kicks in the ribs. Reynolds didn't moan or twitch.

Before the horse could bolt again, the sharpshooter turned and grabbed its reins and then quickly mounted him. The horse whickered and brought his forelegs up in protest, trying to unseat him.

The ring shifted to the edge of his pocket.

The horse reared again, pawing at the air. The sharpshooter held onto his rifle and reins with one hand and grabbed the horn of the saddle with the other.

The ring slipped out of his pocket and fell into the stream.

Using soothing words and caresses, the sharpshooter calmed the animal. After a few minutes, the horse was quiet and merely pawed at the ground to show his displeasure. He bent low in the saddle to stroke the horse's neck. Reynolds moaned.

The sharpshooter pulled up his rifle and aimed at Reynolds' head. He was about to pull the trigger when he heard the pounding beat of someone running, approaching. He couldn't risk another shot and alert the runner of his location. Reynolds would bleed out soon enough. He eased the hammer down and put the rifle back in its sheath. He would leave behind Reynolds' boots. It was wiser to stay on the spirited horse and get away swiftly.

He turned the horse to the stream and splashed through the water, making his way opposite that of the runner. After a few hundred yards the stream narrowed, and the water reached the horse's stirrups. He turned to look over his shoulder as he approached the curve of the stream. Reynold's body was still. A flash of lightning and clap of nearby thunder spurred him to put his heels to the horse's sides. The horse quickened its pace. The pelting rain drowned out the horse's splashing and concealed his retreat.

He was a mile or so away from Reynolds when the rain stopped. He halted the horse, taking a deep breath and savoring his good fortune. The ring had always brought him luck. He felt for his talisman.

The emerald ring was gone.

CHAPTER 1

COMING HOME

Thursday, June 15, 1865

As she looked out the stagecoach window, the hair lifted on the back of Katie's neck. The stage jostled over the ruts in the dusty road as they neared Liberty. The landscape achingly familiar with its empty miles of pastures and only the occasional house or herd to break up the monotony.

Without turning her head, she felt the other passenger's eyes on her. In Katie's opinion, he was rather uncouth. After a brief nod to her as he'd entered the stage, he had curled up on the opposite bench, using his satchel as a pillow, and fallen asleep. He had slept for the entire eight-hour trip from Cleveland, not even awakening for the comfort stops.

The last jostle had probably caused him enough discomfort to awaken him. She could hear his movements as he sat up.

Katie ran her finger over the star carved in the amethyst stone on her necklace. Touching it brought her comfort. She relaxed and let her hand fall onto the open letter in her lap. She had read it repeatedly during her journey home, Andrew's letter of recommendation for a doctor's apprenticeship. It was worth the equivalent of gold to Katie.

The paper crinkled under her touch. Without looking over to the other passenger, she discreetly folded the letter, and put it into her reticule.

A welcome breeze blew through the coach. Katie brushed the stray blonde hairs from her face and tucked them into her bonnet. She could still feel the man's eyes on her. At twenty-three years old, she had seen enough of the world to know when she was admired. She lifted her chin and turned to him.

He quickly turned away. She had put him at about twenty-five or so when she examined him as he slept. "Liberty is only a few miles away," Katie said, "Is that your destination?"

"It is." His eyes met hers. "I hope I didn't snore. I was up late. So many changes in politics since Mr. Lincoln's assassination." He flipped open his jacket revealing several papers in his coat pocket. "I wrote on the train from Columbus, so I can file my story as soon as we get to Liberty."

"Lincoln's death is a terrible loss for our country. Such a good man. And Andrew Johnson . . ." she scoffed. "The man is no Abraham Lincoln. Let's hope he doesn't destroy all that we fought for in this war."

"You follow politics then?"

"Yes. I may not have the right to vote, but that doesn't keep me from sharing my opinions with those who do."

The rear wheel of the stage abruptly tilted due to a large hole. "Oh, these horrible roads!" Katie grabbed the coach window ledge to keep her seat.

"We're lucky we didn't lose a wheel there. It would be impossible for me to write on a coach. I can sleep anywhere."

"You're a writer then?"

"A reporter for *The Liberty Gazette*."

"Do you know Caleb Brown?"

"I am he." He tipped his hat. "At your service, ma'am."

"You are Caleb Brown?"

"Yes, ma'am."

Katie's eyebrows shot up.

"Don't leave me in suspense. How do you know of me?"

"It was your article in the newspaper that led me to nurse at Camp Dennison."

"I wrote that quite a while ago."

"Nursing was my salvation, Mr. Brown. I was despondent after I lost my husband. He died at Gettysburg."

"I'm sorry. A terrible loss, I'm sure."

His response seemed genuine. She liked him. "Thank you. After my husband died, I needed a distraction and a way to help the war effort. Nursing provided both."

"And we're very grateful for your service. Desperate times demand drastic measures. Although having women nurse has become more common. The dire need for nurses and Miss Nightingale's service in the Crimean has changed the old way of thinking."

"We're in agreement on that. Florence Nightingale is my inspiration. I admire her ideas, especially on cleanliness and nutrition for the patients."

"I'm sure that helped secure your position. Begging your pardon, ma'am, but I was told they sought plain-looking nurses. I'm surprised you qualified."

Katie flinched at his boldness, but she recovered herself. "My father's friendship with General Wade probably helped.

I had a letter of introduction from the General. I'm Mrs. Harris."

"Pleased to meet you, Mrs. Harris. Is that the letter you put in your bag?"

"No." She touched the stone at her neck again.

"You're returning home then?"

"Yes." The stage lurched, and Katie grabbed the window ledge again. "My homecoming may be a surprise. The telegraph lines have been down, and mail delivery has been sporadic."

"Telegraph's back up. I received a telegram from Liberty this morning."

"Then maybe my family has received mine."

"I thought Camp Dennison sent their nurses home weeks ago. You're just now returning?"

"I helped a young widow and her children return to Kentucky. My brother is probably already home. Stuart served in the cavalry."

"Stuart Reynolds is your brother?"

"Yes." Katie's eyes brightened, thinking of Stuart with pride and the pleasure of a family reunion in less than an hour's time.

Caleb lowered his head but kept his eyes on hers. "I'm not sure how to tell you this."

Katie leaned forward. "Is it my father? I received word he's been ill."

"No, your brother. Stuart Reynolds was shot about a week ago, not but a mile or so from his home."

"Stuart was shot. Is he all right?" Her voice dark with concern.

Caleb swallowed. "He died, ma'am."

Katie cried out, "No!" She put her hand to her mouth to stifle another cry. She shook her head and her hand fell to her lap, but her voice was shrill with shock. "What happened? How could such a thing happen?"

"The marshal thinks it was bummers."

"Bummers? I don't understand."

"Desperate soldiers who steal food and sometimes horses as they make their way home from the war. We've had problems with them in Liberty, but I've not heard of a bummer murdering."

Katie closed her eyes for a moment, trying to hold back the tears. When she opened them, she turned toward the window. Her thoughts were of Stuart and their last reunion nearly a year and a half ago. He had taken leave to escort her to Camp Dennison. She had been nervous about traveling over two hundred miles from home and anxious about nursing wounded soldiers. Stuart's humorous stories and cheerful disposition had made the trip pass quickly and had quelled her fears.

Her reflective mood turned to one of anger. Stuart was probably eager to share a happy family reunion. The war deaths had been cruel, terrible; but being so close to home and losing his life was somehow crueler. She turned to the reporter. "Who is this bummer?"

"We don't know."

The stagecoach driver blew his horn, announcing their arrival in Liberty. The stage stopped in front of the American Hotel. From her window, Katie spotted Meghan crossing the street to meet the stagecoach. The black ribbons of Meghan's straw hat fluttered behind her. Meghan would know details of Stuart's murder and know if what Mr. Brown had said was true. She said a quick prayer that Meghan would prove him wrong.

The driver opened the stagecoach door and took Katie's hand as she stepped down to the road.

Caleb called out, "Mrs. Harris."

The driver dropped her hand as she turned slightly and looked over her shoulder. "Yes."

"I don't think it was bummers that killed your brother. If there's anything I can do to help find his murderer, please call on me."

He would help her find Stuart's murderer. Was he serious? That was the marshal's job. Nevertheless, she reached out her hand to accept his card. Katie read it silently,

Caleb Brown, Reporter, *Liberty Gazette*
South Main Street, Liberty, Ohio

She slipped it into her satchel. Their eyes met. "Thank you."

Meghan arrived at the stage a little breathless. She kissed Katie's cheek and then held her at arm's length. "I'm so glad you're home."

Katie's tears threatened. It couldn't be true. The reporter must be mistaken. "It's good to be home." Meghan was like a sister to her. "You must have received my telegram."

"Yes, I've been listening for the stage's arrival."

Caleb Brown came around the back of the stage with a dark carpet bag in hand. His eyes focused on Katie. "I meant what I said. Call on me if you wish to pursue this and would like my help." He tipped his hat. "Good day, ladies."

"What was that all about?" Meghan asked.

Katie's eyes filled with tears. "Mr. Brown informed me that Stuart was murdered."

Meghan lowered her eyes. "It's true."

A whimper escaped Katie.

The driver had pulled a small chest and a stained paisley carpet bag from the boot and placed them onto the planked sidewalk. He looked up at Katie, concern evident on his face. "Do you need any help with these, ma'am?"

Meghan took charge. "No, a boy will be by in a few minutes to pick them up." She handed him a few coins. "Thank you."

Meghan took Katie's arm in hers and led her to her dress shop. "You must be parched. Let's have a cup of tea and then we can take the pony cart to Six Maples."

* * *

As Meghan's pony cart came into the yard, Hannah came out to the porch, wiping her hands on her apron. Although technically the Reynolds' housekeeper, Hannah was more like a mother to Katie since her own mother had died days after Stuart's birth. Hannah had worked for the family for as long as Katie could remember. She raised Katie and Stuart as if they were her own, which was why Hannah's own daughter, Meghan, was so like a sister to her. They'd grown up together.

Hannah's jet-black hair was pulled into a bun. Strands of silver now ran through it. Her high cheekbones gave evidence of her Wyandot ancestry, which did not show in her daughter Meghan's more European features. Hannah came down the porch steps to meet Katie and Meghan.

MAE MCGRAW

As Katie stepped from the pony cart, Hannah's round face broke into a wide grin. She pulled Katie in for a hug nearly crushing her against her large bosom. "Welcome home." She released Katie and held her at arm's length. "You have so little meat on your bones. Don't they feed nurses?" She laughed. "We'll take care of that in no time. I have a nice dinner prepared. Your father will be so pleased to see you're finally home." Hannah released Katie and turned to her daughter. "Can you stay for dinner?"

Meghan replied, "Yes, I closed the shop for the day."

"Good." Hannah took Katie's arm again and led her into the house. Meghan took the horse by the harness and said, "If you grab your bags, Katie, I'll take care of the horse."

"Thanks," Katie pulled the bags from the cart and followed Hannah, leaving the dusty bags on the porch.

The kitchen was just as Katie remembered it. She took in the sights that were home. The large table covered with a flowered oil cloth, the sink and water pump under the butter yellow curtains, which softened the window. She ran her fingers over the wooden counter and relished the aroma of fresh bread and bubbling stew. Plentiful food and the comfort of this kitchen were the things Katie had dreamed of while nursing.

"Your brother," Hannah said.

"I know." Katie took a deep breath and ran her hands down her skirt. "Caleb Brown, a passenger on the stage told me."

Hannah held her lips tight for a moment. "So you learned this from a stranger. I'm so sorry." She tilted her head. "I seem to know that name."

"He was the *Gazette* reporter who wrote about the need for nurses at Camp Dennison."

Katie sat down at the table. "He also told me Marshal Gerber believes Stuart was murdered by bummers, desperate soldiers who steal as they return from the war."

"Yes, I'm familiar with the term."

"Mr. Brown doesn't believe it was bummers."

"Does he suspect anyone?"

"I don't know. I didn't think to ask him questions when I first learned of Stuart's passing, but I will." She pursed her lips into a tight line and then said, "You may be sure of that."

Meghan entered the kitchen from the back porch and went to the sink to wash her hands. Over her shoulder she said, "The boys are on their way. I think they've missed you as much as I have."

The mood in the room shifted. Hannah placed a hand on Katie's shoulder. "We'll talk later."

Turning to her daughter, Hannah used a cheerful voice to announce, "Dinner's ready. I was just going to call the boys when you arrived."

Meghan said, "I'll set out two more plates."

"Good," Hannah said. She gently squeezed Katie's shoulder. "Before we eat, let's see your papa. He's already eaten and is working now or trying to."

"How is he?" Katie asked as she stood.

"He's doing poorly." Hannah interlocked her arm in Katie's. "But we mustn't dwell on that today. Your return is happy news."

Katie and Hannah walked through the dining room and living room to Philip's office.

"He can't be very sick if he's working in his office," Katie said.

"We moved his bed down here a few weeks ago." She turned and winked at Katie and lifted her shoulders. "I can't wait to see your papa's face when he sees you." She knocked. "Philip, mind if we come in?"

That was unusual, Katie thought. Hannah had always addressed her father as Mr. Reynolds.

"Come in." Philip Reynolds' voice was weak.

Hannah opened the door with a flourish. "Katie's home."

Philip was leaning back on pillows. Papers piled at each side. Hannah motioned Katie through the door.

Philip moved to sit up straighter and regarded Katie over his wire-rimmed glasses. An affectionate smile lit up his face. "Katie," he whispered as if saying a prayer. He put his hand out to her.

Katie stepped forward. "It's good to be home." She took his hand and kissed her father on the cheek then stepped back to examine him. Formerly a robust man, he had lost weight, which had caused his face to slacken. Her father looked at least ten years older than his fifty years.

Hannah straightened the papers on the bed and moved them to the table.

Philip said, "Bring a chair over to the bedside for a visit, darlin'." Katie took a visual sweep of the room as she moved the two wing-back chairs closer to his bed. An armoire was now set next to a file cabinet. The bed was set up where Philip's desk had been.

Both women sat down as Philip removed his glasses and put them on the bedside table. He turned to Katie. "You've heard about your brother."

Katie noticed his red-rimmed eyes. "Yes."

He paused for a moment. "I don't believe it was bummers. That lazy fool of a marshal is convinced it's bummers because that's the easy way out. We must find out who did this, Katie. I can't rest easy until I know that Stuart's murderer is punished."

"I am of like mind, Papa."

Philip began to cough with his agitation, and Hannah moved to his bedside to put a cup to his lips.

He took several swallows and leaned back against his pillows.

Hannah turned to Katie. "It's a restorative tea. Laudanum's a bitter medicine, but mixed with honey, it's tolerable."

Philip handed the cup back to Hannah.

Katie was familiar with the pain reliever, a mix of alcohol and opium.

Hannah set the cup aside, propped Philip's pillows, and tucked the quilt around him.

"I'll see what I can do, Papa. Mr. Brown that newspaper man said he would help. I'll call on him."

Hannah put her hands on her hips and addressed Philip. "Liam told you not to get too excited, so we'll let you rest a bit and talk later."

Liam West had been a favorite playmate of Stuart's while he was growing up. He had remained a close friend of the family and was now the county doctor.

Philip reached out to take Katie's hand.

She leaned forward and took it.

"I'm pleased you're home, darlin'," Philip whispered. "You must find Stuart's murderer. I'm depending on you."

He held her hand for a moment, then his hand slipped from hers.

Katie took a deep breath to calm herself. She wasn't sure if it was fear or anger that had made her so anxious. The charge to find Stuart's murderer was an unfair burden. That was the marshal's job. She didn't know the first thing about investigating. Where to even begin?

Hannah dimmed the oil light at the bedside, closed the curtains, and motioned toward the door. Katie followed her.

When they reached the kitchen, the savory smell of stew was no longer as enticing to Katie. She steeled herself to be civil with Hannah. Her father's condition wasn't Hannah's fault. "He's lost weight, and it's so unlike him to be in bed at this hour."

Hannah turned to Katie. "Yes, he took a turn for the worst after Stuart's murder, but your being home will restore him to health. I'm sure of it." She paused. "Tonight we celebrate your homecoming."

The kitchen door flew open. Tommy and Billy, Meghan's sons, ran in.

"Auntie Katie's home," the boys cried out in unison.

She hugged them both and kissed the tops of their heads. "Oh, it's so good to see you. I've missed you terribly."

Hannah clapped her hands. "All right, boys, wash your hands before we eat."

Meghan turned to pump the well handle and water soon spilled into the soap stone sink.

Katie sat down at the table, exhausted. The long day on the road, learning of Stuart's death and then her father's plea to find Stuart's murderer, it was too much. She had come home hoping to rest and refresh her spirits. That wasn't going to happen.

CHAPTER 2

GRITTY DETAILS

Friday, June 16, 1865

The morning light shone through Katie's bedroom window awakening her. She must have finally fallen asleep. Even though she had been exhausted, Katie had tossed and turned all night. How would she go about finding Stuart's murderer? Maybe the marshal was right, and Stuart had been killed by bummers who were long gone, and her father couldn't accept that. Stuart would not easily give up his horse. She could envision the theft escalating to the point of gunfire. These men were used to killing.

But then Caleb Brown thought differently. Was he a newspaper man searching for a story or suspicious with good reason? Where would she even start? Damn. The marshal needed to do his job. She angrily kicked off her sheets and then dressed for the day.

"Good morning. Coffee's on the stove," Hannah boomed when Katie entered the kitchen.

Katie poured herself a cup of coffee. Her hands wrapped around the coffee mug. "Tell me everything you know about Stuart's murder."

Hannah leaned her backside against the sink. She shook her head. "Well, Stuart was almost home when he was shot in the chest, right below his shoulder." Hannah put her hand on her upper chest. "The bullet probably pierced his lung. Liam said it was a long-range rifle."

Katie bit her lower lip. That didn't fit with the scenario she had imagined. It certainly didn't sound like a fight over a horse. Maybe Caleb Brown was right. But who would want to murder Stuart? And why?

Hannah intruded on Katie's thoughts, "With Liam's war experience, I'm prone to trust his judgment on that."

"On what?" Katie asked. Had she missed the thread of the conversation?

"Liam thinks a sharpshooter killed your brother with a long-range rifle." Hannah turned to the window as if she imagined the scene there. "Stuart was just left there to die. He may have lingered for a while, according to Liam." Her voice thick as if holding back tears. "Makes me sick to think that someone left him there to die alone, so they could steal his horse and rifle."

Hannah reached for a napkin, dabbed her eyes and turned to Katie. "I know finding these bummers won't bring Stuart back, but I want the murderer to pay for killing him, to pay for ending the life of such a good man." With a catch in her voice, she continued. "Stuart was like a son to me."

Katie got up and hugged Hannah. "I know. He was a good man." She paused. "We need to persuade the marshal to investigate further. Mr. Brown thinks it may have been someone other than bummers. The marshal may have been too hasty in his conclusions."

"Marshal Gerber's made up his mind. And your father doesn't have the strength to do anything about it. Perhaps you can get that lazy marshal off his behind to investigate."

Katie blew out a long breath.

Hannah continued, "The marshal's gullible, no mind of his own. Victor Ross suggested a bummer killed your brother and that was that. Some people are awed by money. Our marshal is one of them."

"Victor Ross. When did he return from the war?"

"Oh, he's been back for a while. Only served for ninety days. You missed a lot of gossip while you were living in Farmingdale. When Mr. Ross was conscripted, he paid his three hundred dollars to buy his substitute, said he needed to tend to his ranch business."

Katie shook her head. "Another man dodging work, just like Marshal Gerber."

Hannah bent to pull a warming plate of bacon and pancakes out of the oven and then put the plate down in front of Katie. "Yes, now let's get you some breakfast. You're all skin and bones, child."

After breakfast, Katie and Hannah walked to Stuart's gravesite. A rectangular fence surrounded the tidy family plot. Katie's mother and grandparents were buried there. And now Stuart. The cemetery was on a hill that overlooked the house, just beyond their apple, plum, and cherry orchards. A big oak tree stood guard behind the far fence wall and shaded the graves. Katie walked alone to Stuart's grave and said a prayer while Hannah gathered wildflowers.

Katie knelt next to the rectangular mound and picked up a handful of freshly turned dirt. Stuart was dead. She couldn't get used to this. She'd never again hear his laughter or see his infectious smile. She covered her face with her hands. Tears came and great gulping sobs. After a few moments, she felt Hannah's hand on her back. Katie wiped the tears from her cheeks. With her head bowed she murmured, "I will find your murderer, Stuart. I promise you that."

Hannah put the flowers on Stuart's grave, and they walked back to the house, lost in their own thoughts. Katie planned her strategy for making good on her promise to her brother and father. She would visit the valley of the murder site. Perhaps she'd find something there. Then she would call on Marshal Gerber and maybe even Caleb Brown.

They walked silently back to the house. As Katie ascended the porch steps, Hannah gently tugged the skirt of Katie's dress, which had lost all its color from frequent washing. "Time to get you settled in with some decent clothes."

Katie called back over her shoulder. "Fashion is the last thing on my mind right now."

Hannah followed Katie as she walked through the kitchen and then up the stairs to her bedroom. "You've lost too much weight. Will any of your clothes fit?"

Katie ignored Hannah's question but turned to face her after she entered her bedroom. "I want to talk with the marshal and Caleb Brown. See what they know. But beforehand, I want to see if I can get evidence that will convince Gerber to make a real investigation."

"How?"

"I don't know. But I need to see for myself where Stuart was murdered. I'm going to take a ride out to the pine valley this morning. Maybe I can find something to ignite that lazy marshal's interest."

"You aren't riding alone to the valley." Hannah said firmly. She opened the door to the large chifforobe in Katie's room. "It's too dangerous."

"I need answers," Katie said.

"Yes, but the first order of business is getting you presentable. Meghan will need to take in your dresses and skirts."

She had only taken two black dresses to Camp Dennison. The rest of her clothes were in the chifforobe or hanging from the attic rafters, covered with sheets to protect them. Hannah's comments triggered thoughts on another task that needed attention.

Katie talked to Hannah's back as Hannah riffled through the dresses, blouses and skirts. "My house in Farmingdale, Hannah. Are the Petersons still renting it?" Katie had rented out her furnished house in nearby Farmingdale to a family when she left for Camp Dennison.

Hannah replied. "Yes, and I haven't heard any complaints so they must be satisfied. I've been depositing their rent money in your account the last few months. Hard for your father to get into the village."

"Thank you." Katie would have to decide whether to move back to her home or stay on at Six Maples again as she had immediately after Paul's death. Hannah might need her help caring for her father.

Katie sat down on her bed. "Do we have someone who could deliver a message to the Petersons? I could pay them a social call on Sunday afternoon and find out their plans."

"I can send a note this morning with Brett."

"Brett Williamson, my former student is working here?"

"He's been working here for the last few months. Good worker."

"He was a good student. Yes, let's send a note." Katie got up and walked over to her traveling chest and opened the lid. She rifled through the trunk and pulled out a pair of dark trousers. "I'll wear these, so I can ride astride when I go out to the valley."

Hannah gasped and put her hand over her mouth. "You can't ride astride a horse." She sat down heavily on the bed.

Katie folded the trousers over her arm. "The hills in the valley are steep. I'm not riding sidesaddle on such a slope, and I certainly can't take a wagon."

"Katie, what will people think?"

"These trousers were given to me by a general's wife. We became friends as the general convalesced. She often saw me riding astride. The general recovered quickly, and they left the hospital. A month later these came in the mail as a gift."

Hannah shook her head. "Scandalous."

"I rode to pick up medical supplies for Camp Dennison." Her hand went to the stone hanging from her necklace. "No one thought less of me. The camp didn't have ladies' saddles, and the path was often too narrow for a wagon. The doctors couldn't be spared for errands. Besides, I find riding astride comfortable and safer."

Katie put the trousers down on the chest and walked over to the window. She pointed to the old barn set far back from the house. "I'll walk the horse to the woods wearing a skirt over my trousers and make a saddle switch there. That way if any of the men are about, they won't see me." She turned back to look at Hannah. "And the family's honor will be saved."

Hannah put her hands on her hips. "I suppose Brett can bring a saddle." A tone of resignation in her voice. "A general's wife gifted you these trousers?"

"Yes. She was quite progressive."

Hannah walked to the window and stood next to Katie, surveying the yard and woods beyond. "I suppose you could make a saddle switch at the old barn." She gave an exaggerated huff. "I'll see if Brett can ride with you after he returns from the Petersons with your note."

"Why do I need an escort? I know where the valley is." She gave Hannah a crooked smile, satisfied that she had caught her out. "I thought you didn't want anyone to know about my riding astride."

"Brett won't talk, and you need an escort. He and his brother were the ones to find Stuart's body, so he may be able to share information with you. And besides, it's just not safe for a woman without a gun."

"So, give me a gun."

"Even with a gun, you would be foolhardy to go out there alone." She shook her head. "If anything were to happen to you, well, your father would never recover."

Katie took a deep breath. How could she argue with that?

Hannah turned back to the chifforobe and removed a white cotton blouse with a high collar from a drawer and pulled a skirt and belt from a hook. "The skirt has belt loops, so you can cinch it at your too small waist." Hannah laid the clothes and belt on the bed. "Brett knows how to handle a gun, which he'll bring along. I'll see to it. Write up that note for the Petersons, I'll find Brett and bring up some pins. We'll see about marking some of these clothes so that Meghan can take them in."

Hannah turned to the window. "Oh, there's Brett." She walked over to Katie's balcony door, opened it and called out, "Brett, do you have time to deliver a note to the Petersons at Rustic Hills?"

"Yes, ma'am," Brett answered.

Katie stepped onto the balcony and called out to Brett. "Good, we'll have a note for you in a minute."

Katie turned to Hannah and whispered, "You know, you can be awfully bossy."

"Hmph," Hannah said as she left the balcony and walked through Katie's room. At the hall doorway she turned back and said, "You best write that note, so we can get on with your alterations."

"The last word," Katie mumbled. "Always have to have the last word, don't you?" Hannah was too far down the stairs to hear her comments, which was probably just as well. Funny how you forget those little annoyances when you're homesick.

CHAPTER 3

MURDER SITE RIDE

Friday late morning, June 16, 1865

Fifteen-year-old Brett stood in the yard with two horses. Brett had been one of Katie's students when she taught at the local school. She could still see the youthful face in the tall gangly adolescent. Brett had been small for his age then with sporadic school attendance, like so many farm children.

Katie had taught at Liberty school for three years before she gave up teaching when she married Paul Harris. Brett had been a polite child and a quick learner. She welcomed his companionship but worried about putting him in danger.

Brett handed Katie a note. She opened it and took a moment to read it.

> Dear Mrs. Harris,
> We would welcome a visit on Sunday afternoon at two o'clock. If this time is not agreeable, please send a message. Otherwise you will be expected then.
>
> > Kindest regards,
> > Mrs. Peterson

"Good." Katie put the note in her skirt pocket, and they walked their horses to the old barn. Brett was as talkative now as he had been in his youth, telling Katie about his work and responsibilities.

"We're lucky to have you working for us at Six Maples," Katie said. "But do you plan to continue your schooling?"

Brett shrugged. Instead of answering, he said, "Be on the lookout for Timber rattlers when we get to the valley. Timbers aren't as vicious as some snakes but be mindful of 'em just the same."

Katie glanced warily from side to side.

"Aww, you don't need to worry yet. Timbers like rocks, like sunnin' themselves. Your horse'll let you know if one's around."

When they reached the old barn, they led the horses inside. Brett took the side saddle off Katie's horse, a chestnut mare, and hung it on the railing. "Mr. Philip's been talkin' about tearin' this old barn down. Lucky for us, he hasn't."

"It's a shame it was never kept up."

"Pretty far from the house," Brett said.

"Yes. Everything was too far from what they called the new-town road. This barn was built about the same time as the original homestead, an old log cabin built by my grandfather when he was a young man."

Brett pulled a saddle from another stall railing. "This here horse is Mouse and you're using my brother Joey's saddle. Hannah said you'd like to use it, rather than the ladies' saddle. That so, Miss Reynolds?"

"Yes, but it's Mrs. Harris now, remember?" She moved to the front of the horse to hold him still while Brett adjusted the saddle.

"Yes, ma'am. Kind of got used to calling you Miss Reynolds when you was teachin', that's all." Brett gave the strap on the horse's girth a final pull. "Makes real good sense you ridin' with a regular saddle goin' up and down them hills."

"That's how I rode during the war," Katie said, "but don't let on to the others."

"Yes, ma'am, I got plenty of secrets."

The thought of his secrets intrigued Katie, but she let his comment go for now.

Brett had turned his head, feigning sudden interest in the floor while Katie mounted her horse. She hiked up her skirt to sit comfortably, her trousers now visible.

Brett glanced up to give her the reins. "You're wearin'" he paused, "trousers."

She took the reins.

He slapped his leg. "Don't that beat all."

Once they were on the path to the valley, Brett talked about recent bobcat sightings. Katie had always hiked to the valley with Stuart, Liam, and Meghan when they were children, never realizing the danger of snakes or bobcats. She vowed to carry a gun in the future and take time for target practice.

They cleared the woods and stopped at the top of the ridge.

"That's the place," Brett said, pointing to the stream below. "That's where we found Mr. Stuart's body, not but a week ago."

There were two paths to the stream that ran through the east side of the valley, one shorter and steeper, the other meandering and more manageable. Katie put pressure to her horse's sides and took the longer path to the valley.

Brett followed until they reached the bottom. He remained on his horse as Katie dismounted.

Katie asked, "Will Mouse be all right here for a bit?"

"Yes, ma'am."

Katie dropped the reins and the horse moved to the stream to drink. "Do you know if the bullet killed my brother immediately? I do hope Stuart didn't suffer much."

"He was shot here." Brett put his fingers in the spot between his shoulder and heart. "Me and Joey, we have our ideas about his murderer if you don't mind me sayin'."

"Yes, I want to hear your theories."

Brett dismounted and dropped the reins. "Beggin' your pardon, ma'am, I think it was a man and a woman."

"A woman?" Katie's tilted her head. "What makes you say that?"

"Well, me and Joey was the ones that found Mr. Stuart."

"I had heard. That must have been hard for you."

"Yes, ma'am. Joey ain't accustomed to seein' dead folk, but me and Joey kept our wits. There was a man's footprints for sure, maybe just Mr. Stuart's. Hard to judge. And small footprints circling the area where Mr. Stuart musta fallen, pretty much the size of yours." Brett pointed to the footprints Katie had made in the clay shore.

"We could see that there was some kind of commotion, like he must have struggled or wrestled with the woman. We reckon she fell right next to his body." He pointed to the edge of the stream. "Her footprints and such was here."

Brett covered his mouth with his hand. "Sorry, I hope sayin' this don't make you too sad."

"I'm fine, but thank you," she said. "Please go on."

"Well, then it rained again while we was ridin' back to Six Maples, hard enough to wash out footprints and such by the time the marshal arrived."

"Did you share all this information about a woman's footprints with the marshal?" Katie asked.

"Yeah, we told Hank. He said he told the marshal."

Hank was the stable manager at the Reynolds' ranch and Brett's boss.

Katie tilted her head, puzzled. "You didn't come back down here with Hank and the marshal?"

"No, ma'am, the boss said we best go back on home for the day. Me and Joey were all right with that. Joey was kind of scared and all."

"Yes, of course."

"Sure riles me up just thinkin' about it. When that woman come down here, well, Mr. Stuart musta still been alive. Maybe she didn't realize he weren't dead yet."

He rubbed his chin, mimicking the gesture of a contemplative old men. "No matter. What we could figure is that Mr. Stuart and that woman musta tussled. There were marks in the clay as if to say so. So that's how I know'd that there was a woman involved in the murder, because of the small footprints on the stream bed."

"Thank you. Your explanation is most helpful. Where do you think the murderer took aim at Stuart?"

Brett glanced up at the ridge. "The shot came from a distance to be sure. The doc even said so." Brett pointed to the ridge about three hundred feet from where they had entered the valley from the woods. "The tracks and the brush were trampled up there. Joey noticed it. The sharpshooter musta been watchin' for him from that eastern ridge. We can go up there if you have a mind to."

"Yes, I'd like to. Why do you think it was a sharpshooter?"

He pointed to the ridge again. "You can get a clear view to this part of the stream from that spot up there. But it would've taken a sharpshooter to drive home a bullet from that distance, don't ya think?"

"You're probably right."

"Once we told Hank and got through all that commotion, Joey was ready to go home. He wanted to tell Ma all about it. Ma was real upset, but before she could start fussin' at us, we decided to come back here. Joey wanted to figure out what happened." He shook his head and smiled indulgently. "He's always a curious one." Brett's eyes grew large. "Sorry, ma'am."

"It's all right, go on."

"By the time we got down here, Mr. Stuart's body had been moved and everybody was gone. It rained hard, so the small footprints was gone too. All that was left was men's prints, probably from the marshal and Hank, but Joey and me still wanted to figure what happened."

"What were your conclusions?"

Brett scrunched up his face. "Ya mean, what'd we figure?"

"Yes, that's what I mean."

"I'll show you."

They walked their horses back to the top of the ridge. Brett stood next to a tall pine tree. "The pine needles were scattered under this tree. Joey noticed it. I had me a look. It wasn't a deer or some other varmint. We could see a man's footprints. Like he stood here. No woman's print up here. And no horse prints, so he must have been walking, probably needed a horse. That's why the marshal thinks a bummer murdered him."

"But you think the murderer or murderers were a sharpshooter and a woman."

"Yes, ma'am."

"Did the marshal come up here to the ridge to investigate?"

"I don't know. They were probably in a hurry to get back to town. Brett glanced at the path. "When it rains a lot, these paths get real slick, lot a clay. The marshal probably wanted to get Mr. Stuart's body home before the rains come again."

His eyes narrowed in concentration. "I'm figurin' with the wind and the heavy rain, things got mussed up by the time the marshal come back the next day. I told Hank all about the woman's footprints and the scattered pine needles we seen on the ridge, but he weren't really listenin' all that much. I don't mean no disrespect or nothin', but Hank said the marshal had already figured who done it. Said the bummer was probably a sharpshooter." He nodded. "We've had some of them comin' through stealing from folks 'round here. Hank tol' me the marshal figures Mr. Stuart was shot for his horse and the murderer was long gone."

Brett swung himself back in the saddle. "They didn't pay me and Joey's ideas no mind at all."

Katie used a nearby boulder to remount more easily. "Well, I am very interested. I want to find my brother's murderer, and I hope I can count on your help."

"Yes, ma'am." He paused as he watched Katie mount the horse. "You ride real good."

Katie settled herself in the saddle. "Thank you. Your theories have been most helpful, but a word of caution."

Katie lowered her voice to a conspirator's level. "For Joey's sake, I think we need to keep this information to ourselves for now. I don't want you getting into any kind of trouble. Don't talk too much about our ride out here." Katie didn't know whom she could trust. "If Hank asks, tell him I just wanted to visit the location where Mr. Stuart died."

"Yes, ma'am."

"Let's say we head back now." Katie pressed the horse's sides and clicked her tongue, and Mouse walked ahead.

Brett brought his horse parallel to hers. "There's somethin' else, I think I should tell you. Somethin' we tol' Hank, but he didn't make much of."

"Yes," Katie said, ducking under a low tree branch.

"It's strange."

"Go on."

"Well, me and Joey found two cards not too far from Mr. Stuart's body. Caught in some brush near the creek. Joey spotted them."

"Playing cards?" Katie asked.

"Well, they weren't regular playin' cards like you would use for poker. Showed them to Hank, and he said not to pay them no mind. Hank figured they blew in from that gypsy camp since them's the kind of cards that gypsy woman uses."

"Gypsies? What did these cards look like? Do you have them?"

"Sure, got 'em back at the house. One's kind of scary, though."

"How so?"

"The one's got a skeleton in a black hooded robe, couldn't see a face for the hood but he only had bones for his hands, and he was carryin' a scythe. It gave Joey the jitters just thinkin' about it. The other card's got a picture of a woman. She's blindfolded and carryin' some dishes on a chain in her left hand and a sword in her right."

Katie raised her eyebrows. The tarot cards that symbolize Death and Justice. Were the gypsies involved in Stuart's murder? "So where are these gypsies? Did anybody talk to the gypsy woman about her lost cards?"

"Do you think she wants them back?"

Katie had to swallow a laugh. "No, it's not that. I wondered where I could visit these gypsies. I'd like to talk with them."

"They were camped a couple of miles from here, about halfway to Wordsworth. Got the best draft horses around."

"Yes, they would have. Maybe somebody in their camp saw something unusual, something that can help us."

"They don't like to deal with regular folks. They're real suspicious, unless you're comin' to buy their horses or gettin' your fortune told."

"Oh, I know. Are they still in the area?" Katie asked.

"Don't know, but the boss might."

"Hank?"

"Yeah, they always camp in the same place. I hear tell Mr. Stuart used to go there regular-like when they were camped nearby." His eyes grew large. "The boss said he was kind of sweet on the fortune teller."

"Stuart was sweet on the gypsy woman?"

"She's real pretty."

"That's interesting. Yes, I think I would like to meet this fortune teller."

"You can ask the boss about 'em."

"No, I don't want to involve Hank in this just yet. Let's keep this gypsy woman another of our secrets. I'll see what Miss Hannah knows. I don't want you to get into trouble with Hank for sharing this gypsy business with me."

Chapter 4

Neighborhood Reunion

Friday, June 16, 1865

Brett and Katie returned to Six Maples, the Reynolds' ranch. Brett took the horses to the barn, and Hannah crossed the yard to meet Katie.

"Learn anything?" Hannah asked as they walked together to the porch.

"What do you know about the gypsies camped nearby?"

"We sometimes buy their horses, but we haven't had much call to work with them lately. Why do you care about the gypsies?"

"I need to visit the fortune teller."

"Don't you have enough to do without such a frivolous waste of time?"

"I think she may know something about Stuart's murder."

"Now don't start involving those poor people in this mess. They have enough troubles without you bringing on more."

"I'm not bringing the law in on this. I want to talk to her. Learn what they know about Stuart. Has the marshal been out to see them?"

"No, and let's keep it that way. Some townspeople don't need much of a reason to run gypsies out of town. Philip's always looked out for them. They sell fine horses at fair prices."

They rounded the corner of the house and mounted the steps to the porch. A horse hitched to an elegant buggy was tied up at the kitchen porch rail. "Whose buggy?" Katie asked.

"Liam's here for Philip." Hannah shook her head. "Oh, I suppose I should refer to him as Dr. West, but knowing him since he's been in short pants...." She sat down in one of the two white rockers on the porch and motioned for Katie to sit in the other. "What brought on this interest in talking to the gypsies?"

Katie told Hannah what she had learned from Brett about finding tarot cards and indications of a woman's presence at the murder site.

Hannah said, "Maybe we should talk to Suzanne."

Katie cocked her head. "Suzanne's the fortune teller. I'll be darned. The last time I saw her she was thirteen or so. According to Brett, she's pretty and Stuart was sweet on her."

"She was a good friend to Stuart."

Katie's hand reached for her amethyst stone.

Hannah focused on Katie's movement and then lifted an eyebrow. "Let me think about a meeting with Suzanne. Maybe something can be arranged."

Footsteps in the side yard drew their attention.

Hannah said, "Seems Liam is through with his examination. He'll want to talk to you about your father."

When he rounded the corner of the house, Dr. Liam West's face lit up when he saw Katie. Liam was as she remembered him, fresh-faced and wholesome. Even as a child, Liam had been compassionate. Liberty was lucky to have him as a doctor.

As he approached the porch, hoofbeats drummed in the distance. All eyes turned to the horseman on the road. As he cleared the trees and turned into the drive, he approached the house at a slower pace, kicking up less dust.

"Humph," Hannah exclaimed. "It's Mr. Ross. Now, what could he want?"

The sun caught the silver in the tassel of Ross's black hat as he dismounted in front of the porch. Liam stepped over to greet him. Both women got up and descended the porch stairs as Ross dismounted. Ross tipped his hat at the older woman first.

Hannah nodded. "Good afternoon."

Then Ross focused his attention on Katie. "Mrs. Harris," he said, gallantly sweeping his hat from his head. He held the wide brim of the hat against his leg. "It is good to have you back."

"Thank you. It's good to be home. The war went on far too long."

"You'll get no argument from me on that account," Ross said. "You're as beautiful as ever. Fortunately, the war has not deprived us of that."

Victor Ross was striking with dark eyes and olive skin. His black pants and boots were a bit dusty from the ride, but his shirt was bright white.

He ran a hand through his sleek black hair. She noticed his high forehead, a mark of intelligence according to phrenologists.

Victor put his hat back on. "I came not only to welcome you home but also to ask if you would dine with me tomorrow. I am very eager to hear all about your nursing experiences and your opinion on an idea I have."

"I am surprised you've already heard of my arrival."

"Your arrival on the stage yesterday was noted because you're an important lady."

She gave him a small cursory smile. There was no cause for her to be harsh, but she also didn't want him to think she could be easily manipulated by flattery. "Although your invitation sounds lovely, I'm afraid I have quite a busy schedule for the next day or so, although I'm sure we can find a convenient time to meet." She did want to know why he was convinced it was bummers who had murdered Stuart. "I have a few things I would like to discuss with you as well."

He gave Katie a dazzling smile. He had straight white teeth. "That would give me great pleasure. For now, I will leave you to your family events and look forward to seeing you again soon." Ross remounted and tipped his hat to the group, giving Katie a last glance.

Katie heart fluttered. He was a handsome man, but he knew it too. All were quiet as he left.

Liam West broke the silence. "Welcome home, Katie. It's good to see you."

"Thank you. So, how is my father?"

"I see you haven't changed, right to the point." Liam chuckled, taking the sting from his comment. "He's resting right now, but I'd like to talk with you about him."

Katie grabbed the front of her skirt, picking up the hem. "It's hot out here. Let's go inside." As they entered the parlor, a breeze blew through the open windows, cooling the warm room.

"I'll get some refreshments," Hannah said.

Katie sat down on the edge of the sofa.

Liam settled into a leather chair and put his medical bag on the floor. They talked for a few minutes about mutual friends, including Dr. Andrew Peyton. Without thinking, Katie touched the amethyst stone on her necklace. Her palms began to sweat. Were tongues wagging at Camp Dennison about her relationship with Andrew? Did Liam know about their indiscretion?

Hannah returned with a pitcher and glasses. Katie sighed heavily, relieved that their awkward conversation could end.

Katie gave a winning smile. "Thank you, Hannah, I'm parched."

Hannah handed glasses all around and then settled on the sofa next to Katie. "I hope you like sassafras tea."

"Yes, thank you." Liam cleared his throat and turned to Katie. "I'm sorry to bring you sad news so soon after your arrival home, but your father has taken a turn for the worse."

Since Philip's room was near the parlor, Katie leaned forward and whispered, "Can Papa hear us from here?"

"No," Liam answered quietly. "He's sleeping by now. I gave him a heavy dose of laudanum to control his coughing."

"I see." Katie looked down at her hands, quelling an impulse to clench them into fists.

"He was recovering from pneumonia, but with your brother's death, his illness has taken hold again. He was greatly distressed." He paused. "I don't like sharing this news. This illness has weakened him considerably."

Hannah let out a small cry, as if suddenly punched.

Katie took her hand.

"Your nursing experience will be helpful," Liam said to Katie. "Give him laudanum to ease his cough. Breathing is difficult for him."

Liam addressed Hannah, "You can also help by continuing to prop his pillows and serving a light diet. That beef and barley soup provides good nutrition." He took a deep breath. "Are his business affairs in order?"

"Yes," Hannah said. "Katie's not yet involved in the business, but Philip will see that she is very soon."

"Good, good," Liam said. "I've made him aware of how serious his condition is, but it's best if you show a brave face and try to make him rest."

Hannah's eyes looked heavenward.

Liam chuckled. "Not always easy, is it?"

"No."

Katie said, "You don't practice bloodletting, do you?"

Liam shook his head. "Many still subscribe to that remedy, but I have read about it extensively. I don't find it to be helpful. In fact, I deem it detrimental to the patient."

"I am like-minded," Katie said, "and relieved to hear that's not your practice."

Liam picked up his satchel and brought it to his lap. "I'm sorry to bring you such dire news, ladies. If there is anything I can do, please send a message at any time. I'll come as soon as I can." He opened his medical bag. "I brought another bottle of laudanum in case it's needed."

Katie's brows drew together.

Liam must have misinterpreted her concern. He said, "Laudanum was in short supply during the war, but my mother has connections." He chuckled. "Allow him to rest.

That's the main thing. I'll be back in a day or two. Do you have any questions?"

Katie said, "I'd rather not give him too much of the laudanum. Can I occasionally substitute brandy? When he recovers from the pneumonia, papa will crave the medicine. Withdrawal is painful."

Liam blew out a breath. "You make a valid point. Patient comfort must be tempered with thoughts for the future. If brandy helps to curb his cough and allows him to sleep, please substitute brandy for the laudanum when possible." He paused. "Rest is also important for his recovery. Philip has been wracked with bouts of coughing when the laudanum is withheld, but coughing is necessary to clear the lungs. It's a fine balance." He stood and picked up his medical bag.

"Thank you." Katie saw him out and returned to the parlor.

She watched as Hannah picked up the laudanum and put it on the tray with their empty glasses. Her shoulders slumped and her movements were slow. Hannah's deep sorrow made her wonder about her father and Hannah's relationship. Perhaps she wasn't the only one with a secret.

Hannah put the laudanum from the tray on a high cupboard shelf, out of the reach of her grandchildren, Tommy and Billy. When Hannah realized that Katie had followed her into the kitchen, she turned, giving Katie a wistful smile of what must be feigned cheerfulness and then pulled out a chair. "Now, what is so special about that amethyst stone you're wearing?"

Katie's thoughts were on her father and Hannah's relationship, so the reference to the necklace startled her. "Why nothing." She pulled on the stone.

"Hmph, you'll tell me when you're ready, I suppose."

Katie sat down heavily on the kitchen chair. "Oh, Hannah, I've been such a fool."

Hannah sat in the chair next to Katie. "What is it, child?"

Katie held the stone between her fingers. "I worked with Dr. Andrew Peyton at Camp Dennison. He gave me this."

"Why on earth does that make you a fool?"

"Because I love him. I love Dr. Peyton and he's a married man."

Hannah gasped. "You didn't do anything inappropriate did you?"

Katie lowered her eyes. "Well, there was a kiss. I'm not sure if it was witnessed by anyone though." She sighed and lifted her eyes. "It happened after a grueling day. I was overcome with exhaustion and sadness, so was Andrew. We had been working together and lost a drummer boy. He was so young. It was heart wrenching. We tried so hard to save him. When the boy's body was removed, I took comfort in Andrew's arms for a moment. I cried and he comforted me. And then we kissed."

Katie bit her lip. "He apologized immediately and said that it would never happen again, but I think others could tell we cared for one another."

In a private moment a day before I was set to leave, he gave me this necklace as a remembrance of our time working together." She held the stone as she spoke. "He told me I was an excellent nurse."

She paused. "I may be a good nurse, but I've decided I want to become a doctor. I had a chance to learn much from Dr. Peyton. When we had the time, he would show me a procedure, such as stitching up a wound, and then I would do the next procedure with his supervision. When we were overwhelmed with injured men, he would let me take care of the more minor injuries. I gained such satisfaction from the work that I want to learn more. I want to learn all that I can about medicine and surgery."

Hannah's eyebrows shot up.

"Andrew agrees. He says I am more than capable. He asked if I would be interested in an apprenticeship with him. Medical schools aren't apt to enroll women. If I can attend lectures and fulfill my apprenticeship, I may be licensed. Great progress is being made in allowing women to practice medicine." She swallowed. "It was a very hard decision, but after much consideration, I turned him down. I couldn't trust myself to hide my feelings for him. When I was about to leave the camp, he gave me a letter of recommendation for an apprenticeship with a doctor."

"You're a woman. How could you even think of becoming a doctor?"

"Some women are pursuing medicine. Andrew told me about doctors Elizabeth Blackwell and Mary Edwards Walker. Both went to medical school. Dr. Blackwell went to Geneva Medical College, which no longer allows women." Katie shook her head. "Dr. Blackwell practices medicine and teaches. Dr. Walker was an Army surgeon, who attended the Syracuse Medical College and was captured by Confederates when she tried to help wounded Virginia citizens."

"I've never heard of them." Hannah tsked. "Nursing has changed you. Think of your father and the Reynolds' reputation. Please don't frighten your father talking about such a pursuit." Hannah got up and began vigorously wiping down the counters.

Katie asked, "Why shouldn't a woman become a doctor? I've tried all the other approved pursuits for women, teacher, wife, and nurse. Why should I be stymied? Some women might prefer to have a woman doctor. I've thought about it on my journey home. I want to help women, allow them to have a choice. I'd treat men too if they'd have me."

"Treating men. Katie, that's scandalous!" Hannah sat back down and took Katie's hand. "You could be a midwife, no harm in that and Liberty needs a midwife. Liam's been delivering the county's babies."

Katie drew her hand away and stood. "Delivering babies would be fine. I have great respect for midwives, but I want more. Women should have someone of their own sex when they're sick with ailments not just when they're having a baby. Men don't always understand women's maladies and some even brush them off as hysteria."

"Liam would never do that! He's an attentive doctor to both men and women." Hannah paused. "As if you're father doesn't have enough to worry about."

Katie sat back down again. "I can't believe it. I tell you I kissed a married man, and you brush it off, but you chastise me for my desire to become a doctor."

Hannah said, "It's too much to bear all at once. I think you handled your relationship with Dr. Peyton like a lady. Things like that occasionally happen and you must forget him, of course. But having you become a doctor, well, that's a lot to take in." She shook her head. "A doctor's apprentice. You have no time for that. Your father wants you to take control of the mill."

"What?" Katie moved to the edge of her chair.

"After Stuart's passing, he and I talked."

"So, my father would have no qualms about my running the mill but would scoff at my becoming a doctor?"

"Kevin Fletcher would run it. Your papa wants you to oversee it. With your brother gone..." Hannah left unsaid that there was no one else.

"If that's his thinking, my father might be more open to the idea of my pursuing medicine than you might think."

Hannah stood. "Philip plans to talk with you about the mill. I think finding your brother's killer and learning about the mill business are quite enough to keep you busy. Don't you agree?"

"For now."

"Let's take care of the business at hand and not fuss about this silly notion of doctoring."

Katie was seething. She had counted on Hannah's support, expecting her to be supportive of her idea that women should have an alternative to male doctors. She needed to get away before she exploded in frustration. "I'm going to check on Papa."

CHAPTER 5

PUZZLING PIECES

Friday late afternoon, June 16, 1865

Katie nearly slammed the door as she entered her father's room but caught it in time. Philip was sleeping. She took a few deep breaths. Hannah's lack of support surprised Katie as much as the realization that her father expected her to run the mill. Was she the family's pawn?

The family dynamics were changing. Hannah was different now, more confident in her authority. Had there been a change in Hannah's and her father's relationship?

With the thought of relationships, Katie's memories of Andrew intruded again. The tenderness in his face as he put the necklace in her hand, the shot of passion when he touched her.

Katie shook her head to shake away her thoughts. She must quit acting like some lovelorn schoolgirl and find her brother's murderer before the trail went cold. Then she could concentrate on her own dream. She stepped over to her father's bedside and put her hand on his.

Her father stirred but didn't wake up. Katie whispered her thoughts aloud, "What made Victor Ross think it was bummers who killed Stuart? And what part do the gypsies play in Stuart's death?"

Philip eyes fluttered for a moment.

"I'm sorry. Go back to sleep, Papa."

She couldn't stay angry with Hannah for long. Hannah cared deeply for her father and had always acted like a mother to her. She was old-fashioned, that was all. Hannah would come around.

* * *

When Katie returned to the kitchen, Hannah was paring asparagus at the table and the sassafras tea pitcher was still on the counter.

"Papa's still sleeping," Katie announced as she poured herself a glass of cold tea. She took a long drink and then turned to Hannah. "Did Victor Ross come on strong or am I imagining things?"

Hannah lifted her eyebrows. "You are worth a lot of money. With your brother gone and your father's illness, you gain quite an inheritance. I think Mr. Ross is interested in your money, this property, and your property in Farmingdale. You need to be careful."

"Mr. Ross doesn't interest me, so there's no need to worry about that."

"Ahh, but he is handsome," Hannah said. "And he has a way with women. They say he may have a woman tucked away in town if you want to believe the local gossip."

Katie had taken a sip of her drink while Hannah talked and nearly choked on Hannah's last comment. "A woman tucked away?"

Hannah pursed her lips. "It is a silly expression, isn't it?"

"Yes." Katie's shoulders fell. Is that what the hospital staff said about her and Andrew? Was she talked about as Andrew's tucked-away woman? She blew out a breath of exasperation. It was a good thing the war ended when it did —for many reasons.

"How about the visit with the gypsies?" Katie asked. "Any thoughts on how I can accomplish that?"

"Not yet."

Katie leaned against the counter. "Brett says he and Joey found the tarot cards for Death and Justice."

"You mentioned that earlier. How do you know so much about tarot cards?"

"Suzanne and I played together as children. She used to practice giving me readings."

"Gypsies are usually wary of gorgios. You may have some advantage in knowing her as a child. Be warned, though, she won't appreciate your asking questions about a murder."

"I can't believe the marshal hasn't talked with the gypsies. What if Suzanne knows something? I can't risk their breaking camp and leaving before I have a chance to ask questions." Katie bit her lip. "You know how restless they are. Who knows when they might leave? I need to talk to Suzanne before it's too late!"

"Now calm down. I'll talk to Hank and see if Brett can be spared to drive you out there tomorrow. I'll tell Hank that Philip wants a new draft horse for the mill. Your father's been talking about it anyway. You could go with Meghan and Brett calling it a little outing to have your fortunes told and a chance for Brett to inspect their horses. With the privacy of a reading, you could ease in a question or two."

"I like that idea."

Hannah cut off the bases of asparagus and put them aside as she spoke. "When we see Meghan tonight, we'll ask if she can spare the time. I would feel much better about this with Meghan at your side."

"Do you think the gypsies could have murdered Stuart? Maybe I shouldn't put Meghan and Brett in such danger."

"I don't think that Suzanne is a danger to you. She is far more likely to be an ally than an enemy."

"Stuart and Suzanne." Katie shook her head. "I wonder how Papa would react to that news?"

"I don't think telling Philip about Stuart's dalliance with Suzanne is necessary. Some things are better left unspoken."

Katie smirked. Hannah had always addressed her father as Mr. Reynolds. Perhaps there was a change in their relationship? Thinking this, Katie blurted, "It seems everyone in this family has secrets."

Hannah mumbled, "Hmph."

"You have secrets too," Katie said.

"Whatever are you talking about?"

Katie mentally cringed. She wasn't ready to confront Hannah about her relationship with her father, so she brought up a long-held question instead. "Well, your husband's disappearance, I often wondered about that as a child. You never talked about him. Meghan doesn't even remember him."

"Meghan was only a year old when he left."

"What happened?" Katie sat down. "Am I being too nosy?"

"No, it used to bother me, but the years have softened the pain and embarrassment." Hannah let out a long sigh. "John

Cunningham died. Well, at least I think he's dead. He was a trapper, so he would go off for months at a time and leave me here in Liberty. We were too much trouble, he said." Hannah's eyes took on a sad far-away look. "A burden, he called us."

Hannah returned her gaze to Katie and her voice became clipped. "Well, one spring he never came back. I couldn't marry again even if I had wanted to. I wasn't sure he was dead."

"Oh, I'm so sorry."

"He drank too much and was hurtful when he did. I married him because he would have me, and then I wouldn't be a burden to anyone else. For all my troubles, I was rewarded with a beautiful daughter and eventually a lovely home here. I have a good life."

Hannah paused for a moment and then made a shooing gesture with both of her hands. "Now go on. Wash up for supper. Meghan will be here soon, and we have much to plan."

* * *

The next morning, they left for the gypsy camp. Katie could smell their arrival before she could see it, an odd mixture of horses and the yeasty aroma of baking bread. Brett was holding the reins with a light touch. Meghan sat in the middle of the bench; her posture straightened as they entered the camp.

Katie nudged Meghan. "Are you all right?"

"I've always been a little afraid of the gypsies. Liam teases me about that."

"So, you call Dr. West by his first name?"

"Well, we always did as children. Why wouldn't I?"

"Sounds like you've renewed that relationship since he came back. You're a widow and he is a bachelor."

Meghan didn't acknowledge or deny this, but Katie didn't miss the small smile that played across Meghan's lips.

The woods thinned out to a clearing. A swarthy man stepped out from behind a large tree, startling them with his sudden appearance. He swayed as he approached their wagon. The horse reacted by pulling its head back and stopping the cart.

The man calmed the gelding with a touch. With his eyes focused on Katie, he said, "You're a long way from home." His English accent was heavy, and his words slurred.

Brett answered, "Good morning, Mr. Danior. It's me, Brett. I work for Mr. Philip at Six Maples."

"Hmph, this war's given a boy a man's job. Risky caring for two beautiful women all by yourself, don't ya think, boy?" Then he smirked. "You have horse business?"

"Yes, sir. Hank asked me to check out your draft horses, see if you have any for sale." He looked over at Katie. "The ladies here want to see the fortune teller if she's willin'."

Danior acknowledged each woman with a nod. His eyes lingered on Katie.

Katie kept a neutral face, but Brett must have sensed her uneasiness because he asked again, "Is Miss Suzanne seein' visitors?"

Danior licked his upper lip, continuing to stare at Katie. He waited a few beats before answering. "You fine ladies want to know more about your love lives?" He let go of the horse's reins. "Wait here."

With the advantage of the wagon's height, Katie had a good view of the camp. Two wagons were set up near a cooking fire where baking bread nestled in the coals. Other wagons were scattered so that they were more secluded. Danior walked to a wagon at the edge of the woods and knocked on the bright yellow door, which was outlined on all four corners with white curlycues.

A child's squeal of delight brought Katie's attention to the children, who had stopped their play to stare at the wagon's arrival, but now they returned to their games. Colorful laundry dried on nearby bushes. In summer such a nomadic life might be pleasant, but what did the gypsies do when winter came? She'd never wondered about that as a child. The gypsies always came to Liberty during the warmer months.

Danior waved and walked toward their wagon.

Brett called softly to the horse and shook the reins. As they neared Danior, a breeze kicked up bringing with it the smell of his unwashed body and alcohol.

Danior led their horse by the harness to the dark green gypsy wagon. "Fortunes by Madame Lovell" was painted in yellow scroll on the wagon's lacquered sides. At the edge of the woods, Suzanne's camp was isolated from the others.

Danior stopped the horse at the van's door. Brett jumped down and held his hand out to help Katie step down before Danior could intercede.

"Wait here." Danior's mood shifted to sullen. "Madame Lovell will call when she is ready." He turned and motioned for Brett to follow him and walked away.

Brett turned to go. Katie grabbed his arm and whispered, "Be careful around those horses with him. He's been drinking."

Brett nodded and walked quickly toward a makeshift corral. Danior turned and gave another lusty glance back at Katie while he waited for Brett.

When they were out of earshot, Katie said to Meghan, "He makes me anxious."

"Why is that?" the voice behind Katie asked.

Katie turned. Suzanne, no longer the girl Katie remembered, was striking. She had a trim figure, almond-shaped eyes, an olive complexion, and thick glossy black hair.

"Please don't take offence. I'm fearful because he's been drinking," Katie said.

"Your observations are true enough. He drinks too much. "Do you want your fortunes told?"

"I'm Katie Harris, Stuart Reynolds' sister. I would like to ask you a few questions."

Suzanne lifted an eyebrow. "I can tell fortunes if that is what you seek."

Katie sighed. "Yes, we would like our fortunes told."

Suzanne lifted her chin toward Katie. "You first." Suzanne turned sideways in her wagon doorway and gestured for Katie to enter.

Once inside, Suzanne motioned for Katie to take a seat on the bench at a table covered in heavy green linen that fell to the floor. Tarot cards were neatly stacked on the corner of the table.

When Suzanne sat down, her foot brushed against the tablecloth, revealing a large well-worn book that lay open on the floor. The pages were handwritten with a few diagrams of plants. Katie did not have time to see more.

The Roma woman casually covered it with the draping tablecloth and turned to Katie. "You are Stuart's sister, Katie Reynolds. We played together as children."

"Yes, my name is Harris now. I'm a widow." She paused. "I am investigating my brother's murder."

"I know nothing of that. I can only reveal what the cards tell me."

"Fair enough. Tell me what your cards reveal about Stuart's murder."

Suzanne pierced Katie with her gaze as she shuffled the cards. Tension was evident in her stiff posture. She placed the tarot cards in the center of the table. "Divide the cards."

Katie split the stack in two.

Suzanne picked up the cards and put what had been the bottom on the top of the stack. Then proceeded to lay the cards down in rows, some facing up and others down. She flipped cards as she spoke. "You are in love with a man, but you cannot marry him."

Katie's eyes widened. "How could you know that?"

Suzanne smirked. "The cards."

"Do the cards tell you anything about my brother's murder?"

Suzanne ignored Katie's question and continued to flip cards. "I see great sadness for both you and your love." She lifted her head. "And tension in your shoulders and hands. Are you estranged from him?"

"Please, I'd rather not say. The cards say nothing about my finding Stuart's murderer?"

Suzanne's eyes narrowed. "You are a puzzle, like your cards." She pointed to a card that pictured a heart with three swords running through it. "This is a warning of conflict and violence. There may be grave danger in what you seek." Suzanne swept the cards back into a pile. "Beware."

"Is that it? Can't you be more specific?"

Suzanne shuffled the cards. "No, I cannot." She put aside her cards.

"The reason I wanted to talk with you is that two tarot cards were found at my brother's murder site."

The gypsy sighed. "Stuart came to see me when he returned home from the war. Before he left, I read his cards. I warned him of danger. The death card came up. I gave it to him as a reminder to be cautious." Suzanne's eyes welled up. "I begged him to stay with me another day. He laughed and said he had survived four years of war and would be damned if he could not survive the last few miles home. Then he told me about your disappearance. He was worried about you."

"My letter explaining my delay never reached my family. I never meant to worry Stuart. I helped a young widow with small children. The war was over and the casualties manageable, so I traveled with her to her home in Kentucky."

"Your war caused much pain and confusion."

"The Justice card was also found at the murder site. Did you or some other gypsies follow Stuart home?"

For just a second, Suzanne's eyes widened, but she quickly masked her surprise with a neutral façade. "I told you I gave him the Death card, so that he would be cautious."

"But what of the card that symbolizes justice?"

"That is all the cards tell me." Suzanne said.

"Do I need to involve the authorities to get answers from you?"

"No." She took a deep breath. "I will ask others what they know. Come back again. I will help you if I can." She stood. "I will see your friend now. There will be no charge."

* * *

Having returned from the gypsy camp, Katie and Meghan settled in with Hannah in the kitchen. Hannah poured coffees and set them down in front of the women. "What news from Suzanne?" Hannah asked as she joined them at the table.

Meghan stirred cream into her coffee as she spoke. "I'm to have success in my business."

"No surprise there," Hannah said. "You work hard enough."

"And," Suzanne said, "an old friend will become more intimate."

"I wonder who that could be?" Hannah winked.

Meghan blushed.

Katie said, "You didn't tell me that. Who do you think she means?"

"Who knows if it's really true?" Meghan said. "And I certainly didn't want any young ears hearing about that."

"Oh, Brett. You can trust him to keep a secret." Katie shifted her gaze to Hannah. "Hmm, another secret?"

Hannah ignored Katie's reference to their early conversation. "What else did the gypsy have to say?"

Meghan had recounted Suzanne's other predictions as Brett drove them home, so Katie gave the rest of Meghan's recitation only half of her attention. She did notice that Meghan left out a warning Suzanne had given about snakes. Katie abhorred snakes. When Meghan had relayed the snake prediction on the way home, it had made Katie's skin crawl. It seemed an important warning to omit, but she probably didn't want to alarm her mother.

Meghan addressed Katie. "Please tell us what happened when you talked to Suzanne. You hardly said a word in the wagon."

"I needed the time to think."

Katie turned to Hannah. "Suzanne asked me to come back. She planned to talk to the others in her clan to learn anything more about the day Stuart was murdered. Did you know Stuart had stopped at the gypsy camp to see Suzanne before making his way home?"

Hannah shook her head.

"He did?" Meghan asked. "What did she say about his visit?"

"That she read the cards and warned him." Katie pulled a small, folded paper from her skirt pocket. She glanced at it. "I've been keeping notes. Stuart was found on Thursday afternoon, the ninth. So he spent Wednesday night, the eighth, at the gypsy camp and was shot sometime early on Thursday."

"What does that tell us?" Meghan asked.

Katie glanced over at the desk in the corner. "Do you have a pencil?"

Hannah got up from the table and pulled a pencil out of the drawer of her desk. She handed it to Katie.

"Thank you." Katie wrote as she spoke, "I'm just trying to put together a timeline." Katie read aloud as she wrote, "Wednesday, June 8, Stuart stopped at the gypsy camp." When she'd finished writing, she said, "Suzanne cared about him."

Hannah said, "I believe they secretly met when their clan camped near Liberty. What else did she say?"

"Very little. Suzanne's book and the Justice tarot card puzzle me."

Meghan leaned across the table toward Katie with her hands out, palms up. "What book?"

"See if you can make any sense out of this. I saw an old book on the floor of Suzanne's wagon or vargo. Vargo's what she calls her wagon."

Hannah and Meghan nodded as if they were aware of this fact.

Katie tapped the pencil on her chin. "The book was open to an illustration of plants and written in some language other than English. It wasn't Latin."

Hannah asked, "Romanian?"

Katie shrugged. "Anyway, Suzanne tried to hide it from me, nonchalantly. She flipped the tablecloth over it."

Meghan rolled her eyes. "I think Suzanne likes to come across as mysterious."

"I think it was more than that," Katie said.

Hannah said, "Maybe she's a medicine woman and that is her book of rites." As a woman with a Wyandot heritage, Hannah readily believed in a shaman's power, so the equivalent in a Roma was easily accepted.

"Very well, but if Suzanne's some kind of medicine woman or a shaman, as you call it, then you'd think she'd stick with plants and medicinal potions, not tarot cards. I'm assuming that it was Suzanne who left the Justice card." Katie put one finger in the air. "First because she uses tarot cards and admitted to giving Stuart the Death card." Katie then lifted the second finger. "And second, I could see her seeking justice. I sure wouldn't want to anger her." She tightened her lips, then said, "Could Suzanne have felt betrayed by Stuart and murdered him in retaliation?"

Hannah shook her head. "I don't think so."

"Humph. Then there's her warning. She told me to beware. Like she's warning me off investigating this."

"Suzanne warned you?" Meghan asked.

"Yes, no specifics. Just a general warning." Katie lifted her hands and wiggled her fingers, eyes wide and said, "Beware."

Meghan laughed.

"I want to go back to the gypsy camp tomorrow, if possible," Katie said.

Hannah shook her head. "Certainly not on Sunday."

"Monday then."

"I don't know, child. It may be too dangerous. See what your father thinks."

Katie nodded. "He's worked with the gypsies for years. I'll see if he can give me some history, but first I must wash up from that dusty ride. She walked to the door and then turned back to Hannah. "One more question. How long has Papa been ill?"

Hannah lifted her eyes to the ceiling. "He started showing signs of the illness in early spring, sometime in late March." Hannah brought her focus back to Katie. There were tears pooled in Hannah's eyes. "He was tired all the time and had a bad cough, but Liam didn't diagnose him with pneumonia until early April."

"When did everyone in town learn about Philip's illness?" Katie glanced at Meghan. "You can probably answer that."

"About the time we learned of the war's end, mid-April."

Katie wrote this new information on her timeline.

Meghan put her hand over Katie's paper, and Katie stopped writing.

Meghan said, "Suzanne told you to beware. You really do need to be cautious."

"No, what I need to do is find out who killed Stuart before the trail gets too cold. We deserve answers, and the marshal's not providing them."

Katie paused, then added, "I believe papa's recovery depends on it."

From the other room came the sound of coughing and Hannah stood. "I need to check on your papa."

Meghan gathered their coffee cups and brought them to the sink. She began washing them.

Katie added a final note to her list. "I don't suppose we can do much tomorrow. What about church and Sunday dinner. Does your mother still make Sunday dinners an event?"

Meghan turned and leaned back against the counter. "Actually, Mama's planning a bigger than usual celebration on Sunday night. Liam's been invited."

"What are we celebrating?"

Her eyes lit up. "It's a secret."

"Oh, so you know?"

"I think you'll find it's happy news."

Katie tilted her head to the side. "Does it concern you?"

"I think you'll find it to be good news, and I'm not telling you anything else." Meghan turned her back to Katie and finished washing the dishes in the sink.

"Then I need to see Suzanne on Monday. I can go with Brett in the afternoon. Would you be able to meet me on

Monday morning when I talk to the marshal? I could sure use your support. You know him better than I, and it seems to me he's a lazy slug."

Meghan chuckled. "Sure I can do that. I'll give Tricia some of my work."

"Who's Tricia?"

"She's my assistant. She's an excellent seamstress. I'll get a little work done this afternoon, and I should be able to carve out an hour or so on Monday morning. The marshal's office is right next door to Liam's new office. Instead of coming and going house to house, his mother set him up in a doctor's surgery where patients visit him when their illness allows travel. Liberty has grown and Liam is far too busy, so Mrs. West's idea is helpful, one of the few." She smirked.

As she was saying this, Hannah returned to the kitchen. "Speaking of the doctor, what did Liam's apprentice want with you last night?" Hannah asked Meghan.

"While I was here last night dropping off the boys, Dr. Stephens stopped by."

"He hardly just stopped by, Meghan. Your boys told me that a man rode in here like a house was on fire while we were with Philip."

"Dr. Stephens is a bit prone to histrionics, but rightfully so in this case. Tricia had been attacked and very upset. Liam thought it would be helpful for Tricia to have a friend by her side, so Dr. Stephens was the messenger. I said good night to the boys and left." Meghan grimaced. "Sorry I didn't get a chance to say goodbye to you, but I was concerned. And Mama, thank you for watching the boys."

"Yes, yes, so what happened?" Hannah asked.

"Someone hit her in the face and then stole her reticule, although it only contained a few coins. She said it was too dark to see who it was. Poor thing, she had to get three stitches in her lip. Liam put in tiny stitches, so it should heal without giving her much of a scar. Liam thought having a friend with her would be comforting."

Hannah put a bowl of butter on the table. "What's this town come to when a woman can't walk safely down the street?"

Meghan sighed. "Liam sent a note to the marshal."

Hannah placed sliced pumpkin bread on the table. "Makes me fearful with you and the boys living in the village. Why don't you just move out here with us?"

"Mama, I'm fine. I'm safe. Liam and I don't think it really was a stranger. I know she sees a gentleman occasionally. I think he supports her. He may have been the one who hit her, and she was too embarrassed to say so."

Hannah shook her head. "Who's the man?"

"I don't know. She hasn't ever said anything to me about him, and I would feel awkward asking. I do know she can't support herself on what little her husband left her beyond the house. I pay her for her help at the shop, but she spends most of that on new clothes."

"Did she lose her husband in the war?" Katie asked.

"No, he was injured in battle. He lost two fingers, one being his trigger finger, so he was sent home. It was before Gettysburg, wasn't it, Mama?"

"Hmph, some were a bit suspicious of that."

Katie nodded. It was not that uncommon for a man to shoot off his own trigger finger to get out of serving.

"After recovering, Sean McDowell came home and married Tricia. Less than a year later, he fell off his horse going over a jump and broke his neck. It was terribly sad."

Hannah said with a sniff of disapproval, "Racing horses over a jump, you might have said. The man was drunk and foolish."

"Yes, but Sean McDowell was also handsome and delightful. I can see why Tricia fell in love with him. But Mama's right, it was his foolishness that caused the accident."

"What about Tricia's family? Is she all alone then?" Katie asked.

Hannah said, "Her folks are dirty and lazy. Tricia's the best of the bunch."

Meghan said, "Although Tricia is beautiful and naturally graceful, she comes from a large and poor family, the Donnelleys. They're not any help financially or supportive in any way, more jealous than otherwise. Her husband used to gamble and race when he wasn't working, but he was a hard worker."

Hannah said, "He won enough to buy that little house in town. Sean McDowell did have some luck racing horses against fool-hardy gamblers."

"What a sad story," Katie said. "Does she have any children?"

Meghan answered, "No, they were only married for a short time before the accident." Meghan stood. "I need to get the boys home. I've got plenty to do this afternoon." She went to the door and called for the boys.

Katie glanced at her notes. "I'm almost convinced Suzanne was at Stuart's murder site."

Meghan asked, "You don't think she killed Stuart, do you?"

"No, but that book she hid bothers me. Suzanne didn't say that she gave the Justice card to Stuart when he left her camp, but it was at the site when Brett and Joey returned. That's another loose thread." Katie sighed. "Monday when I go into town, I'll ask the marshal what he's learned."

CHAPTER 6

SURPRISING NEWS

Sunday Afternoon, June 18, 1865

Katie and Hannah met Meghan and the boys for mass at St. Martin's on Sunday morning. After the service, many parishioners gathered in the churchyard to welcome Katie home. A smaller group began to move to the church hall for coffee and sweet breads. Hannah and Meghan left for home.

Katie stayed to visit with several old friends. Caroline, a childhood friend, had promised Katie a ride home.

Mrs. Dubois, Liberty's biggest gossip, crossed the room and made a direct line toward Katie's circle of friends. "Welcome home, Mrs. Harris," Mrs. Dubois said. She then addressed the others, "Do you mind if I speak with Mrs. Harris alone for a moment?"

Without waiting for an answer, Mrs. Dubois nudged Katie to a quiet corner. "I know you're friends with Dr. West," Mrs. Dubois said.

"Yes, he's a family friend," Katie acknowledged.

"Then you're just the one to tell the doctor about Dr. Stephens."

Katie's brows furrowed, showing her confusion at Dr. Stephens's name.

Mrs. Dubois pursed her lips with impatience. "He's Dr. West's new assistant. Well, you know we are all so pleased with Dr. West, but his assistant!" She huffed. "The man is abrupt in his manner and seems to know little about stomach ailments."

Katie listened but didn't respond. Any comment she made would be repeated at teas and luncheons throughout the village. If Mrs. Dubois was not happy with Stephens, his days as a Liberty doctor were numbered. Mrs. Dubois and her circle of matrons were influential and could make his life miserable.

While Mrs. Dubois rattled on about other social infractions made by Richard Stephens, Katie thought about how this news might affect her future. If Dr. Stephens chose to leave Liberty, perhaps there would be a place for Katie to step in as Liam's apprentice. She could learn much from Liam as her proctor while she attended medical lectures at the Western Reserve College in Hudson, only a few hours' journey. Yet she, too, could fall into the same gossip trap. How would these gossips take to the idea of a woman doctor in Liberty? Katie grimaced at the thought.

Mrs. Dubois tilted her head. "Mrs. Harris, are you well?"

"I'm fine. My shoes are just a bit tight." Tight shoes would suffice as a reason for her scowl. Her feet were just fine, but the explanation satisfied Mrs. Dubois. This was not the time nor the woman with whom to share her thoughts about pursuing a medical education.

Katie returned home, so filled with coffee and bakery that she declined dinner. She soon set off to visit the Petersons.

Katie's visit to her home in Farmingdale was couched as a social call since it was Sunday, but she did learn that the Petersons hoped to continue leasing Rustic Hills.

Katie's Rustic Hills home and property were quite valuable. As an only child, Paul had inherited the property from his parents, who had died shortly after Paul and Katie married. With Paul's death at Gettysburg, it was now hers to lease or use.

Katie made the decision to stay with her father and Hannah at Six Maples for the time being, and she let the Petersons know that. The couple showed an interest in purchasing her property, so Katie had much to think about as she returned to Six Maples in the late afternoon.

When Katie came into the dining room, she found Hannah bustling around the table, fussing with flowers and place settings. Seeing Katie, Hannah burst into a radiant smile, then spread out her arms, palms up to show off the table with its centerpiece of dark red peonies. "Billy and Tommy picked these."

The contrast of red flowers and green leaves against the white tablecloth was stunning. "The flowers are beautiful." Katie turned to Hannah. "And so are you! Who fixed your hair?"

"Pshaw." Hannah looked away, but the timid smile and the flush of her face revealed her satisfaction with the compliment. "Colleen did it." Katie remembered Colleen. She had been one of her students and would be about sixteen now.

Hannah continued, "Although she's helping us with dinner, she loves to fix hair." Hannah walked out to the hall and stopped at the mirror. She pushed back a stray strand of hair. Satisfied, she turned back to Katie. "Your father wants to see you."

Katie smiled, rarely had she seen Hannah so excited. "Very well, I'll go change out of these dusty clothes."

"No, just go in. He has important news to tell you." Hannah took Katie by the shoulders and pivoted her toward Philip's room.

Katie walked down the hall. At the door, she paused and turned her head toward Hannah.

Hannah made a shooing gesture with her hands.

Katie gave a light knock on the bedroom door. "Papa, may I come in?"

"Yes," he answered.

Philip's bed was empty. Where was her father?

She heard a soft chuckle.

She turned toward the sound. Philip sat in one of the wing chairs in front of the window, a cup of tea on the table.

Hannah was right, her return had already restored some of his vigor.

"Please sit down," her father asked. "I have news to share before our supper tonight."

"I'm so dusty. How about if I stand?"

Philip waved a hand toward the bureau. "The bottom drawer has bed sheets. Put one over the chair."

Katie went to the bureau and pulled a sheet from the drawer. She walked over and spread it over the chair as she spoke. "You're looking much better today."

"Must be your return home. I worried so about you, darlin'."

"I'm sorry for that." She sat down, releasing a puff of dust.

Philip gave a little cough. "Where have you been?"

I went to Rustic Hills and called on the Petersons. They plan to continue leasing my home, may even buy it." She sighed. "I don't know if I can stay there without Paul. It brought back so many memories."

Philip sipped his tea.

They were both silent. Katie was lost in thoughts of her short marriage to Paul. All their dreams to fill the large home with children ceased when he died at Gettysburg. She had been pregnant with their first child and miscarried after learning of his death.

She shook off her melancholy thoughts and brightened her voice for her father's sake. "Hannah says you've got big news."

He took her hand. "Hannah and I have married."

"Today?"

He laughed and then coughed. "Certainly not. I wouldn't have put the burden of this illness on her if I had known. It was at Christmas, before I took sick." He coughed and took a sip of his tea.

"That's wonderful news. But why all the secrecy? Why doesn't everyone know?"

"We wanted you and Stu to know first. Before everyone else in town that is. Meghan knows." His voice became raspy. "I'm so glad you're pleased."

"Oh, I am, Papa, I am. It's just this is so sudden for me."

"Yes, I suppose." Philip settled into the back of the wing-backed chair. "Hannah and I have teased each other about it for years, in private, of course. War is a great incentive to live life more fully. The only advantage to war."

Katie squeezed his hand.

"Oh, I sound like some doddering old fool, I know, but it's true. If you ever love someone again, Katie, then act on it. Don't mourn Paul's death for too long. Life's for living not grieving." Philip cleared his throat. "I speak from experience, you know. When I lost your mother, I thought I might as well die too, but I couldn't. I had you and Stu to care for."

Philip's words caused Katie to lose herself in her own grief. Her emotions were still raw after the visit to Rustic Hills. She was plagued by conflicting emotions, mourning Paul, her lost child, and now loving Andrew. Had she fallen in love with Andrew just to ease her sorrow? The question had been on her mind for days now.

Philip's lips tightened and he lowered his eyes. "It takes time, darlin'." He took her hand. "I know you're still grieving, but good times will come again. I promise."

"Well, we have reason to celebrate tonight. Tell me how you proposed?"

Philip released her hand and took a small drink of tea before he spoke. "Hannah and I were sitting down to dinner with Meghan and the boys on Christmas day. Conversation turned to the rest of our family, namely you and Stu and how you might be spending Christmas." Philip drank more tea. "And it finally hit me. We are a family, all of us, you, Stu, Hannah, Meghan, Tommy, and Billy. I think of you all in that way, so why not make it all legal and proper between Hannah and me?"

Katie gave her father a warm smile as she settled back into the recess of her chair.

"I shared my thoughts with Hannah that evening when we were alone. She agreed, so we married and off we went to Cleveland to celebrate." She moved to the edge of the chair and turned his way. "What did the townspeople say? I'm sure Hannah worried herself to death thinking of the gossips in town. Taking a stage together for Cleveland." She lifted her hand to her mouth feigning shock. "Scandalous."

"It's none of their damn business." Philip cleared his throat. "Excuse my frightful language, darlin'. I get so tired of the gossip in the village. For Hannah's sake, we fabricated quite an elaborate story about Hannah's need to take care of some business for the church. Father Kelly married us and helped with that charade."

The tea concoction must have been making him drowsy. He leaned back into the chair and closed his eyes while he spoke. "And January's such a slow time at the mill." He opened his eyes again. "It was an easy stretch for folks to believe that I was merely traveling along to help her negotiate the travails of the big city."

"Oh, I think you like the intrigue too, because, really, it would have been all right to write to me with the news."

"We made a pledge. We didn't want anyone outside the family to know before you and Stu, and we agreed that it would be best to tell you in person. We wanted to celebrate our marriage with a fine supper once you and Stu returned and to tell you then." Philip's cough was harsh and long.

Katie stood. "Are you all right?"

"Yes, yes, I'm fine." He finished off the drink. "This tea is soothing."

Katie nodded. "Hannah's always been like a mother to me. This is such good news." She sat back down again. "Tell me about the wedding if it won't cause you too much difficulty."

"It was just a small ceremony at St. Martin's. Father Kelly married us, of course. Meghan and Carl Schneider were our witnesses. Meghan's neighbor, Carl, has become like a second father to Meghan. We knew we could trust him with our secret." He paused. His face revealed the pleasure of his memory, and then his attention returned to Katie. "Hannah and I spent the following week in the city, sightseeing, dining, and dancing." Philip's voice became low now as he suppressed his cough. "Best decision we ever made."

A quick knock on the door frame turned their attention there.

Hannah peeked in.

Katie rose from her chair and kissed her father's cheek. "Congratulations!"

Hannah walked into the room with a sly smile.

Katie hugged her and whispered, "I'm so happy for you." Then she stepped back from her embrace, still holding Hannah's arms. "It's wonderful to be able to call you mother!"

"So now you know." She turned to Philip. "She's happy, yes?"

"Yes," Katie said, answering for her father. "I am very happy."

Hannah gave Philip a triumphant smile. "Good. Now I must be off to check on our supper preparations."

When Hannah left the room, Katie walked back over to Philip's chair. "You've loved her for many years, haven't you?"

Philip took Katie's hand. "I have, darlin'. I've made things right for Hannah's future too. According to my will, you'll be sharing our family's holdings with her." He talked low now, suppressing another cough. "Paul left you comfortably provided for with your house in Farmingdale, so Hannah will inherit this house, this land, and the horses. You'll inherit the mill."

Katie paused for a moment. "I'm delighted with your decision."

"Good. I want to take a short nap, so I can be at my best for our celebration supper."

Katie picked up the sheet from the chair and put it aside then took her father's arm and helped him into bed. By the time she had straightened his blankets, the laudanum in his tea had worked to check his coughing. Philip was snoring as she closed the door.

When Katie reached the kitchen door, Hannah was giving instructions to Colleen and Sheila. Sheila was another of Katie's former students.

Hannah turned to Katie, "These girls are a godsend, helping me with the heavy cleaning and gardening, and making this evening special."

Katie greeted the girls and then turned to Hannah, "Can you spare a moment before I dress for supper?"

Hannah's gaze took in Katie's disheveled hair and dusty clothing. "You need to get ready, and I need to give the girls a few last-minute instructions. I'll be up to your room shortly, but only for a few minutes. I need to get ready too."

BITTER MEDICINE

Once in her bedroom, Katie took off her skirt and blouse and used the wash basin to clean up. Feeling refreshed, she set about putting on a clean chemise. A beautiful sea-foam colored dress lay on her bed. She tenderly moved it aside when she sat down to put on her stockings. Hannah must have laid out the dress. She remembered wearing it with Paul at her side and caressed the silk of its voluminous skirt.

For a wistful moment, she thought about Paul. She had been so deeply in love with him. They had been happy in their courting and there had been no great challenges to keep them from marrying. Now life and love had become so complicated. With that thought, Andrew came to mind. She touched her lips, remembering their one kiss, and then she grabbed the pillow off the bed and hugged it, knowing he would never be hers to cherish.

Katie's thoughts were interrupted when Hannah knocked. "Come in."

Hannah walked in and pulled the dress off the bed and held it up by the shoulders. "Will this do for dinner tonight?"

The dress had a deep V-neck and was cinched at the waist with a diamond-shaped insert. The fabric shimmered when Hannah moved it.

"I'm a little thinner in the waist now than when I wore it last. I think Meghan will need to take in that insert. Or I can just forego a corset, which wouldn't bother me one bit."

"Humph. In no time at all, I'll have you back to a wholesome weight. You're skin and bones, child. Meghan has already altered the dress, so you'll need to wear a corset." She reached into the chifforobe, gathering Katie's undergarments and laid them next to the dress.

Kattie said, "I told the Petersons I would be staying at Six Maples for the time being. They were relieved. I think they'd like to buy Rustic Hills." She stood when Hannah held up the corset.

Katie slipped the corset over her head and turned her back to Hannah who tugged on the strings as she spoke. "Your staying with us here at Six Maples is wonderful news. Your father will be so pleased. You must tell him tonight at dinner. It will give us even more cause for celebration."

That realization quieted Katie, her dream to study medicine slipping away. Helping her father run the mill as he recovered was the right thing to do. Was studying medicine even feasible? A woman doctor. Hannah had scoffed at the suggestion. Would everyone else too? What would her father think?

No. It was wrong to hold someone back because it makes you uncomfortable. Surely she could convince Papa with that argument. He was a reasonable man.

Hannah had finished buttoning up Katie's dress and came around to face her. "Your dress is beautiful, but your hair's a fright. I'll send Colleen up to fix it." Then Hannah positioned Katie in front of her full-length mirror.

Katie gasped. She had forgotten just how well the color and cut of this dress complimented her figure and skin tone.

Hannah stepped behind Katie and spoke to her reflection in the full-length mirror. "Yes, I agree. You're breathtaking."

It had been some time since Katie had dressed so elegantly. When Hannah left, Katie turned from side to side, and chewed on her lower lip as she examined the dress in the mirror, pleased with the results. If only Andrew could see her tonight.

* * *

Hannah was seated in the parlor and Katie was descending the stairs when Sheila opened the door. Liam West stepped into the room.

The doctor took off his derby upon entering and seeing the women. "Mrs. Cunningham, Katie, so nice to see you."

Katie turned and winked at Hannah, knowing that Liam would soon learn Hannah was no longer Mrs. Cunningham.

After the greeting, Hannah led Liam to Philip's room for a brief examination. Katie heard Meghan's coach arrive and pulled back the draperies. Carl Schneider stepped out in a top hat and suit, looking quite debonair. He put his hand out to assist Meghan from the coach. Katie was sure that Meghan was wearing the height of fashion, a charming pink silk dress with a white hat and matching pink ribbon.

The boys moved stiffly in their short pants, jackets, and starched shirts. Tommy took the overnight case from the driver. Billy made a scrunched-up face as he tugged at his collar while Mr. Schneider paid the coachman. Meghan and her boys planned to stay the night. Mr. Schneider would return to town with Liam.

Soon the boys were playing jacks in the kitchen with Mr. Schneider while all three women were settled in the parlor with a glass of wine, talking about how clever Hannah and Philip had been in concealing their marriage. A few minutes later Philip and Liam joined them in the parlor. Liam congratulated Hannah on her marriage, evidently Philip had shared their news with him during the examination.

Mr. Schneider came into the parlor from the kitchen. "I'm just not as good at jacks as I was in my youth. The boys beat me hands down."

The women laughed and Hannah poured the men each a glass of whiskey.

Taking his glass, Philip said, "Time to celebrate."

Liam lifted his glass. "To the happy couple." They raised their glasses in the toast. They chatted as they finished their drinks, and then Philip took Hannah's arm and they walked into the dining room. Katie glanced at her father. His face revealed the effort it took to put on a show of health and vigor.

During supper, Katie noticed the exchanges between Liam and Meghan. Something more than their friendship was revealed in the flashing glances and focused attention whenever one or the other spoke. She could remember doing the same with Andrew as they ate in the mess. She had a tickle of pleasure at the memory.

The seating had put Hannah and her father at each end. Meghan sat between her boys on one side, and Mr. Schneider, Katie, and Liam on the other. Toasts were again raised to the bride and groom and to the war's end.

It was a delightful supper with no mention of Philip's health or Stuart's murder. Hannah was radiant in a midnight blue dress. Katie learned that Meghan had designed it.

Katie noticed the evidence of her father and Hannah's relationship. Her father often glanced at Hannah to check her reaction to something said. At one point during supper, her father lifted his glass to Hannah in a silent toast. Hannah had answered his toast with a coy smile. They were in love, and looking back, Katie realized they had been for so long.

How foolish it had been to wait and deny themselves the pleasure of marriage until now.

Probably society's stigma, Philip a man of European descent marrying a woman who was half Wyandot. If Stuart had known of their father's marriage to Hannah, would he have kept his relationship with Suzanne a secret?

Thinking of lovers kept apart brought to mind thoughts of Andrew again. Katie gave a heavy sigh. The click of silverware on china and the buzz of conversation covered the sound from all but Meghan, who glanced toward Katie.

Katie gave Meghan a quick look of reassurance; her thoughts then focused on Meghan. She and Liam were obviously attracted to each other, so what kept them apart and friends rather than lovers? Meghan was a couple of years older. Was it the age difference that caused their reluctance? Or did they fear a shift in their relationship might lead to a rift in their friendship?

Maybe it was Meghan's Wyandot heritage. Her maternal grandmother was Indian. Was it Liam's mother's prejudice that kept them apart? Mrs. West would undoubtedly value society's opinion over marital happiness. Perhaps Liam shared his mother's bias. Observing the two as they talked across the table confirmed that was not the case. All signs pointed to their attraction for one another. They shared the same feelings as she and Andrew. She had not imagined Andrew's attraction to her.

As she took a sip of her water, Katie's eyes suddenly widened with a revelation. Society's stigma of divorce was the reason why Andrew was reluctant to pursue their relationship. Andrew was a good man, the type of man who would discount his own happiness for the sake of his wife's reputation. Of course, that was it. How foolish she'd been. The possibility made Katie choke on her water bringing everyone's attention to her at the table.

Philip grasped her hand. "Are you all right, darlin'?"

Katie put her other hand to her throat. "Yes, I'm fine." Katie raised her eyebrows and lifted her chin to let them know that she was not in danger of choking. She was much happier with her epiphany. Katie ate and drank the rest of her supper with relish. Andrew did love her.

CHAPTER 7

FLASHBACKS AND FUTURE DREAMS

Monday, June 19, 1865

It was ten o'clock in the morning and the little village bustled with business. As Brett drove the wagon into town, Katie considered the old buildings that lined the street. Many needed minor repairs and paint. Being homesick at Camp Dennison, Katie had glamorized Liberty. Reality asserted itself as she surveyed the village square. A few small trees offered little shade, and the fence surrounding the square was shabby. Liberty was hot, tired, and dusty.

Brett stopped the wagon in front of Meghan's shop. The boy jumped down from the wagon, pulled a small stool from under the seat, and helped Katie step down.

"Thank you." She released his hand. "Do you have Hannah's and Hank's lists?"

"Yes, ma'am." He pulled two folded papers from his back pocket.

Katie glanced at the dual-sided clock that hung from the corner of Schneider's dry good store. Meghan had told Katie this was her neighbor's latest addition to his storefront. He was very proud of it and checked it often against his pocket watch. "Come back at noon and we'll have lunch," she told Brett.

Brett glanced at the clock and then turned to Katie and tipped his hat "Yes, ma'am." The village streets were filled with horses and wagons. As Brett left, his wheel cut through a pile of manure.

Katie coughed from the pungent smell and the body odor of the three men who had walked past. The odors reminded her of a far worse smell, wounded men after a battle. The stench of unwashed bodies, carbolic, and seeping infection. The combination of these present smells brought back the memory of Chattanooga—

In her mind's eye, she was once again hurrying through the aisles of the hospital tent with Andrew urgently calling for her help in the surgery. She relived the distress of ignoring the injured men in their cots, some lying on the dirt floor, and others propped up against tent poles. There were too many injured men. Too much suffering. She couldn't attend to the men who reached out to her, crying out for water and attention.

Her body reacted as if she was once again back in the chaos of Chattanooga, a rapid heartbeat and shallow breathing. Katie grabbed the nearby post and lowered her head to ease her dizziness. She once again visualized the man whose cheek had been blown off. She gasped for air as if she were suffocating.

Hearing the chatter of nearby children, the memories began to fade, and her heartbeat slowed. Her breathing was nearly back to normal. She shook her head and checked Schneider's clock. Only a few minutes had passed. She stood taking deep breaths. She would push on, just as she had at Chattanooga.

Katie scanned the area, discreetly from left and right. Everyone was going about their business. No one had noticed her reaction. This was not the first-time uncontrolled memories of Chattanooga had overwhelmed her. She wanted desperately to control her mind and her body's reaction to them. Was it guilt because so many men had died that caused those memories to overwhelm her? She had worked non-stop for two days after the battle, rarely stopping to eat and taking only one short nap. She and Andrew saved many soldiers. She had even stepped in when Andrew's hands were too slick with blood to finish surgery. She could do that, so why couldn't she control these painful recollections?

She swallowed hard and composed herself, lifting her chin and the hem of her skirt. She let go of the post and stepped up to the sidewalk. By the time she got to Meghan's shop her breathing had returned to normal. Her hands still shook slightly as she reached for the door, but not noticeably so. She would be all right now.

The little bell above her tinkled as she opened the dress shop door. Meghan called, "Come on in, Katie."

Three pastel dresses in varying stages of completion hung from the weave of a wicker-walled cubicle. All the bright colors made her feel drab. Hannah insisted she wear a dark skirt and blouse when she came to town, clothing appropriate for a sister mourning her brother.

Meghan came from behind the screen panel with a teapot in hand and set it on the table. "You're adorable in that hat."

Katie was wearing a broad-brimmed straw hat with black satin ribbons. Meghan had given it to her last night, suggesting that Katie needed to replace the battered bonnet she had worn while traveling.

"Yes, very feminine. Thank you. It's nice to be able to pay attention to fashion again."

Katie scanned Meghan's shop, feigning nonchalance after the frightful memories of war. Bright bolts of fabric were stacked on the shelves behind the highly polished wooden counter. A delightful contrast to the hospitals she had worked in. Bright colors made a difference, she thought, even Miss Nightingale had pointed out the need for color and light for healing, which probably worked well for buying too.

Meghan led Katie over to a table. "I saw you ride in with Brett a few minutes ago. I thought you might like some tea as fortification before we went to see the marshal. Besides with the morning rush, I'm parched."

"Sounds wonderful, I am a little nervous about this meeting. I want answers and some men don't like to see women involved in such things."

Meghan chuckled. "Oh, I know. Even though I am a businesswoman, the other shopkeepers in town often treat me as if I were a fragile child instead of a competent adult. Except for Mr. Schneider, of course."

"Yes, Philip says he's like a second father to you."

"He is, but then so is your father. I'm very lucky to have them both in my life."

"And now you may have another good man in your life," Katie said, referring to Liam West.

Meghan blushed and busied herself with tea things.

Katie covered a half-smile at Meghan's reaction with her hand. Meghan's friendship with Liam was blossoming into the romantic realm, but it seemed Meghan wasn't ready to talk about it.

They settled themselves at the little table outside the kitchenette. As she poured Katie's tea, Meghan asked, "Did you learn anything from Philip about the gypsies?"

"Nothing that helps find the murderer. He knew that Stuart sometimes called on Suzanne when they camped nearby." She tilted her head. "Am I the only one who didn't know about that little romance?"

"Katie, you had a teaching career, a whirlwind marriage, a home six miles away, and then spent over a year and a half nursing. You've missed out on a lot."

"I think I may just sell my house in Farmingdale. It was Paul's family home. We loved living there, but I'm a widow now." Katie shook her head. "There are too many memories. I'm thinking about moving to Liberty."

"It would be wonderful to have you nearby."

"Not right away. I'll stay at Six Maples for the time being. I have so many things to consider." Katie took a sip of her tea. "Philip mentioned a new will was drawn up by his lawyer, Harold Overmeyer."

"A well-respected attorney here in town."

"He recently changed his will. I'm to inherit the mill and he wants me to become more involved in the business."

"Well, that's good, isn't it?"

"I don't know. Katie lifted her chin as if in defiance. "I want to become a doctor and that requires education and time. I'm not sure if I'll be able to run the mill and study medicine."

Meghan said, "You want to be a doctor?"

"Yes. I loved nursing and I watched as doctors treated soldiers' injuries and diseases. When the doctors were overwhelmed after a battle they shouted instructions so that I could do their work. And I did. I was meant to do this, Meghan. It's my calling. Besides women deserve to be doctored by a woman if they choose."

"Yes, of course," Meghan said. "I just never imagined a woman doctor."

"It makes sense though, doesn't it? Some women might feel more comfortable having another woman tend to her ailments."

Meghan crinkled her brow. "So, you'd be a midwife?"

"I would deliver babies, yes, but women have other needs as well. I would be more than happy to doctor men too. If they'd allow me."

Meghan blushed and took a sudden interest in her teacup. "Oh, for heaven's sake, what a prude you are." Katie shook her head. "As soon as I find Stuart's murderer, I'm going to start attending lectures. The preceptorship route is my choice, which requires at least three years as an assistant while attending a variety of medical lectures before sitting for the exam." She paused. "Know any good doctors who might take on an apprentice?"

Meghan sat back in her chair. "A woman doctor, here in Liberty, that'll be a shock."

"You're a Liberty businesswoman," Katie continued.

"Yes, in a business traditionally run by women."

Katie pursed her lips, then said, "Oh, Meghan, don't be like your mother and argue with me."

"So my mother knows. She'll be worried about the gossips."

"She thinks it's utter nonsense for me to pursue medicine, yet she doesn't bat and eye at the idea of my running the mill."

"Good point. Did you mention that?"

"In Hannah's world, I would be more like a figurehead than a manager at the mill."

"I expect that had your blood boiling."

Katie grimaced. "Your mother is old fashion, but she'll come around. I think."

"Does your father know?"

"No, not yet."

Meghan blew out a breath. "That won't be easy."

"I know, but I'm hoping he'll take the news better than Hannah." She paused. "Getting back to the mill operation. They're building wagons there now. During the war that side of the business was very profitable."

Meghan's gaze swept around the room. "Philip's been generous with the mill's profit. He and mama gave me the money to set up this shop. I didn't know how I would support myself after Tom died. Setting up this business helped to allay my worry as well as my grieving. It would have been years before I would have been able to afford the sewing machines, fabric, and accessories. I'm very fortunate."

They finished their tea. Meghan locked up the shop and the women walked to the marshal's office. A man slouching against the corner of the hardware store watched their progress while he chewed on a wooden matchstick. Katie glanced his way as they approached him, and he tipped his hat.

Meghan must have sensed Katie's apprehension. She linked Katie's arm in hers as they passed him.

Katie glanced back at the man as Meghan opened the door to the marshal's office. The man caught her eye and tipped his hat again. Katie shuddered. Her instincts signaled danger.

CHAPTER 8

MARSHAL GERBER'S THEORY

Monday, June 19, 1865

"Good morning, ladies." The marshal swung his feet from the desktop to the floor while sliding a dime novel into the top drawer. He stood. "Mrs. Harris, welcome home."

He turned to Meghan and touched his index finger to his head in a small salute. "Mrs. Turner, always a pleasure. "Has Mrs. McDowell recovered from her unfortunate attack?"

"She seems to be recovering. Although it is rather frightening to learn we have someone so vicious in our little village."

"I stopped at her house to get more information. She couldn't offer much in the way of a description. It was dark you see. It's hard to be a woman on her own. I told her next time she had an evening errand to let me know. I would be happy to escort her. Being the marshal, I feel it's my responsibility to protect her."

Hearing the marshal's last comment prompted Meghan to direct a mischievous smile Katie's way, but she quickly suppressed it with a gloved hand and a cough. Liberty's gossips had it that the marshal showed a keen interest in Tricia's welfare, some said with romance in mind.

"I have asked around," the marshal continued, "but no one seems to have been in the area when she was attacked. I'll be sure to give that alley more patrol in the evenings."

Katie walked toward the window that overlooked Liberty Street. "That's good. Now, about my brother's murder."

The marshal's face took on such a study in gravity and seriousness Katie wondered if it was a façade.

"Yes, I'm sorry for your loss. Please sit down." He made a sweeping gesture toward the chairs. "Can I offer you coffee?"

Meghan sat down. "None for me, we just had tea."

Katie had glanced outside to confirm the suspicion that she'd been followed. "None for me either, thank you, but I would appreciate it if you could tell me the name of the man out there."

As the marshal moved toward the window, Katie studied the slouching man. He was holding a matchstick and reaching in his pocket, probably for a cigarette case. The man saw her gazing through the window at him and threw the matchstick on the ground.

Katie stepped aside to allow the marshal to see her view.

He looked. "Where?" His brow furrowed as he turned to Katie and stepped back.

Katie stepped up to the window again. "Oh, he's gone." Katie put her hand to her mouth and scanned the streets for his whereabouts.

The marshal cocked his head and gave her a look.

Katie flipped her hand feigning an air of indifference. "Oh, well. I thought I knew him and felt bad that I had forgotten his name." She walked over and sat down. "I'm sorry to have bothered you with that."

"No matter, happy to oblige." He sat down behind his desk. "What would you like to know about this terrible business?"

Katie explained her desire to hear all that the marshal had learned about her brother's murder.

The marshal listed the series of events Brett had relayed and finished up his litany with his theory that theft was the motive. He put both palms on his desk and stood. "Of course, I will continue to investigate, but the murderer is probably long gone by now."

"Well, I plan to investigate this too," Katie said. "May I count on your cooperation?"

The marshal shook his head. "Not the work for a lady, if you don't mind me saying so."

"I feel I must pursue this. May I count on your help?"

He sat back down and blew out long breath. "Yes, of course."

Katie said, "I understand you've put a notice in *The Liberty Gazette* in an effort to find information."

"Yes, sometimes a witness will come forward."

"Please let me know if you get any leads from that."

"Nothing so far."

Katie nodded. "I would like you to ask for a second request through *The Gazette*. In this one, let's note Stuart's horse's markings. Perhaps if people know the horse's color and markings we might learn more. Do you agree?"

"Well, you know, that's a good idea. Why don't you write something up? Bring it around and I'll sign it. Paper goes to press on Thursday."

"I'll do that."

As they walked back to Meghan's dress shop, Katie kept a keen eye out for the man with the matchstick. He had disappeared.

Meghan had a fitting appointment, so they said their goodbyes and Katie met up with Brett.

Katie and Brett walked across the square to the Liberty Café.

As they were seated, Brett said, "This is the first time I've eaten in a restaurant. Three different dinner choices, isn't that nifty?" He was reading the hand-written menu when the waitress approached. "I'm partial to the roast beef and mashed potatoes." Brett looked up from his menu, recognizing the girl. "Sarah," he said, "I didn't know you worked here." His face suddenly flushed.

"So nice to see you, Sarah," Katie said. Like Brett, Sarah had been one of Katie's students and was about the same age. With cornflower blue eyes and blonde hair, she had been an attractive child, and the same features served her well as a young lady, which Katie could see was not lost on Brett. "I'll have the same," Katie said.

"Yes, Miss Reynolds." Sarah's eyes flashed to Brett. "So nice to see you."

Brett flushed again. It took him a moment to compose himself, but he recovered well enough to carry on a bit of small talk with Sarah when she returned with their dinners.

Katie thought trips into town with Brett would have to include dinners this summer. From Brett's lingering looks when Sarah walked away, Katie was pretty sure he was smitten with the young waitress.

After dinner, Brett sat on a bench under the bank's awning, while Katie stopped to see the manager. When she left the bank, she and Brett walked as they consulted Hank's list. Reading over the list, Katie nearly bumped into Victor Ross. "Oh, I'm so sorry," she said. She moved aside. "I shouldn't read and walk at the same time."

Victor lifted his hat in greeting. "No harm done. Good afternoon, Mrs. Harris."

Katie nodded. "Mr. Ross."

"I was going to ride out to Six Maples later today, so this fortunate meeting may save me that delightful errand."

"What can I do for you?" A bit of exasperation was evident in Katie's voice. She had little patience for such flattery.

"I would like to invite you to supper on Saturday evening at the American Hotel. I have a proposition that would benefit many in our town. Your expertise in its planning and organization would be most helpful."

"I'm not sure of my commitments."

Victor motioned toward the bank bench. "Then would you agree to sit here and talk for a moment?"

"Yes, of course." She turned to Brett. "You have Hank's list. Would you mind going to the blacksmith's without me?"

"No, ma'am."

Katie put a few coins in his hand, and the boy tipped his hat and left.

She and Victor sat on the bench. After asking about her family, Victor finally got to his point. "I would like to organize a charity ball to benefit those who have not served but have suffered from the war."

"Widows and orphans?"

"Yes."

"What a wonderful idea!" She immediately regretted her enthusiastic reply. She needed to solve Stuart's murder. Planning parties was not going to get her results.

Victor laid out his plans for music, dancing, and light refreshments. He planned to take care of all costs and donate the proceeds to the needy families in Liberty. The advertisements were already posted in the shops.

Katie was touched by his generosity. "It sounds like you have everything planned. What can I possibly do to help?"

"First of all, accompany me," Victor said. "We can talk about the particulars on Saturday night while we have supper. I have other ideas as well."

"Mr. Ross, you do wear me down." She chewed on her lower lip while she took a moment to consider the idea. "Let's plan on having supper then. If I have some obligation, I'll send a message with my regrets. Will that do?"

"Yes. May I pick you up at six?"

"That would be fine."

"We now have a theater in town. Perhaps you didn't know that. I thought we could see *Black-eyed Susan* then have a late supper."

"A theater! Liberty is becoming cosmopolitan."

Victor made a move to stand but stopped when Katie remained seated.

She said, "I'm curious. Why do you think my brother was killed by bummers? Do you have any evidence?"

"It's only common sense," he said. "Bummers have been stealing from the outlying farms and ranches of the village. These men are desperate for food and horses as they make their way home, and they're used to killing."

"But you have no evidence?"

"Now, now, a lady like you shouldn't be concerned about such things anyway. That's the marshal's job."

"Stuart was my brother. I have a very keen interest in finding his murderer."

"This is a sordid business and not the type of dealings meant for a lady." He paused. "You must leave such things to men."

His patronizing attitude was annoying. She took a deep breath. "The marshal seems to have dismissed Stuart's murder as unsolvable. I mean to find out who did this."

Ross shook his head. "I can't see you worrying your pretty head about such matters. I'll tell you what. I'll talk to the marshal about investigating this further."

She checked her anger at his condescending comment, knowing she needed to know more, and this man might be able to help her. With a couple of glasses of wine and a romantic setting, Victor Ross might be more forthcoming.

Katie stood. "Well, thank you for that. I will see you on Saturday. Perhaps by then you will have learned something more from the marshal."

* * *

Katie was quiet as Brett drove the wagon back from the village. Her mind was racing. She needed to get a description of Stuart's horse for the newspaper posting. Maybe she could talk to Caleb Brown when she dropped it off. She also wanted to revisit the murder site. She needed something that would convince Marshal Gerber to resume the investigation.

As a last resort, she could show him the tarot cards Brett found in the valley as a ploy for further investigation, but that would target the gypsies. She shuddered, thinking of the prejudices she might flame with such a report. She needed something else. She could always remind him of Brett's discovery of a man's footprints under the pine tree on the ridge and a woman's footprints near the water's edge — details he seemed to have ignored. Unlike the marshal, she would take her time, consider all evidence, and thoroughly scour the valley.

Six Maples came into view as they rounded the bend, a white house with green shutters. Their homestead was aptly named: the maple trees dominated the landscape. The leaves of the tall, spreading trees kept the house and front yard shaded and cool. As they neared, Katie imagined a cold drink on the porch with her feet up and a medical book in hand as the perfect way to spend the afternoon.

She sighed. Her dreams would have to be put on hold. She turned toward Brett and asked, "Do you have time to saddle up Mouse for me when you're done unhitching the gray?" She used her chin to point to the gelding pulling the wagon.

"Where you goin'?" Brett blurted out. Then he raised his eyebrows, and his eyes grew large. "If you don't mind me askin'?"

Katie reached over and pulled the front of Brett's hat down. "I'm just going to ride out to the valley. I want to get a sense of the place, be alone to think about my brother. Can you understand that?"

Brett pushed his hat back. "You stay sad for a while when you lose someone important. If a ride out there makes you feel closer to him, then you gotta do it."

"You're very perceptive."

His brows furrowed in confusion.

She explained, "You're aware of people's feelings."

"That's 'cause of my pa dying. He died in camp. Measles. We lost him a year ago."

"Oh, Brett, that must have been hard for you."

"Yeah, and even harder on ma, but she can rely on me and Joey."

"I'm so sorry."

They rode on for a few minutes in silence and then Katie said, "No need for the pretense of a side-saddle. Hannah said the men won't be in the barn this afternoon."

"Yes, ma'am, you sure use big words. What did you call it, pretense?"

"Pretense means pretending. Brett, I do wish you'd take time for more schooling. I could spend evenings with you and Joey if you're too busy during regular school hours."

He scrunched up his face and glanced over at Katie. Facing forward again, he said, "I'll think on it and talk to ma."

Katie face brightened in satisfaction. She'd chip away at his reluctance. "Good."

"This war sure has changed things. You goin' out to the valley alone and actin' so independent and such. Sure wish more women were like you." He kept his eyes on the horse's back and slapped the reins.

Katie turned to Brett. His face had flushed. She thought he was a little embarrassed about giving her a compliment. Maybe there was hope in the next generation of men, who might be more appreciative of women's capabilities, like doctoring.

Brett brought the wagon up to the kitchen porch. They unloaded the sugar, flour, salt, and other supplies they had purchased in town for Hannah and put them on the counter in the kitchen.

Hannah walked into the kitchen as Katie and Brett brought in the last of the packages. "I saw you come in," she said. "I've been reading the newspaper to Philip, but he's fallen asleep."

Brett tipped his hat. "Afternoon, ma'am." Then he turned toward Katie. "I'll put Hank's things in the barn and go saddle up Mouse."

"Thanks." Katie turned to Hannah. "How is he?"

"Resting now. His good days are often followed by exhaustion. He overdoes it."

Katie turned to the counter and picked up a bag of salt.

Hannah retrieved two cups. "Just let that set on the sideboard for a minute. I'll get to it later. Sit, sit. You must be thirsty after that dusty drive."

Katie drank her coffee while she explained to Hannah all that she had learned in town and planned to do.

Hannah said, "The charity work with Victor Ross might be helpful. You might learn more about what Ross and his people have to say about Stuart's death, although your dining with him might not please Philip much."

"Why is that?"

"Oh, Philip's always civil with Mr. Ross, don't get me wrong. It's just that he's mentioned more than a few times how the man didn't do his duty during the war. Paying three hundred dollars to avoid serving. He bristles a bit whenever he's around your Mr. Ross."

"My Mr. Ross! Hannah, I'm just having supper and seeing a play with him."

"Yes, and you be careful. He has a reputation as a ladies' man."

Katie chuckled. "I am grateful for your concern. After being on my own and nursing rough men, well, I think I can handle Mr. Ross."

"Hmph," Hannah said before taking a sip of her coffee.

A horse's snort had Katie out of her chair. She walked over to the window and pushed aside the curtain. Brett had Mouse saddled up and hitched to the back-porch post. "I'm going out to the pine valley and then to the gypsy camp to see Suzanne."

"That may not be a good idea. You going alone."

"I'll take my new gun. Brett has already warned me about the rattlers, bobcats . . ."

"And murderer," Hannah added.

Katie raised her eyebrows. Yes, a murderer too." She left the kitchen and called over her shoulder from the stairs. "I'll be careful."

In her bedroom she slipped on her trousers, and then hid them with her skirt. After pulling her boots back on, she opened the nightstand drawer and pulled out a five-inch pearl handled pistol.

Katie studied the gun so intently that the knock on the door made her jump. "Come in."

Hannah opened the door and then leaned on the door frame. She glanced at the gun in Katie's hand. "You know how to use that?"

"Not really. Philip gave it to me the other night, said I might need it, but he was tired and didn't do much explaining." She turned the gun in her hand. "It's so small. I'm not glad to be carrying a gun, but I can see their necessity. I'll ask Brett to show me how to use it." She paused. "Unless you know."

Hannah walked toward Katie and put out her hand. Katie put the gun in Hannah's palm.

"It's a Pepperbox. Where are the cartridges?"

Katie pulled open the nightstand drawer and drew out a box, which she opened.

Hannah put four cartridges on the nightstand. She pointed the gun toward the window. "One click rotates the firing pin. The second fires the gun." She pulled the hammer so that it clicked once and pointed it toward the window. The firing pin rotated whenever Hannah pulled the hammer. "That's how the gun works. It's breach loaded." She cocked the hammer and then pressed a button under the barrel and slid the barrel forward. "Did you see how I did that?"

"Let me try."

Hannah handed the gun over.

Katie practiced and then gave the pistol back. Hannah picked up a cartridge from the nightstand and held it up. "These are twenty-two caliber shorts, so there's less powder in the bullet, accurate for about ten to fifteen feet. So it's only for short range. And here's an important bit of advice: if someone is dangerous, do not let him get close. Shoot him while he's too far to grab this out of your hand and use it against you."

Hannah loaded the four cartridges into the chamber and shut the barrel. Then she opened the barrel again and tilted the gun so that the cartridges dropped into her palm. "Now you do it."

Katie repeated the loading and unloading of the gun. "Whew, this is a process. How did you learn to fire a gun?"

"Your father gave me a similar one and taught me how to use it. Trust me, this is much simpler than the old ball, primer, and ramrod days. Take some practice shots out by the old barn. I'll talk to Brett. He'll help."

Katie pointed the gun at the open window. "Papa thought I should have it. Stuart's murder probably got him thinking about the possibility of an attack on me."

"He had that gun ordered for you months ago. The war causes us to think hard about protection and rightly so. You need to be careful. Someone out there killed Stuart and now you're asking questions."

Katie brought the pistol back down to her side and gingerly put the gun in her pocket. She picked up the leather satchel and put the box of cartridges inside it. As she was pulling the strap over her head, she said, "I talked to Papa about possible grudges or rivalries concerning Stuart, but he couldn't think of any. How about you?"

"No. The marshal thinks Stuart's crossing the valley made him an easy target." Hannah pursed her lips. "I would feel better if you would at least take Brett with you. He's an ace shot."

"No, I want time to think."

Hannah shook her head in disapproval. "Very well." She pursed her lip, then said, "Best to put that gun in your saddle bag when you're riding and keep it with you when you're on foot."

CHAPTER 9

TROUBLE IN THE VALLEY

Monday afternoon, June 19, 1865

After shooting practice with Brett, Katie rode to the valley alone. She tethered Mouse to a tree on the ridge and walked down the valley path, closely examining the brush for torn cloth or other evidence. Finding none, she sighed in frustration. Too much time had passed. If only she had come home sooner. She sat on a large flat rock near the stream.

As she peered at the water, the sun reflected off a small shiny object wedged beneath a rock. Katie took off her shoes and stockings, rolled up her britches, and waded into the water. Using one hand she gathered up her voluminous skirt, with the other she reached for the shiny object and drew it out of the water. It was a silver ring with a large emerald surrounded by tiny diamonds.

"Jesus, Mary, and Joseph," she exclaimed, as she held it aloft. The silver band would fit on a large man's finger. Who could it belong to? The murderer?

The bottom of her skirt fell into the water. "Damn."

98

A voice rang through the valley from the ridge. "What a fine surprise!"

Danior, the lecherous gypsy who had led them into the camp on Saturday, stood with his arms akimbo.

He had large hands and gypsies seemed to prefer silver. Was this his ring? Had he come back to retrieve it? She drew in a breath and the hair on the back of her neck rose in alarm. Was he Stuart's murderer? What possible reason would he have to come to the valley except to search for the ring.

She tucked the ring into her skirt pocket. "Damn." She'd left her gun in the saddlebag. Mouse was tethered to a tree over three hundred feet away up on the ridge.

Danior walked briskly toward her, grabbing small tree branches and bushes as he descended.

The heaviness of panic rose in her chest. She took a deep breath to bring herself under control. She turned her back to Danior, sat down on the large rock nearby and quickly fastened her stockings and pulled down her pant legs. She swiveled her seat on the rock so that she was now facing him and glanced up after buckling her shoes. Danior had stopped to watch.

Her heart was racing, but she would mind her own business and casually walk up the steeper path to avoid him. Danior was taking the longer path that traversed the valley. He stopped and stumbled, grabbing a bush to right himself. She realized he was drunk.

She kept her head down, paying close attention to the path as Danior drew parallel to her on the other path. The paths came close at this point.

She picked up her pace as she headed toward the ridge. Danior stumbled as he crossed the brush between the paths. He was now following her up the steeper path. She gained a few more feet and then glanced over her shoulder.

Danior paused to catch his breath. "I thought I recognized your horse, a fine horse for a fine lady all alone talking to the fish." He laughed.

So Danior had heard her exclamation when she found the ring. Had he been there early enough to see her retrieve the ring from the stream and put it in her pocket? "This is the location of my brother's death. I feel very close to him here as if I could talk to him." She turned back toward the hill and resumed her climb.

"Maybe you need somebody to hold you until you feel better." He quickened his pace and Katie matched his speed. Her skirt heavy with the stream water slowed her down, allowing Danior to reach her. He grabbed her by the arm and pulled her toward him. His foul breath nearly made her retch. She pulled away, but he kept a tight grip on her arm. "Or maybe you just need some fun, some Roma fun to cheer you." He pulled her closer.

Katie tried to pull away, but Danior's grip was strong. "Let me go," she shouted. She moved to the side causing him to have an awkward grip on her arm and she broke free. She scurried up the hill, wondering if she would faint from hyperventilating. She concentrated on controlling her breathing. The path near the top of the ridge was steep. To gain speed, she used both her hands and feet to climb.

Katie felt a tug on her skirt. Was she caught on some brush? She turned.

No, Danior had pulled on the hem of her skirt. She stumbled and fell against the hill but quickly pushed herself up.

She wasn't quick enough.

Danior fell on top of her, pushing her back down. He shoved her face into the dirt. A small rock connected with her cheekbone, but she hardly felt the pain. Her mind was sharper and the adrenalin coursing through her body made her feel stronger. She'd feel the pain later, but for now she was glad for the advantage it gave.

Danior turned her over and was soon on top of her. He grabbed both her hands and pulled her arms above her head with one hand. She pulled one hand away and he tried again using both of his hands to secure her hands. His grip was strong. He secured both of Katie's hands again in one hand and used the other to bring her skirt up to her thighs.

His breath nauseated her as he tried to kiss her. She turned her head to the side and tried to push him away with her body. He was too heavy to move.

"No!" she screamed.

Danior moved his hand from her thighs to cover her mouth and nose. She had trouble breathing and wildly shook her head. He removed his hand.

She gulped in the air.

He adjusted his hold so that he held her arms with the crook of his arm and elbow. His hand then went up her skirt to her waist. She kicked and cried out, "Leave me go!"

Danior covered her mouth with his to muffle her cries, trying to kiss her. She clamped her mouth shut. Danior's other hand fumbling with the buttons of her trousers.

"What's this?" Drink had rattled his thinking enough that the buttons on her trousers under her skirt caused him confusion. He reared up to look, relaxing his grip on Katie's arms.

It was just the break Katie needed. She freed her arm and gave his chest a hard, fast shove. He rolled down the incline a few feet before he was stopped by a large angular rock. The point hit him squarely in the back. There was a change in his heavy breathing. The rock had knocked the wind out of him. But a moment later he surged to his feet again, angry now and more determined than ever.

Katie scrambled up the hill again. Her foot caught on her water-soaked skirt and made her trip. She righted herself. She was near the top of the ridge. Mouse whinnied and stomped, frightened by the conflict. Would the horse break her lightly tied reins and run?

As she reached the crest of the ridge, Danior grabbed her skirt and then her hair. She lost her balance and fell back against him. He was even more aggressive now and flipped her over, pushing himself on top of her.

This part of the hill was pitted with rocks. Two of them were digging into her back. Again, he pulled her arms above her head, covered her mouth with his, and lifted her skirt and fumbled with the buttons on her trousers. Katie slipped one of her hands free. Danior was so intent on the buttons, he didn't notice. She reached down to her side. Her hand closed over a fist-sized rock. She worked to dislodge it from the dirt. Danior continued to struggle with the buttons and finally ripped them off. His hand reached into her trousers as she clawed at the dirt with her fingers.

She finally dislodged the rock and gripped it.

Danior pulled away. "You're a feisty one, aren't ya?"

When he tried to kiss her again, she lifted the rock and smashed it against the back of his head, once, twice, three times. She watched as his eyes shifted from surprise to oblivion. His body became slack. He fell to her side, unconscious.

Katie pushed herself away from him. Was he dead?

She glanced at his chest, which rose and fell. She hadn't killed him. She took several deep breaths to quiet her nerves.

She climbed the steep incline to the top of the ridge. Danior's horse was tethered to a tree. She walked over and released it, giving it a slap on the rear. The horse bolted, taking the path that led back to the gypsy camp.

Her trousers kept slipping over her hips because she had lost two buttons during Danior's attack. She glanced back at Danior who was still unconscious and lifted her skirt to tuck the waistband of her trousers into the waistband of her petticoat. She walked over to Mouse and untethered her reins with shaking hands. Coming off the adrenaline rush, Katie's legs shook, which made Mouse skittish. Moving Mouse near a large flat rock, she stood on the rock and used her hands to guide her left foot into the stirrup, and then grabbed a hold of the saddle's pommel and swung herself into the saddle.

Mouse craned her long neck toward Katie, ears back. Once she was seated, Mouse shot forward.

Glancing behind to check on Danior, she was relieved to see he was still unconscious. She was safe for the moment. Mouse galloped on the path for home.

As frightening as Danior was, he was not a problem anymore, and running away wasn't going to solve any mysteries. She still had many questions and Suzanne might provide answers. Should she return to the gypsy camp? Katie slowed the horse to a stop. Leaning over in the saddle, she hugged Mouse's neck and made soothing noises. "It's all right," she whispered, wondering who she was trying to convince, the horse or herself.

A pounding of horse hooves in the distance caught her attention. She sat up. A rider was coming her way. She could see the dark outline of a tall man on horseback. He wore a broad brimmed hat, but he was too far away for Katie to make out his face.

The rider slowed his pace then stopped. Had he seen her? His horse reared up as he turned sharply, and then he galloped off in the same direction he had come. "That was odd, and a bit suspicious, wasn't it, Mouse?" Had her presence interrupted a meeting between Danior and the rider?

Calming the horse had calmed her. Her hands had stopped shaking, making it safe to pull the gun from her saddlebag and put it in her pocket. She switched her hands on the reins and felt for the ring in her other pocket.

In the struggle with Danior, she had nearly forgotten about it, but the ring was still safely tucked away. A ring so valuable and unique might lead her to the murderer. The first person she'd ask about it would be Suzanne. The ring could very well belong to Danior. But if that's what had brought him back to the valley, what had brought the mysterious rider?

Katie waited a few minutes and drank from her canteen. Her nerves were settled now, and she was feeling more confident with her gun as protection. She turned the horse around. Avoiding the ridge, she took another path to the Roma camp. She needed to talk to Suzanne.

* * *

Suzanne was pulling sun-dried clothes from a bush when Katie rode into the camp. The men were busy with a variety of tasks, checking the wheels of their vardos, brushing down horses, and pulling down the temporary fencing. The men stopped their work and turned to follow Katie's movements. Her hair was disheveled and her skirt wet and torn.

Suzanne watched Katie as she approached and then turned and scowled at the men. Some shrugged their shoulders and returned to work. Others turned to their tasks but gave a backward glance to Katie. When she neared Suzanne, Katie dismounted. In a low voice she said, "Danior attacked me by the stream where Stuart died."

Suzanne's face shifted. The lines of her mouth and eyes changing quickly from the tension of alarm to the softening contours of sympathy. "Are you all right?"

"Yes." Katie pushed stray hairs from her face with a dirty hand. "I'm fine."

Suzanne took the reins from Katie and tied Mouse to a nearby tree.

"Would you send someone to check on him? I knocked him unconscious with a rock." She paused. "At least I think that's all I did."

Suzanne smirked. "He has a hard head. He will live." She turned to the group of men taking down the makeshift corral. "Tomas."

Tomas turned to give Suzanne his full attention. He walked towards the women, donning the shirt that he had grabbed from a nearby post, and buttoned it as he approached. Tomas was tall, lean, handsome, and quick to respond to Suzanne's summons. Was he in love with Suzanne, Katie wondered. How had Tomas felt about Stuart's visits?

Suzanne adjusted the freshly dried clothes to the crook of her arm. "Would you go pick up that drunken Danior? He's fallen off his horse again. Last seen in the pine valley, the valley with the shallow crossing."

Tomas glanced at Katie and then nodded. He called to the men. "I'm off to get that fool, Danior."

The men grumbled in acknowledgment as Tomas walked toward the line of horses tethered at the edge of the camp. The rest of the men went back to their work. Danior's horse returned. Tomas was in no rush to retrieve Danior, but he took Danior's horse with him when he left.

Suzanne took Katie by the elbow and directed her toward her vardo. "We will go inside. We can talk in private, and you can wash up."

Herbs, pots, and dishes were stacked on a small table in the corner. Everything was in disarray, where before it had been tidy.

Suzanne placed the clean clothes she had gathered on a bench and motioned for Katie to take a seat at the table. The vargo had a Dutch door. Suzanne closed the lower portion and drew a curtain over the upper half. A small breeze blew through the light fabric giving some relief from the heat. Suzanne lit a lamp. "Please sit."

As she did, Katie glanced at the floor where the old book had been during her previous visit and jostled the floor length tablecloth for a peek below. The book was gone. She glanced up to see Suzanne watching her. Suzanne said nothing as she poured water from a pitcher into a large bowl. She put the bowl, a small cloth, a hand mirror, and a comb in front of Katie. "You should wash your face and fix your hair."

Katie looked in the mirror. "Oh, I am a fright."

Suzanne nodded. "Is that dirt or a bruise on your cheek."

"A bruise," Katie replied ruefully. Danior pushed my face into the dirt. My cheek connected with a rock."

"He should be sent packing. The pig!"

"Agreed, just don't send him from your clan near Liberty," Katie said as she delicately washed the bruised area of her face.

Suzanne poured her a small glass of whiskey. Katie tasted it tentatively at first and then finished the whiskey in one more swallow. After refreshing her face and hair, Katie pulled the emerald ring from her pocket. "I found this in the shallow crossing where Stuart was murdered."

Suzanne's eyes widened. "That may be valuable."

"Have you ever seen it before?"

Suzanne shook her head.

"Stuart wasn't wearing it?"

"I would have noticed such a ring. Where did you find it?"

"Half hidden under a rock in the valley stream. You're sure it's not Danior's or Tomas' ring?"

Suzanne pursed her lips. "No, I would have told you."

"I just wondered why Danior would revisit the valley where my brother was murdered. What would bring him there?"

"Who knows? If he's drunk, he was probably searching for you. After this stupidity, we will keep him close to our camp, so you will be safe." Suzanne picked up the bowl of water and cloth, pulled aside the curtains, and threw the dirty water toward the grass on the side of the vardo. She scanned the surrounding area before she turned back to Katie. "A bit of advice, I would not flash that ring around too much. It may be a way to identify the murderer, but it may also cause the murderer to react in fear."

"Probably good advice. Thank you."

Suzanne put her hand out. "May I see it?"

Katie handed Suzanne the ring.

Suzanne brought out a magnifying glass from a nearby drawer and inspected the gemstone. "This is very valuable indeed. She slid the ring across the table to Katie. "I told you once already to beware, now I will repeat my warning. Do not act as your brother did and ignore me. I saw grave danger in your cards. Be cautious."

Katie gestured to the floor beneath them. "The big book that was on the floor when I had my fortune told interests me. May I see it?"

"A family book, my mother gave it to me." She shrugged. "A book handed down for many generations. Few know of it, and I would like to keep it that way. My mother died last year. She was a Shivani."

Katie's face must have shown her confusion at not understanding the word.

"A Gorgio word. 'Shivani' would be a gypsy witch."

"So your mother's book contains spells."

Suzanne shook her head. "Spell is a strong word. I learned much from her, but not all that she knew. I will tell you this since I have involved you in my, as you call it, spell. Stuart spoke very highly of you. He admired your spirit and intelligence. I used one of my mother's incantations to entice you to seek justice for Stuart, to find his murderer."

"Hmph, there was no need for that. I would have done so anyway."

Suzanne lifted an eyebrow as if in disbelief. She got up and moved the Dutch door curtain aside, checking outside again. She returned to her seat and lowered her voice to a whisper, "I am not yet as skilled as my mother, but I promised Stuart that his murderer would be found and punished. It is only right. I could not heal his physical form, but I could give him peace. He and I seek justice, not revenge. That is why the tarot card for justice was found in the valley. I used it as I recited the words to make you seek his murderer."

Katie bit her lower lip remembering Brett's observation. The woman's footprints Brett saw at the stream's edge were Suzanne's. "So you were with Stuart when he died."

Suzanne sighed. "Yes."

"Do you know who killed him?"

"No, I do not." Suzanne sat forward, her body leaning over the table. "I would tell you if I knew, even if it was one of my clan. Do you not understand that I loved your brother? That I too grieve for him?"

Suzanne gripped Katie's hands. "I found Stuart after he had been shot. I cradled him in my arms as he took his last breath." Tears threatened. "I asked him if he knew who shot him. He said the man stood on the ridge with his back to the sun. Stuart could see only the man's outline. He was tall and wore a hat with a large brim. That is all he could tell me."

Katie's eyes widened. "How is it that you were in the valley?"

"I was gathering herbs nearby." Suzanne paused for a moment, focused on her hands, and then lifted her chin. "No, that is not true. I followed him as he made his way home. I was frightened for him. I had seen terrible danger in the cards."

Katie's voice grew loud with excitement. "Did you see any evidence of the murderer?"

"Shh, please talk quietly." Suzanne stood and pushed back the curtain on the door again.

"I'm sorry," Katie said.

Suzanne released the curtain and returned to her seat.

Katie composed herself folding her hands on the table like an attentive student. "So, you are a witch?"

Suzanne nodded. "Like my mother, I am a Shivani." Suzanne motioned with her head toward the door and the men outside. "They do not like me practicing my craft with Gorgio. Some in my clan are jealous of my power, as they were of my mother. So I am cautious. No. I did not see the murderer. I walked my horse, searching for herbs while I followed Stuart. He was far ahead of me."

"You came upon him at what time?" Katie asked.

"Shortly after he would have arrived at the stream, late morning. I knew the place where he would be crossing. It is a familiar route. The stream is wide but shallow there."

Katie mused, "So a good spot to ambush Stuart if the murderer knew he would be coming home."

"That is probably so, but I saw no one in the area when I arrived. The thief was quick to steal away with Stuart's horse and gun. Stuart died in my arms, but I had to leave him. I was too afraid. My people are blamed for crimes we do not commit."

"Like murder? "Were all your people accounted for?"

Suzanne's eyes grew dark, her voice flat, "Yes."

"How about Danior? Where was he? Stuart's horse was taken, and we both know Danior has a way with horses."

"I will find out. See if anyone remembers seeing him with a new horse that day. I was very upset when I returned. My people will remember more of what happened on that day because of it."

"Would you recognize Stuart's horse if you were to see it again?"

Suzanne stared at the table with concentration evident on her face. "Mostly black, with four white feet." She shook her head. "We have no horse with markings like that."

"Danior could have hidden Stuart's horse or sold it." Katie straightened her posture, anger welling up with Suzanne's lack of answers. "Danior tried to rape me. I'm sure the marshal would be interested in knowing that. I wouldn't put it past Danior to murder Stuart for his horse and saddle."

"No! Please do not bring Gorgio! I will ask about the horse and Danior's whereabouts on that day. Unlike your family, many Gorgios treat us like dogs. There could be a mob lynching. The innocent might suffer."

"I ought to prosecute him if not for myself then to save some other poor woman from an even worse outcome."

"I will tell the elders what happened. He will suffer consequences. I promise."

Both women were silent for a moment.

Katie blew out a long breath. "I'll trust you to take care of this matter within your clan. But in return, you must help me."

"I will talk to the men to be sure Danior was sleeping off his drink when Stuart was murdered. He may have been jealous of Stuart, but he is not a murderer."

"Danior was jealous of Stuart? Is Danior in love with you?"

Suzanne made a face of disgust. "I would have nothing to do with that pig, and he knows it."

Katie could believe that..

In the distance children yelled to one another and a woman laughed. Suzanne stood. "You must go now. The women are returning with their strawberries. They already think I spend too much time with the Gorgio."

Katie stood and paused at the vardo's door.

Suzanne's eyes grew wide, and she took ahold of Katie's arm. "Wait. Something else may be important. It is about a didicoy. He may live in Liberty."

Katie turned back to Suzanne. "Didicoy?"

"Only half Roma. The man's father was Irish." She let go of Katie's arm. "Milo is with another clan; it was he who told me about a didicoy he rode the rails with as a boy. When our clans meet for festivals, Milo tries to impress me. So I pass his comments off as big talk. Now I am beginning to wonder."

"This friend, he may know something about the murderer?" Katie asked.

"Perhaps." Her hands made a shooing gesture. "Go now. I do not want you here when Danior returns. Come see me tomorrow. Come with the man buying the horse. I will tell you more then."

CHAPTER 10

GYPSIES FLEE

Tuesday morning, June 20, 1865

Katie walked into the kitchen and put her straw hat on the hook near the porch door. She turned around to address Hannah. "The gypsies left." She shook her head. "I can't believe it."

"I'm not surprised." Hannah removed the coffee pot from the back burner of the stove. "They can't risk staying nearby after Danior's attack on you yesterday."

Hannah lifted the coffee pot slightly in Katie's direction.

"Yes, please." Katie walked to the kitchen sink, gave the pump a few pushes, and washed her hands. Florence Nightingale's pronouncements on cleanliness caused Katie's handwashing to become a habit. She turned toward Hannah as she dried her hands. "Hank was mad as a March hare. He wanted nothing further to do with the *gyppos* as he called them."

Katie sat down and Hannah gave her a cup of coffee.

"Hank makes a good point." Katie's eyes narrowed. "Who does that? Who tells you to come out and buy one of their horses and leaves before the sale? I told Suzanne I wasn't going to make trouble for them."

Hannah gave a gentle smile. "They have too much history on their side that tells them otherwise. Did Hank give you a better description for Spirit, Stuart's horse?"

Katie pulled a well-worn piece of paper out of her pocket and put it on the table. "Yes, I'll write that description for the newspaper." She paused. "Here's the real problem. At the first sign of trouble, Suzanne runs. So how can I trust her?"

"They're frightened." Hannah brought a plate of asparagus from the sink over to the table and sat down in front of the cutting board. "Your family is prominent in Liberty and Danior attacked you. Suzanne may be influential in her clan, but she's not in charge. They have a council of men that make decisions."

Katie lifted her shoulder. "Of course, they do. Why would a woman have any say?"

Hannah picked up on Katie's sarcasm. "The war has changed you, child." She paused. "Colleen told me this morning there's talk around town about how you insist on doing the marshal's work, men's work."

Katie chuckled. "Sounds like I ruffled the marshal's feathers."

Hannah looked up from her work. "There's been talk."

"Let me guess, Henrietta Debois, the biggest gossip in the county and her horsey-faced daughter."

Hannah chuckled, "Yes, I'm afraid so."

"I am not going to let those women stop me. Oh, and besides I can't stop." Katie tilted her head. "Suzanne put a spell on me."

"What?"

"A spell so that I find Stuart's murderer. She told me that yesterday."

Hannah shook her head. "If that's so, I'm glad of it."

Katie sighed. "How about giving me a bit of credit for my own wish to seek justice?"

Hannah took Katie's hand across the table. "I do wish you'd be more discreet though. The talk in town . . ."

"How in all that's holy am I supposed to be more discreet? First, you're glad I'm searching for Stuart's murderer and then you ask me to be more discreet. You need to make up your mind."

"Shh, please you'll wake your father." Hannah patted Katie's hand. "I just worry about your reputation."

"I know, but I have to ask questions, or I'll never learn anything." Katie blew out a long breath, composing herself. "The ride with Hank did have some merits. We had a nice long chat once Hank got tired of cussing out the gypsies." Katie took a sip of her coffee. Hannah's coffee was strong, so Katie doused it with cream and stirred it as she spoke. "Hank said that Stuart's passing was really hard on Liam."

Hannah picked up an asparagus spear and methodically cut off the end, her eyes focused on the vegetables as she talked. "Stu and Liam had been friends for many years. I can't remember a time when Liam didn't spend his summers in Liberty. Can you?"

Katie shook her head. "Good memories. We looked forward to his visits as soon as school let out. It was cause for celebration when Mrs. West would come to Liberty in her fancy carriage for a visit with her brother. We knew we'd have Liam for three months."

"Stuart was always a bit sad when Liam returned home in September," Hannah said.

"I'm sure he hated to see Liam go, but I suspect it was the beginning of the school year that brought on Stu's autumn melancholy."

"Stuart never took to schooling the way you did. He was good for Liam though, who tended to be too serious. Stuart knew how to have a good time. It was a nice balance."

"All that seriousness paid off. Liam is a good doctor. Meghan swears by him."

Hannah smiled. "He learned from the best. Old Doc Coughlin may not have known all the latest techniques and medicines, but he was honest, and his patients trusted him. Liam has plenty of old-timers that need to be coaxed a bit when it comes to new ideas. And after so many summers here, Liam knows how to handle Mrs. Dubois and her lot." She shook her head. "I do feel a bit sorry for Dr. Stephens, Liam's new assistant."

"I know of him." Katie tilted her head. "Why do you feel sorry for him?"

"The women in the Dubois circle are making his life miserable with their complaining and gossip."

"Mrs. Dubois cornered me at the church coffee to complain about Dr. Stephens. That woman can be a formidable force in this town."

Katie tilted her head. "I'm puzzled by Papa's grudge against Mr. Ross for not re-enlisting. Liam never enlisted in the war. He signed on as a contract surgeon, but Papa doesn't hold that against him, as he does with Mr. Ross."

"That was a different situation. When Doc Coughlin died, Liberty needed a doctor. Liam returned to fill that need. But privately, I also think he'd had his fill of war doctoring."

"I did miss a lot while I was away." Katie stood.

"And where are you going now?"

"Out to cause more gossip."

"You really do need to watch your p's and q's, young lady."

"I'm going into town to talk to Liam. I want to see if he knows of any old grudges or motives for Stu's murder."

"Sit down and relax. Liam will be here for dinner tonight. Mr. Overmeyer's bringing over your father's new will. Liam and Mr. Schneider are to be witnesses. I'll ask them both for supper, which I'm sure they'll accept. And you can talk to Liam then." Hannah chuckled. "Although Liam's mother won't like that, two suppers here in one week! And Mrs. Dubois will be the first to tell her about it. She writes to the woman often, and she brags about their friendship." Hannah shook her head. "Mrs. Dubois is always trying to curry favor with Mrs. West."

"How would Mrs. Dubois know Liam's whereabouts?"

"You'd be surprised what that woman knows."

"Maybe I'll call on her some time so she can tell me who killed my brother."

"If she knew, it would be all over town." Hannah paused. "Mrs. West has been after Liam for a visit home, and he's begged off with excuses about his busy workload."

"Mothers do like to see their sons. I can't say that I blame her for that."

"There's a bit more to it. In her eyes, it's fine if he must work in Liberty for a time to gain experience, but she fears he's getting too settled." With a slight catch in her throat, Hannah continued. "Her plan is to have him move back to Cleveland. Since the war's ended, she's become even more insistent."

Katie sat back down. "You've talked to her?"

"Meghan's told me about the contents of the letters Mrs. West sends to Liam."

"Isn't that interesting. Meghan knows the contents of Liam's letters. Hmm." Katie paused. "And if I'm not mistaken, I'd say you don't like the woman."

Hannah's hands rested on her cutting board. "Bertha West is arrogant and pompous. How such a delightful young man came from her upbringing is a surprise to me. If Mrs. West has her way, Liam will marry the daughter of one of her friends and set up a practice in Cleveland."

"Doctoring in Cleveland among the wealthy might be easier and would certainly be more lucrative. Doctoring is not an easy life here in Liberty. I would imagine far more fulfilling, though."

Hannah lifted her eyebrows. "Are you still thinking of pursuing this silly notion of becoming a doctor?"

"I am." Katie turned on her heels and left the room.

* * *

Katie arrived at the town jail in the pony cart right after the marshal had returned from lunch. She found a nice shady spot for Mouse and tied her up at a post near the square. She could see Liam tonight, but she still had business with the marshal. Within a few minutes, the marshal had signed off on the article describing Stuart's horse and assumed she would deliver it to the newspaper office herself. His manner was brusque, bordering on rude.

She walked over to *The Gazette* office, a small-framed white building with a dark green door and awnings. Katie waved to two acquaintances across the street and called out, "Good afternoon." Instead of returning her greeting, one woman whispered to the other, and they both turned away.

Katie had attended school with these women. She slowed her step as she took the three broad stairs to the newspaper's entrance. She didn't like to think she was affected by the snub, but it saddened her. She lifted her chin in defiance.

When she walked through the door, Katie was hit with a strong inky smell. The newspaper reception area had a four-foot-high counter, which ran across the width of the building. Sunshine streamed through the long, streaked windows, making a bright work area for two young men. A dull pounding in the backroom drowned out the little tinkering bell that should have announced her arrival.

A teenage boy looked up from his sweeping. He propped the broom in the corner by an unlit stove and then walked to the counter. "What can we do for you, ma'am?"

"First of all, I have an article from the marshal's office that he and I would like to see published. The marshal assured me that could be done. He signed off on it."

"Yes, ma'am. We begin printing this week's paper on Thursday morning."

Katie took the article she had written from her reticule. She handed it to the boy.

His lips moved as he silently read it.

MAE McGRAW

Marshal Gerber has recently learned information regarding Stuart Reynolds' murder. The murder is still unsolved, but it is suspected that Reynolds' horse, Spirit, may be in the area. The horse is a chestnut gelding with a blaze. Its back legs have socks, and the front have coronets. If you see this horse, please report its whereabouts to Marshal Gerber. Your report may be given anonymously.

The boy folded the letter. "Very good, ma'am. I'll see that Mr. Weeks gets this."

"Thank you." Katie lifted her chin. She had an idea. "Do you keep the files of old newspapers at this location?"

"Yes, ma'am, five cents an hour. We have a room in the back."

The boy walked over to the swinging doors built into the counter and with a flourish opened one side of it. "This way, please."

Katie followed the boy through a wide aisle divided by the desks. When one of the young men working turned her way, a finger's width of blue ink followed his cheekbone where he must have touched it with an ink-stained finger. Her mouth curved into a smile, and then she bit her lip to hide her amusement. The other man must have seen her reaction. He looked over at his colleague's face, pointed, and laughed. The drum of the presses muted their words and laughter.

Once beyond the desks, the boy stopped and opened a door on the right that led to a small room with two chairs and a large scarred wooden table. Once inside he pulled the door closed. Katie welcomed the slight reprieve from the pounding noise, which had increased as they approached the back of the newspaper office. "Is it always so noisy in here?"

"No, ma'am, but we're running a pamphlet today. What dates are you interested in reading?" With a flourish of his arm he offered Katie a seat.

"I would like to see the newspaper from June ninth."

The boy nodded, departed, then returned and handed the newspaper to Katie. She glanced at the headline. "Stuart Reynolds Found Murdered in Valley."

"Thank you." Katie swallowed, holding back the sorrow triggered by the headline. "I'm trying to learn more about Stuart Reynolds' murder. He's my brother." She checked the by-line. "Caleb Brown wrote this article. May I speak to him?"

"He's not here right now."

"Will he be back soon? I can wait."

The boy lowered his head. "No, he probably won't be back until evening. He's out covering the horse race in Wordsworth."

Katie gave him a tight smile, and then said, "You wanted to go with him."

"Yes, ma'am."

"If you think Mr. Brown will be in the office tomorrow, I'll come back then."

"He'll come out to see you. You're out at the Reynolds place, aren't you?"

"Why, yes, I'm staying with my family."

"He'll probably stop out tomorrow. He wants to interview you about your war nursing."

"Oh, I see."

"Let me know if you need anything else."

"Thank you." Katie picked up the newspaper. Caleb Brown reported Stuart had been shot in the shoulder from a distance. She scanned the article and read an account similar to what Brett and Marshal Gerber had reported. "According to Dr. West, Stuart Reynolds had bled out by the stream's edge. He died shortly after the fatal shot."

Katie visualized Stuart's death scene at the creek bed. She leaned back in her chair, her hands gripping the armrest. Her anger at the injustice renewed. Regardless of gossiping women and a reluctant marshal, she would find Stuart's murderer. Stuart deserved justice.

She stood. She had nothing more to learn here. Katie returned the newspaper and paid the boy. She needed refreshment and solace. A cup of tea with Meghan would help on both accounts.

* * *

Meghan was at her sewing machine when Katie arrived at the shop. "Welcome," Meghan called out. "What brings you into town two days in a row?"

"Research. I was over at the marshal's and then the newspaper office. Do you have time for a cup of tea?"

"Yes, tea's warming on the stove." With her hands filled with fabric, Meghan directed Katie to the tea with the movement of her head. "Pour yourself a cup."

Katie stepped through the curtain to the little kitchenette which doubled as the shop's dressing room.

Meghan called Katie from her sewing machine. "I'll be done here in five minutes. Pour me a cup too."

Katie was fixing their tea behind the curtain of the kitchenette when the little bell above the door rang.

"Oh, Tricia, good afternoon," Meghan said.

Katie peeked through the split in the kitchenette curtain. So this was Tricia. The woman with the stitched lip and the secret lover. She was certainly beautiful even with a swollen lip.

"I've finished hemming the dresses you gave me," Tricia said.

Meghan got up from her sewing machine. "And so fast too. I didn't think you'd have these done until tomorrow."

Meghan took the wooden handles of the large cloth bags that Tricia offered, pulled a dress from it, and then hung it on a high rack with other colorful dresses at various stages of completion. Tricia did the same with the dress in the other bag. Meghan examined the hems. "You do beautiful work. Let me get money out of the register to pay you." Meghan walked to the register and opened the drawer. "Can you stay for a cup of tea?"

Katie was just about to announce herself when Tricia spoke. "No, I must be going."

"Wait, I have another dress for you to hem." Meghan closed the register.

"I'm so sorry, I know I promised to help you with the hand sewing, but I can't now."

"Is it your bruised lip? Are you in much pain?"

Tricia put her hand to her lips. "No, the stitching's itchy, but Dr. West said that would happen." Meghan walked over to Tricia took her hand and put coins in Tricia's palm. "Do you need more money? Just let me know what you think is reasonable. We can work something out."

"Oh, no, that's not it at all. You pay me well enough." Tricia studied her shoes. "I love the work. It's just that I won't be able to do it anymore. I'm afraid that I can't tell you why." Her voice thickened. "I can't."

Katie busied herself with their tea while she eavesdropped on their conversation. The teapot was on a table near Meghan's showcase window. A full-length screen of white shutters allowed Katie to see the sidewalk and street through the wooden slats. A man was standing in front of Meghan's dress shop. She could only see his profile. He looked familiar, but she couldn't place him. Was this Tricia's lover?

Meghan said, "Tricia, please tell me what's wrong."

Tricia's voice lowered as if she was holding back her emotions. "I'm sorry. I can't. I hope we can remain friends."

The bell tinkled as the door opened and then closed.

Meghan called out, "Katie, did you hear all that?"

Katie didn't answer Meghan. She didn't want any sound to alert the man to look toward the window. Meghan's footfall approached. Katie turned at the screech of the drapery rings when Meghan pulled back the curtain to the kitchenette.

"What are you doing?" Meghan asked.

Katie put an index finger to her mouth and then spoke in a whispered voice. "I think this is Tricia's lover. Hmm, maybe not. Tricia didn't acknowledge him when she left. Is he following Tricia? Yes, he is following her. Come here. If you look through these little slots, you can see him. Hurry, he's walking away now."

Meghan walked to the window. "Yes, so? No one can see in. I've checked. I use this room as a dressing room because you can't see in from the sidewalk, the distance is too great."

"Wait, look. It's that man again from yesterday and he followed Tricia." Katie took Meghan's arm. "While you were talking with Tricia, the man with a matchstick waited, standing right outside this window."

"What man with the matchstick?"

Katie gave a heavy sigh. "The man who just followed Tricia now. It's the same man who watched us go into the marshal's office yesterday."

Meghan put her hand to her mouth. "Is he watching us?"

"No, he isn't watching us." Katie pinched her lips, exasperation evident in her tone. "He's following Tricia. He wasn't out there when I arrived. I was about to pour our tea, and I heard heavy footsteps. I peeked through the slats and saw the man's back at the edge of your picture window. Since I thought it would be awkward to step out when you and Tricia were talking, I watched him for a few minutes."

Meghan grabbed a little basket of sewing articles. "Let's go."

"Where are we going?"

"I'm going to follow Tricia. If anybody asks, I'll say she forgot her sewing basket. I have a very vicious pair of scissors in this basket that she or I can use if necessary."

"I'll go with you."

Tricia was walking fast, so Katie and Meghan fell behind walking much slower, not wishing to draw attention to themselves. "I wonder if she's in any danger. She's been acting odd lately."

"How so?"

"More secretive than usual. She's always been a private person, but even more so lately. And then that attack the other night. Well, her explanation didn't ring true."

They reached the tree-lined walkway to Tricia's little white house. Pots of red geraniums were on each side of the door. Starched white curtains draped in each of the front windows.

Meghan glanced around. "I don't see the man that was tracking Tricia, do you?"

Katie turned and scanned the woods across from Tricia's house. He could be hiding in those trees. He had dark clothes and may have slipped in while we approached the curve in the road."

Meghan knocked urgently on Tricia's door.

Tricia came to the door, her eyes and nose red from crying. She seemed startled to see the women and then her eyes widened as she scanned the street. "Why are you here? You must go away."

Meghan handed the basket to Tricia. "You forgot your sewing things." Meghan stepped aside so that Tricia could see Katie. "Katie and I are going to the café for tea. Would you like to join us?"

"Mrs. Harris," Tricia said, "Oh, it's good to finally meet you. Mrs. Turner talks about you all the time." And then Tricia glanced beyond the women and drew back inside her doorway.

Katie turned to see what had frightened the woman. Nothing seemed amiss, so she turned back to the door.

Tricia's posture changed. Her eyes wary. "I'm sorry. I'm very busy."

Meghan mouthed, "Are you alone?"

Tricia nodded.

Meghan quietly asked, "Is someone watching the house?"

Tricia mouthed the word yes.

Meghan gave a pretended laugh and spoke more loudly than necessary. "Well, here's your sewing basket. It has your good scissors inside, so I wanted to bring it back right away." Meghan whispered, "Are you safe?"

Tricia's lips tightened and she whispered. "Yes." She swallowed hard and then Tricia spoke louder, her voice quivering with what Katie thought was fear. "Goodbye, ladies. Thank you for bringing my sewing basket."

Tricia closed the front door quickly.

Meghan took Katie's arm in pretended nonchalance. "Let's go have that cup of tea at the diner."

Katie played along with Meghan's bravado as they walked.

Once inside, the chatter of patrons and clatter of dishes were calming. Katie said, "Let's get that table by the window. I want to see if that man follows us."

Once seated at a table near the window, Katie slightly parted the window's blue and white gingham curtains to get a view of the street. "It may be that matchstick man who's frightening Tricia."

"Maybe," Meghan said.

Their discussion was interrupted when the waitress stopped at their table. They ordered their tea. Katie surveyed the surrounding tables, satisfied that the women at nearby tables were only interested in their own conversations.

"What are we going to do?" Meghan whispered.

Katie pulled the curtain aside. The street was busy, but she didn't spot the man who had followed Tricia. Katie released the curtain. She turned to Meghan. "Let's wait a bit, and then we'll go back and see if Tricia's still okay."

Mr. Schneider suddenly appeared at the table, startling Katie. He glanced at Meghan. "Good day, ladies."

Meghan said, "Oh, I didn't see you when we came in."

Meghan and Mr. Schneider talked business for a few minutes while Katie nudged the curtain to get a better view of the street. Tricia's tracker was riding his mount down the center of the road. As he passed, he glared at Katie. She gave an involuntary gasp and moved her hand, allowing the restaurant's curtain to fall back in place, shielding her from the matchstick man's menacing stare.

Both Schneider and Meghan turned to Katie, evidently waiting for an explanation for her loud gasp. Katie bit her lower lip and then said, "I just saw an old friend on the street. I'll have to catch up with her later."

The waitress arrived with their tea, and Schneider said, "Enough about business, I'll leave you ladies to your tea."

"Before you leave," Meghan said, "I wonder if I could ask a small favor."

"Yes."

"Would you have one of your boys take a few things over to Tricia McDowell's house?"

"Of course."

"Thank you," Meghan said. "I'll bring a basket over to the store within the hour."

Once Schneider was out of hearing range, Katie said, "That horrible man rode by."

"I thought so." Meghan rolled her eyes. "You're so discreet."

"I couldn't help it. He's frightening."

Katie glimpsed Meghan's lapel watch. The clock was upside down making it easier for Meghan to read. "It's nearly four o'clock," Katie said. "I need to get back to the house. Liam's coming to dinner."

Meghan reviewed the check and laid a few coins on the table. "I'll send Tricia some yarn and a couple of crochet hooks with a note buried beneath asking if she's all right. I can tell the boy to wait for her written answer. If we learn something is wrong, we'll get the marshal out to Tricia's house."

"Be careful, Meghan. My instincts tell me that man reeks of danger."

Chapter 11

Conflicting Emotions

Wednesday, June 22, 1865

The next day, Hannah had business in town, so Katie was keeping an eye on her father. She entered Philip's room and found him sleeping, his breathing shallow and erratic. He stirred when she set the coffee tray on his nightstand, then opened his eyes.

"Good morning, darlin'." Her father's drowsy eyes let her know that Hannah had given him a hefty dose of laudanum.

Katie opened the draperies and walked back to the bed. "How are you feeling this morning?"

Philip blinked at the sunlight. "Fine, fine, but a bit tired. I'm afraid I overdid it last night signing off on the will." He paused. "It saddens me to take your brother out of the will and that weighed on me a bit. I hope you're comfortable with my decisions."

Katie stood at his bedside. "Of course, I am. I have my own home, Papa. I'm delighted that you and Hannah married, and it's only right that she has an inheritance. But I do hope that doesn't happen for a long, long time."

Philip took Katie's hand. "I hope so too. I want to knock this illness into a cocked hat and be done with it."

"And you will."

Philip released her hand and moved to a sitting position in the bed, coughing a bit with the exertion. He reached over to the bedside table for his glasses and some papers, but the movement triggered a harsh cough.

Katie helped him prop his pillows to ease his breathing and poured him a cup of coffee. "How about if you drink your coffee while I read those papers aloud?"

He drank coffee and listened intently to yesterday's account of the mill manager's report. Philip put down his coffee and put on his glasses. "Let me see those figures." After a few minutes, he handed the papers back to Katie. "Write a note to Fletcher approving his request to hire a new man."

Philip took off his glasses. "You have much to learn about the mill, but not today. Tomorrow, we'll talk." Philip coughed hard for a few minutes and brought a handkerchief to his mouth, muffling his voice. "There is something I'd like you to do, though."

"What's that?"

He removed the handkerchief. "Go to the mill sometime today or tomorrow to see Kevin Fletcher. Let me know what you think of him. I trust him to be fair and firm with the men while I'm recovering."

"I can do that." She had much to do today, but she could fit a ride to the mill in her schedule if Hannah returned soon.

Philip reached for his coffee "Fletcher's a bit humble. I like that in a man." Philip finished drinking his coffee before continuing. "He's a crack shot with a gun, but he never shows off. You know the type." Philip put the mug back on the nightstand.

Katie sat up, alert to the crack-shot comment.

Philip went on talking, unaware of Katie's reaction. "More important I want you to assess how he runs things in my absence. Assess his management with a mind to our family's reputation." Philip coughed but then continued. "Fletcher understands the business well enough, but we also need to find out how he treats our people now that I'm not there. Talk to some of the old-timers."

Katie answered, "Of course." With Stuart and Philip out of the way, it would be easy for Fletcher to skim money off the mill's profits. A powerful motive if he was a greedy man. She'd take a hard look at Kevin Fletcher.

Philip continued, "Find out if Fletcher listens to the men when they have an idea, if he's firm when a man is lazy, and if he keeps the mill safe. That's important to us."

"I can do that."

"I must get some rest now. We'll talk more about this later, I promise."

Katie returned to the kitchen. The barn dog barked, and Katie assumed Hannah had returned. She stepped out to the porch to greet Hannah but found Victor Ross leading his horse to the water trough. "Mr. Ross, this is a nice surprise."

He lifted his broad-brimmed hat in greeting. "Mind if I water my horse?"

She gestured with a sweep of her arm towards the horse trough letting him know he was welcome to do so.

Victor held the reins slack as his horse drank. "Returning from town, I saw the Turner boys hanging by their knees on a high branch. I didn't want them to get hurt, so I suggested they climb down and practice their skills on a lower branch."

"Oh, thank you. I was going out to find them. I'm hoping they can help me find Brett. I need to have a note delivered to the mill."

"Oh? You're already running the mill." He gave her a charming smile. "I thought they would let you have a few days to recover."

"Nothing like that, although I'll probably be more involved in the mill's operations soon if my father has his way."

Victor's smile faded and his face became more serious. "How is Mr. Reynolds?"

"He has good days and bad but still manages the business from home, thus the note for the mill boss."

Victor nodded in acknowledgment. "More good days than bad, I hope."

Katie moved her hand in a so-so gesture. "Well, thank you for letting me know about the boys. I think I'll walk out there. It's a beautiful day, isn't it?"

"May I join you?"

She shrugged. "As you like."

Victor tied the horse to the railing and then they walked down the drive. "I saw Hannah in town today," Victor said.

"Yes, she has some business to attend to."

"She appeared worried and distracted when I greeted her. Everything all right?"

A slight breeze stirred and lifted Katie's straw hat. She secured it as she spoke. "With my father's illness, Hannah has increased responsibilities. She's very busy, but happy now that the news is out."

"What news is that?"

"Oh, I suppose it will be all around the village in no time anyway, so I can't see any harm in sharing it. Hannah and Philip married. They chose to keep the news quiet until I returned."

The muscles in Victor's jaw tightened. "But he's so ill. Why would he marry her now that he's dying?" Victor's tone was edged in anger.

Katie stopped walking and stared at him. "I beg your pardon."

Victor swallowed hard. "I'm sorry. I only meant that I'm surprised. I hope you will accept my sincere apology for such a callous remark."

Katie walked, remaining silent as she tried to parse out Victor's reaction to her father's marriage. It seemed as if he took it personally. Victor kept pace with her.

After a few minutes, she turned to him. "If you must know, they married at the beginning of the year. My father didn't become ill until spring."

"Perhaps I should go," he said, "although I am truly sorry for making such a callous remark."

Katie stopped and glanced up at him. "I do have to accept the fact that my father is ill." They continued down the drive. "I suppose it does seem odd his marrying Hannah now after all these years, but my father had no idea this past winter what sad news the spring would bring."

"I do apologize, Mrs. Harris. I hope you'll forgive me. You have had more than your share of heartache since arriving home from the war. I certainly don't want to add to your distress."

"You're forgiven, Mr. Ross."

He lowered his head. "Thank you."

She could hardly stay angry when he was so contrite. They reached the end of the drive and walked along the road. Katie spotted Tommy and Billy and waved. The boys jumped from a low branch and came running.

"Auntie Katie, we were so high we could see town," Billy yelled excitedly, quickly reaching Katie. He stood in front of her.

"Please don't climb so high next time. It's dangerous, especially dangling from your knees upside down."

Billy's eyebrows shot up and his mouth formed an O in surprise at Katie's knowing, so she explained. "Mr. Ross saw you when he was coming from town."

A quick glance with slanted eyes from both boys showed their distrust in Victor Ross for snitching.

Katie tousled Billy's hair. "Hmm, that's several miles. Have you boys seen Brett? I need a note delivered to the mill."

"Oh, I can take it," Tommy said.

Billy pulled at Tommy's sleeve. "We were going swimming."

Tommy brushed him away.

Katie shook her head. "I'll take you both to the mill some other time. Today I need Brett's help."

Tommy kicked a small stone. "Brett's in the barn. We'll go get him for you." Both boys ran off.

Victor asked, "Are you still available on Saturday for dinner and the play?"

"Oh, yes."

He adjusted his hat in place as he spoke, "I'll be here Saturday at six o'clock with the carriage. If that's all right?"

"That will be fine." As they walked back to the house, the tension in her shoulders and neck made her pause. Was this the right thing to do? Was she wronging her deceased husband's memory and even Andrew by accepting Victor Ross's invitation? What would Mrs. Dubois and her friends say?

Weighing her conscience and possible gossip would stifle her goals. She must find Stuart's murderer and suffer the small consequences of Mrs. Dubois and her ilk. "*How little can be done under the spirit of fear.*" Florence Nightingale had said, and it was true. If she was to accomplish her goals, she must not act cowardly. Information from Victor might bring her closer to finding Stuart's murderer.

They arrived back at the yard. Victor spoke as he untied the reins of his horse. "You're very quiet this morning. Is everything all right?"

"Oh, I'm fine, just thinking."

His eyes met hers and held them for a moment.

He had beautiful dark eyes. To control the flutter in her chest, she took a deep breath. In one fluid motion Ross was in the saddle. He glanced her way and touched the brim of his hat. "Ma'am," and then he turned the horse toward the road.

Katie's feelings for him vacillated. He was certainly handsome and attentive. She couldn't figure out why she was so apprehensive about Saturday's dinner. Was it her personal feelings about courting too soon or something else?

* * *

Katie was just entering the kitchen after checking on Philip when Hannah burst into the kitchen from the porch door. She clutched an opened letter. "We finally got the mail you sent from Kentucky." She put the letter on the table, turned to prime the pump handle, filled the kettle, and put it on the stove.

Katie sat down at the kitchen table and unfolded the paper smoothing it out on the table. "It's about time my mail came through."

"That poor woman."

"What woman?" Katie asked.

"I read your letter. The young mother you helped return home after her husband died, the one with three children."

"Yes, such a sad case."

"I was so excited when you returned home, I didn't give the cause of your delay much thought. Such a shame that the poor woman's husband died. In your letter. . ." Hannah pulled the letter toward her from the opposite side of the table and began to read aloud, "You said, '*I had written to Fanny when her husband was convalescing, thinking he would soon be going home.*'"

Katie said, "We all thought her husband would soon be able to travel. Since Fanny had no one to watch her children, she brought them along to Camp Dennison."

Hannah nodded and spooned tea into the tea ball and then placed it in the pot. She picked up Katie's letter and resumed reading it aloud.

> "*The soldier died from his wounds the same day the war ended. Fanny was so distraught with grief that I worried about her ability to make the trip home, so I decided to travel with her. I'm sorry this letter is just reaching you now and that you may*

have been worrying needlessly. I had written another letter weeks ago explaining my plans and asked Fanny's older boy to mail it. I found my unsent letter under his mattress. He had forgotten to mail it and was too ashamed to tell me."

Hannah paused for a moment.

"It gets worse," Katie said. Hannah met her eyes, then continued.

"The family lives on a remote farm. I worried about the woman's health and her ability to take care of the children in such isolation, the oldest being only ten and the youngest three, so I stayed on. Three days ago, Fanny's parents arrived, and I made plans to leave. This is the first time I've been able to get a letter off. Mail delivery in the area has been sporadic ever since the war's end."

The low rumble of boiling water caused Hannah to glance up from the letter to attend to the kettle. She got up, poured the boiling water into the teapot, and sat down again.

Katie said, "This war has been hard on so many. What Victor's doing, the charity ball, it's a good thing. I can't help but like him more for it."

Hannah raised an eyebrow. "I suppose." She glanced toward the back bedroom. "Everything all right with Philip?"

"Yes, we have been talking about the mill business."

"He worries. I stopped at Meghan's shop to compose a letter to that man from the Pinkerton agency, paying off his bill in full and canceling his services. His expenses are outrageous." Hannah poured herself a cup of tea and added sugar. "I feel like he was taking advantage of Philip's fear for you."

"Papa had a Pinkerton detective searching for me?"

"We were all very worried about you."

"I am so sorry for the worry and the money wasted. I'm not partial to Pinkerton. I've heard the man is quite arrogant. I'm not surprised his firm charges a fortune for services."

"You've met him?"

"No, heard of him and his ways from a friend." Katie turned an empty mug in circles on the table. What about Tricia? Has Meghan learned anything new?"

"No, Meghan called on Tricia about eight o'clock this morning. That horrible man was slowly walking his horse down the street."

"What happened?"

"Meghan said that Tricia greeted her warmly when she first opened the door but then caught sight of the man and her demeanor changed. She thanked Meghan for the muffins and closed the door."

Katie ran her hand through her hair. "It's like she's a prisoner."

"Indeed, I caught up with Meghan as she returned from Tricia's. We walked back to her dress shop and moments later Victor Ross arrived."

Katie straightened up alert. "He stopped here too. Said he saw you in town, but he didn't mention his stop at Meghan's shop. Whatever did he want?"

"Hmm." Hannah sipped her tea and glanced at Katie. "More tea?"

"Yes, please. So why was Victor at Meghan's? That's odd isn't it?"

Hannah poured the tea. "What's odd is your reaction to any mention of him? You aren't taken in by that man's charms, are you?"

Katie clicked her tongue. "No."

"He is quite the lady's man. You need to be a bit wary."

"All right. Why did he stop at the dress shop?"

"He has a rip in the leather seat of his coach. He wants Meghan to repair it, preferably before Saturday night."

"I see."

"Oh, wait, I nearly forgot. Besides the letter from you, there was also a letter *for* you at the post office."

Katie's heart leaped, thinking it was a letter from Andrew.

Hannah pulled a letter from her reticule and handed it to Katie. The letter was written in a woman's hand. Katie's spirits sank. She glanced up at Hannah as she unfolded it and read. "*Monday, June 19, 1865 — Mansfield, Ohio*"

She glanced at the signature at the end of the letter. "This is from Suzanne. They must have left the camp right after I told them about Danior. How was this letter delivered so quickly?"

Hannah shrugged. "The local stage runs three times weekly with mail. Suzanne's timing was right."

Katie began to read the letter silently.

Hannah pursed her lips and drummed her fingers on the table.

Katie picked up on Hannah's impatience. "Shall I read it aloud."

"Please."

"Dear Katie,

"I am sorry we left so quickly. After hearing what happened to you, the elders decided that Danior is to remain under lock and key at night and be watched closely during the day for a year's time. He is to drink no alcohol. He cannot control himself, so they must control him. It was also their decision to leave immediately. There is too great a risk for what the Gorgio call justice when a crime is committed by a gypsy.

"Please excuse the inkblots and jumps of my pen. I am writing this as we travel. Tomas took the reins, so that I could sit at my table and write to you. I have much to say."

Katie put the paper down in her lap. "Tomas again. I can't help but think he is in love with her."

"Quite possibly."

"Hannah, do you know what that means?"

"She'll marry someday?"

"Well, yes, that's possible, but the more important point is Tomas would be jealous of Stuart's visit with Suzanne."

Hannah grimaced.

"Tomas is rising higher on my list of suspects."

"I see."

Katie lowered the paper.

"What else does Suzanne say?"

Katie picked up the letter and continued.

"I cared deeply for your brother. I knew in my heart that we would never be together, but he was a

good man. His murderer must be found. I have information that may be helpful. You have been kind, so I must tell you to beware of a didicoy who may live in or near Liberty. He is dangerous to you simply because you are Irish. I will tell you the reason why, but first some background."

"The didicoy is half gypsy and gorgio, right?" Hannah asked.

"Yes." Katie turned to the next page of the letter.

"Unfortunately, I do not know his name. It was years ago that I learned of his story from a family friend, Milo, a gypsy who had befriended this didicoy. I was skeptical and brushed the story off as nonsense at the time but remember it still because the man my friend spoke of had planned to settle in Liberty, a frequent destination for our clan.

"I have written the story below just as it was related to me. Remember though, it is an old story.

"Suzanne's quite educated," Katie said. "Where did she get such an education?"

"Stuart used to loan her books."

"My brother gets more and more interesting." She continued reading.

"The didicoy was the son of a poor family who settled in an Irish area of New York, a vicious part of that city. He was teased as a child and made fun of by the many Irish in the area because of the foods

that he ate and the customs of his mother. They were cruel, these Irish children, going so far as to set their dogs on him when he ran errands for his mother. Because of their taunting, he grew to hate all Irish and became ashamed of his heritage. When he was only twelve, he left New York and began to travel on the rails. He wished to be successful so that he could show up his Irish antagonists someday.

"A handsome young man, this didicoy soon realized he could steal greater sums when he blended in with first-class passengers on trains, so he learned to imitate the speech and mannerisms of the wealthy.

"One day he stole $10,000 from a businessman— the satchel had been handcuffed to the mark's wrist, almost an advertisement to a thief like this didicoy. The money provided the means to make a new life for himself as a gentleman. The didicoy had set his sights on Liberty. He told my friend Liberty was a small town with unsophisticated German immigrants. When my friend last saw this thief, it was on the eve of his departure. He was celebrating and had let his guard down with too much drink.

"I am sorry that I do not know this didicoy's name. My friend did not refer to him by name. I wanted to tell you because I fear for you. My intuition tells me you must beware of this man."

Katie put down the letter. "Does anybody come to mind as this didicoy?"

Hannah shook her head. "How many years ago did he move here? If he even moved here. Did Suzanne say?"

Katie perused the letter. "She doesn't mention a time, just that she was told the story years ago. Who knows when this all happened? That's why a meeting with her would have been so much better. I could ask questions."

Hannah had been slicing pumpkin bread while Katie had been reading. She spread butter on a slice as she spoke. "If he came to Liberty, let's say five years ago, with that kind of money, people would be talking. I don't recall any fancy gentleman's arrival."

"She doesn't say anything about his coming within the last five years only that she learned his story from a friend years ago. Of course, this whole story could be a ploy to make me less suspicious of Tomas."

"It's too much. I can't keep it all straight."

"I understand it gets complicated. That's why I like using my list, it helps keep everyone straight." She shook her head. "I can't imagine Tomas was happy seeing Stuart visiting with Suzanne, so regardless of Suzanne's story, Tomas remains high on my list of suspects."

Hannah sighed. "Suzanne's letter says a young man with money came to Liberty. I'm going to have to think about that for a while. Sheila and Colleen are coming this afternoon to do the laundry. I'll ask them about it. They live in the village and hear more gossip than we do out here."

"They're too young. This happened long ago. What about Meghan?"

"She was busy with her husband and babies. No harm in asking though." Hannah took a bite of her spicy bread. "Hmm, this is good. Have some?"

"No, thanks." Katie's head was spinning. She needed time to sort things out. She pulled a folded paper from her pocket, unfolded it, spread it on the table, and reviewed its contents. Katie added unknown didicoy with a question mark and a few details from Suzanne's letter. She boldly underlined Tomas's name, which she had added after the visit to the gypsy camp.

She needed time to think without interruption. "I'm going to take a ride to the pine valley again."

CHAPTER 12

A SURPRISE GUEST

Wednesday afternoon June 21, 1865

When Katie descended into the valley, she noticed the ten-degree drop in temperature, a welcome relief on a ninety-degree day. She dismounted and let the horse drink at the stream. She scanned the valley. After her encounter with Danior, she had become more cautious.

If it was a gypsy who killed Stuart, Danior and Tomas were likely suspects in her mind. Tomas was tall and lean, the description Suzanne gave for Stuart's murderer, but both men had shown a romantic interest in Suzanne and a reason to be jealous. Stuart had been so cavalier about his romance. What had he been thinking? Jealous men could be dangerous.

Katie let go of Mouse's reins and sat down on the large rock near the stream. She pulled her timeline from her pocket. The didicoy suspect frustrated her. Had this mystery man even come to Liberty? Was Suzanne telling the truth or trying to misdirect her suspicion of Tomas as a suspect? She could at least explore the idea of this didicoy. Within the last decade or so, many people had settled in Liberty and the surrounding area, buying farms and ranches. Liberty's population had exploded since she was a girl.

Brush rustled on the other side of the stream. Katie quickly pocketed her suspects list, mounted her horse, and pulled out her gun.

A man in a pork-pie hat emerged from the brush. One glance at Katie's gun and he put his arms up. "Whoa, lady, don't shoot." The man kept his hands in the air as he focused on Katie's gun.

Katie asked, "What are you doing here?"

"I mean you no harm. I'm Caleb Brown, a reporter for the *Liberty Gazette.*"

She tsked. "I remember you quite well, Mr. Brown."

"Seth said you'd stopped by the newspaper office yesterday and that you were willing to give me an interview. I called on you at Six Maples, and they told me you had taken a ride out to, well, to this valley, so I thought I could talk to you here." He paused. "Mind if I put my hands down?"

Katie nodded and moved the gun to her pocket. "This is an odd place for an interview."

"The paper goes to print tomorrow afternoon, and I wanted my story to get into this week's *Gazette.*"

"All right, you may have your interview, but stay on that side of the stream."

"Yes, ma'am. I've been here before. I reported the story of your brother's passing, so I knew the location." He glanced over his shoulder. "I left my horse back in the clearing. Trees and bushes have become overgrown along this path. No need for both us to get scratched up." Caleb took off his hat and focused on it, running his fingers along its brim. "I'm truly sorry for your loss, ma'am."

A perspiration band circled his head when he took off his hat. It caused an indentation in his dark poker-straight hair.

"Thank you," she said. She lifted her chin, motioning to the large flat rock on the other side of the stream. "Take a seat there if you'd like. We can hear one another from across the water just fine."

Caleb returned his hat to his head and sat on the rock. He brought out a pencil and tablet from his pocket. His tan linen coat was wrinkled from wear, but Caleb had an untidiness to him that Katie found endearing.

He rested his right ankle on his left knee and propped his notepad on his thigh. "It's quiet and cool here. Not a bad place to conduct an interview."

Her shoulders relaxed. "I'm not sure if my experiences are exciting enough for a story, but we can give this a try."

"Oh, I've talked to a few people who admire your nursing service." He lifted an eyebrow. "You DO have some admirers. I hope you don't pay attention to gossip mongers. Jealousy mostly."

Katie grimaced.

"Anyway, I think you're fascinating." He spoke with enthusiasm in his voice. "What could be more interesting than a woman's perspective on the battlefield?" He paused. "I hear you occasionally accompanied Nurse Clara Barton to the front."

"Then my experiences have been exaggerated. Did you serve?"

"As a war correspondent not as a soldier. I worked with Brady."

"Matthew Brady," she said, "the Civil War photographer?"

"Yes, I don't want to take up too much of your time, but would you mind if I asked you a few questions?"

"I do want to try to solve my brother's murder. You said you would help me when last we spoke. Are you still willing?"

"Yes, of course. Your brother was ambushed here, but the question is by whom and why?"

"Anything else you can tell me that you didn't include in the newspaper? I read your article."

He tightened his lips and then spoke, "There is one thing."

"Yes." She leaned forward in the saddle.

"Seems trivial but bothered me just the same. Your brother's boots were left here." Caleb pointed to the shoreline. "Whoever murdered your brother didn't take his boots and that just doesn't make sense. For soldiers returning home, a good pair of boots would be prized."

Katie nodded. "I see your point."

"I gave it only a cursory thought when I wrote that article, but it's bothered me ever since. I told the marshal about my suspicions, but he dismissed it as irrelevant, saying they just must have been frightened and skedaddled. I think it's pertinent and it's the main reason I don't think it was bummers."

"That is telling. Stuart probably took his boots off to cross the creek. We always did as children. You get a better foothold on slick rocks with your bare feet. If you're wearing boots, well, one misstep and your boots are filled with water."

"Other than the boots, there's not much else to tell. I came down here as soon as I heard, but it had rained heavily. The marshal's men were taking your brother's body up to the ridge. They were very respectful, but all that rain made it difficult to learn much from tracking."

"Any theories on what may have happened?"

Caleb scanned the trees on the right behind him, the path leading toward Wordsworth.. Most people use this path, coming to Liberty from Wordsworth if they come on horseback. Your brother was reported to have been in Wordsworth, my sources say. I was there yesterday for a horse race."

"Seth told me. He wanted to go with you."

"I know, but he was needed at the presses, a pamphlet to run." He pointed his thumb to the path that led to Wordsworth. "Anyway, the path through these woods would be the shortest route to Six Maples from Wordsworth. If anyone knew he was coming home and wanted him dead, well, this would be the place to lay an ambush."

"Who would have anything against my brother?"

Caleb tightened his lips and then said, "Your family has money and jealousy escalates during hard times. Stuart Reynolds was a war hero and had a lot of luck with the ladies, if you don't mind my saying."

"My brother had a bit of growing up to do, I'm quite aware of that. But murder?"

He lifted his eyebrows. "War does crazy things to people."

She nodded in agreement. "Do you have any inkling as to who might have had a reason to kill him?" She lifted her shoulders. "What would they gain?"

"Sometimes the only gain needed is revenge."

"So you think revenge may be the motive, but you don't have anyone in particular in mind as a suspect."

"No, can't say that I do. But I know a lot of people, and I'll keep my ears and eyes open."

He paused, looking at her intently. "I'll do my best to help you out."

She sighed. "Thank you. That's more than the marshal has to offer. He feels investigating my brother's murder is not a suitable pursuit for a lady and has let all the gossips in the village know his opinion."

"Hmph," Caleb announced. "The gossips in the village didn't see what war can do. They don't have the same experiences and insights you have."

"You're very kind." She adjusted her seat on the saddle. "Let's get on with this interview then."

He glanced at his notes. "I understand you had some experience on the front lines of battle."

"Yes, shortly after I arrived in Cincinnati, Camp Dennison. I had finished my nursing training in early November. Scouts warned that trouble was brewing in Tennessee, so I was sent there to nurse in a make-shift hospital. I arrived before the Battle of Chattanooga, which was fine with me." Katie shrugged. "Dangerous, but I didn't care if I lived or died at that point."

Caleb had been writing furiously and then looked up, compassion evident in his face.

Katie continued, "I think your mind protects you in difficult circumstances. When nursing at the front, I felt outside of myself as I worked. On the evening after the Battle of Orchard Knob, I went into the field with a surgeon after the fighting had ceased, or so we thought. We were premature in our arrival and found ourselves in great danger."

"How so?"

"I was tying a tourniquet around a young man's arm. We had succeeded in stopping the flow of blood, but then moments later the man who had assisted me in applying that tourniquet took a bullet to the chest. He died in my arms." Emotion overwhelmed her. She took a moment to compose herself.

Caleb put the pencil behind his ear. "You never actually served with Nurse Barton though?"

"No, I have never had the honor of working side by side with the angel of the battlefield, as she was called. Chattanooga was my only frontline experience, three of the most horrendous days of my life. My nursing largely took place in the hospital at Camp Dennison."

Caleb's mouth tightened and his face showed distaste. "I've seen what that was like." He pulled his pencil from behind his ear and resumed his writing posture. "You've been home now for nearly a week. Do you miss your work as a nurse?"

She adjusted her seat, and the saddle leather creaked with her movement. "Yes and no. I miss the camaraderie I had with the others, the nurses, surgeons, and soldiers, but it is a joy to be home."

Caleb finished writing her answer and their eyes met. "What was your reaction to learning of your brother's passing?" His face showed his sympathy for her situation.

She replied, "Grief and anger mostly, but that's not what I want you to put in the paper."

"Oh, what would you like me to say?"

She swallowed and paused for a moment. "I am saddened and distraught at finding such a good man murdered after serving his country. I will use the energy from that grief to find my brother's murderer." She paused.

Caleb had his pencil lifted. He was waiting for her to continue while she was thinking about how to trap the murderer using the ring. She was sure the ring belonged to the murderer. Would it be too dangerous? Once again Nightingale's words came to mind. *How little can be done under the spirit of fear.*

She took a deep breath. "I would like you to help me set a trap. The murder took place here and I have been scouring the area for evidence. I found an emerald ring with a silver band large enough to fit a man's finger."

Caleb said, "The murderer, according to Marshal Gerber, is some desperate soldier who has come to find killing too easy. Hardly someone who could afford such a ring or leave behind a pair of boots."

"I think it was someone local. I think my brother's murderer took advantage of those recent reports about bummers. None of the soldiers returning home have killed. Bummers steal food, boots, and horses."

"Your brother's horse was stolen."

Katie's lips tightened. "Stuart's attack doesn't fit with the usual way bummers operate. They steal at night out of desperation. No one's been murdered for their horse. They steal horses from barns in the night or while the horses are grazing in fields, not by accosting a fellow soldier returning home."

"A valid point. Have you shared that logic with the marshal?"

"Little weight my opinions have with the marshal."

"I'm afraid your right." He lowered his pencil. "May I see the ring you found?"

"No, it's in a safe place until it's needed."

"I see." He lifted his pencil again. "Anything else you'd like to add?"

"Yes," Katie said. "The paper comes out on Friday morning."

"We send a few copies to Schneider's store late on Thursday evening, but for most folks Friday morning's when they get the newspaper."

"How about if you put a notice in the paper at the bottom of your article letting the townspeople know that I'm calling for volunteers to come out this Saturday to search this valley. Ask that the volunteers meet me in the yard at Six Maples at eight o'clock, we'll ride out here together and search for any evidence the murderer might have left behind. And Hannah promises a hearty breakfast when the searchers return. The murderer probably knows he's lost his emerald ring. He'll come out here sometime on Friday after he reads my request for volunteers so he can search for the ring beforehand."

"That may work." Calib tapped his pencil against his cheek. A cue that he was thinking, Katie surmised.

"I'll write it up, but only if you'll allow me to accompany you. In good conscience, I couldn't let a woman alone, even one so competent as yourself, take on a murderer."

She sighed and opened her mouth to speak.

Caleb put his hands up in protest. "Beggin' your pardon, ma'am, but I'm not sure I've ever met a more willful woman. But I can be stubborn, too, and I will not put your life in jeopardy and leave you to encounter danger on your own.

You let me come with you on Friday morning or I don't print your request for a search party."

She shook her head and gave him a playful smile. "You drive a hard bargain, Mr. Brown."

He nodded. "How about I meet you at Six Maples at eight o'clock on Friday morning."

"What time on Friday morning are the papers available in the village?"

"Aside from the fifteen or so that we send over to Schneider's store, the newsboys start regular delivery on Friday morning about seven o'clock."

"Let's make our meeting at Six Maples at half past seven, and we have a deal."

"All right." Caleb stood and put the pencil and notebook back into his misshapen pockets. "You've got plenty of starch. I bet you were a fierce advocate for the men you nursed." He paused. "If there's nothing else, I'm going to get back. I have a deadline." Caleb took in the surrounding woods. "You all right here?"

"I have a gun. I'm fine."

"Yes, ma'am, then I'll see you at Six Maples on Friday morning, seven and a half sharp." He tipped his hat and turned to go. His long strides took him quickly out of sight.

With this plan set in motion, Katie found herself thinking about Tricia's plight. She needed to learn more about the man worrying Tricia. Maybe Stuart's murderer and Tricia's nemesis were one and the same. Where was that mysterious man staying? At the American Hotel? Maybe a few glasses of whiskey would loosen his tongue. Caleb could help her with that.

"Mr. Brown," she called out.

Although the trees were thick nearby, she could hear the swish of the brush and tree branches on the opposite side of the stream. He emerged at the stream breathless, "Is anything the matter?"

"I just thought of an idea. Would you be able to find out more about the man who stalks Tricia McDowell?"

"I've heard about a scoundrel in town. Is that the woman he's been bothering?"

"Yes, Mrs. McDowell works or did work for Meghan Turner at her dress shop. The poor woman has suddenly quit and seems to be held prisoner in her home with this scoundrel, as you call him, standing guard. He hides in the woods or parades up and down her street and frightens her with his very presence. I would like to know more about him."

"Yes, ma'am, I'll ask around."

This time, when Mr. Brown disappeared into the woods, Katie watched his departure in silence.

CHAPTER 13

ACCIDENT AT THE MILL

Wednesday afternoon, June 21, 1865

When Katie returned from the pine valley, she had a light dinner and asked Brett to take her to the mill. She intended to make inquiries about the mill manager Kevin Fletcher's leadership during her father's absence. Brett drove their wagon through a well-worn path thick with trees. The screech of the saws let Katie know they were approaching their destination. A white-washed wooden structure came into view. It butted up to the west branch of the Rocky River, which provided steam power for the saws.

Coming toward them from a left fork in the road beyond the mill were two draft horses pulling a wagon with several large tree trunks shorn of their branches. The wide doors of the mill entrance were open. Several men stood ready with ropes and pulleys to unload. "Where does the road to the right lead?" Katie asked Brett.

Brett had stopped the horse to make way for the loaded wagon. "That road leads to the west side of town."

"Been too long since I've been out here."

"That road to the left takes you to the new clearin' that's probably why you got puzzled."

Once the road cleared, Brett pulled their wagon alongside the mill and followed Katie through the mill's main door. The noise was too loud to carry on a normal conversation. When the workmen spoke to one another, it was in brief shouts. Katie wondered about the long-term effects of the mill's noise on the workmen. The cannons and heavy artillery affected a man's hearing during battle, and one means of protection was cotton or beeswax in their ears. She would recommend such earplugs as these for the mill workers when she talked with her father.

Inside the building, Katie and Brett took the flight of stairs that led up to the mill office. At the railed landing, a man was just leaving. He acknowledged them with a nod and held the door open. Katie was grateful to close the door, which muffled the high squeal of the saws.

She glanced to her right. Three large windows across the long side of the office allowed a view of all the intricacies of belts and pulleys that moved the newly felled trees through the saws. She had a bird's eye view of the workmen below. On the opposite side of the office, the windows offered a contrasting view of young trees in their natural splendor and the curve of swift-moving water. The open windows also gave a welcome breeze that ruffled a few of the papers on Fletcher's desk. After he moved a paperweight to stay a pile of papers, he rose to greet them.

Fletcher came around the desk. He was a tall man with a thick head of steel-gray hair and vivid blue eyes. Suzanne had said Stuart's assailant was tall and lean. And Papa had claimed Fletcher was a crack shot with a rifle. She'd keep that in mind.

Katie also noted Fletcher's slight Irish brogue as he welcomed them. Since reading Suzanne's letter, she was now more aware of the many Irish her father employed in their predominately German village.

After their greetings, Katie stepped toward the window overlooking the mill. "You have a wonderful vantage point for watching the men and machinery at work."

"You would certainly know, Miss Katie." Fletcher finished his sentence with a lilt. "You were here often enough as a wee lass. When I used to work on the floor, I remember you coming to visit." He glanced toward the window and then back to Katie. "You would wave to me."

Katie bit her lower lip and nodded, reminded of this childhood memory.

"Won't you sit down, Miss Katie? Begging your pardon, it's 'ma'am' now, isn't it?" Fletcher motioned Katie to a seat. She sat, but Brett stood near the door with his hat in hand. "I've missed the place," she said, then turned toward Brett. "Why don't you sit down?"

Brett glanced at Fletcher for approval.

Katie saw the exchange. "Brett's been my driver and filling me in on many of the changes since I've been away."

"Ah, yes, the war. Say what you will about its many drawbacks, and I'm no warmonger, mind you, but the war's been profitable for us. We've expanded into the wagon business, and war requires a lot of wagons. Your father's a lucky man."

"I suppose in some respects."

Fletcher frowned. "I'm so sorry about the loss of your brother, ma'am. He was a right good man."

"Thank you."

His eyes were steady and there was an ease to his actions that Katie liked, but she wasn't ready to dismiss him as a suspect. She stood and regarded the men working on the mill floor. "We've made some structural improvements," she observed.

"Yes, ma'am." He walked over to the window and then seemed to notice Brett again. "Son, why don't you run down to the stream and fetch us three bottles of the cider near the shoreline rocks?" Fletcher glanced at Katie. "How about joining me for a cold cider?"

"That would be most welcome."

"Be right back," Brett said as he opened the door, momentarily letting in the screech of the saws.

Katie wanted to know a little more about Fletcher's rifle skills. "Did you serve in the war?"

Both took their seats again.

"No, I'm a bit too old for that kind of work. I tried to join up, but they didn't need my old bones. So, I did what I could here."

"And we're grateful for your knowledge and experience, which only comes with age, I might add."

Suddenly the rhythm of the saws and the scream of the blades stopped and there were shouts from below. With the fluid motion of a much younger man, Fletcher was out of his seat and at the window overlooking the mill. Katie stood to see its cause. With a hurried, "Excuse me," Fletcher was brushing past her and down the stairs to the mill floor.

Katie scurried through the office door and out to the landing, gripping the railing as she leaned over to better see the problem. A group of men parted when Fletcher arrived. A log had fallen on a man. Men had removed it, but the injured man was clutching his leg. The machines were winding down. Just then, Brett returned to the mill floor with the bottles of cider.

"Get the wagon," Fletcher yelled to Brett. He pointed to a wide board and directed the men to use it as a stretcher.

Katie started to descend the stairs; maybe there was something she could do to help. Her dress caught on a loosened nail in the stair railing, and she nearly fell. She managed to remove the fabric from the offending nail without ripping her skirt. She lifted her skirt high as she took the rest of the stairs more slowly. She emerged from the building and into the sunlight.

Brett was seated on the wagon bench by the mill's entrance. Brett called down to her. "I think Joseph's busted his leg up pretty good. Fletcher told me to get him to the doctor. That all right with you, Miss Katie?"

"Of course."

Fletcher and the two men carrying Joseph on a plank emerged from the mill and approached the wagon. As Katie moved toward the back of the wagon, a large man came up behind her. "May I help you into the wagon, ma'am?" he asked.

"Yes, please, I would like to make the injured man as comfortable as possible." She glanced at the big man beside her. "Someone called him Joseph. Is that his first or last name?"

"First name, ma'am."

Katie moved to the wagon's high step and put her hand out for the big man's support; instead, he swooped her up and gently set her down in the back of the wagon. Katie was taken aback by the ease with which he lifted her. The wagon's sides did not allow her to see much of the ground. She shifted to the side, not only to get a better view, but to make room for the injured man. A moment later, two more men raised the plank Joseph lay on and placed him beside her on the bed of the wagon. He moaned in pain with the movement. Katie gently cushioned his head and leg with blankets provided by the mill workers.

The man's trouser leg had been torn open. Katie could see that the bone in his calf had pierced the skin. She shifted another blanket over his leg. Joseph didn't need to see the damage. He could feel it.

Brett climbed into the back of the wagon with her. Fletcher gave brisk orders. "Matthew, you ride with Paul in the front. You can help bring Joseph into the doctor's surgery."

The wagon leaned to the side as Matthew, the big ginger-haired man who had set Katie in the wagon, climbed onto the bench beside the driver. He turned around and glanced at the injured man.

As the wagon lurched forward. Matthew produced a whiskey flask from the inside of his leather vest. He reached back and handed it to Katie. "This might help."

Katie took the flask. She put the bottle to Joseph's lips and dribbled a few drops into his mouth.

Joseph swallowed and then said, "Don't let 'em cut off my leg."

"Dr. West will take good care of you." Katie was sure Liam would do his best. A cast of plaster of Paris might be available so long as Liam had been able to procure the gypsum from France. If he needed supplies for his medical office, Bertha West would see to it that her son got them.

"Not much farther," the driver said.

Katie looked around to get their bearings. She could follow their progress with her view from the back of the wagon. They were coming into town from the west. Once they passed Tricia's house, they would soon be at Liam's office.

The driver turned to Katie. "How's Joseph holding up?"

"As well as can be expected." Katie glanced up again as she answered and caught sight of Tricia's tormentor. The horseman's eyes narrowed as he recognized her. "Damn," she whispered.

Brett looked up at her. His eyes wide. Katie tilted her head toward the horseman. "Do you know that man?"

"No, but it looks like he's gonna follow us."

Katie's stomach clutched.

The horseman stopped and tied his horse to the rail outside the saloon. He turned and glared at Katie. She refused to give him the satisfaction of turning away, although a shiver ran up her spine and the hairs on the back of her neck alerted her to a primal danger.

The wagon turned and she lost her view of the man. Joseph moaned with the jolt of their wagon's stop, and Katie directed her attention back to him, offering another swig from Matthew's flask.

Matthew and the driver brought Joseph into the surgery, still using the board as a stretcher. Katie remained with

Joseph while they talked with Stephens, Liam's apprentice. Liam came through the door a few minutes later, drying his hands. He walked over and stood by the patient.

"Dr. West," Joseph grabbed the doctor's arm. "Don't cut off my leg."

Liam peeled back the blanket and examined the wound. "We won't have to amputate," he said assuredly.

Joseph took a deep breath, visibly relaxing with the news.

"Get the chloroform," Liam said to Stephens. "We'll use a plaster cast to set the bone."

As Stephens reached into the cupboard, Katie turned to go.

Stephens said, "This is the last of the chloroform."

Katie turned, surprised at the deficiency, and saw Liam's eyes narrow. "That's odd."

With Joseph settled, Katie left the office and returned to the wagon. She found Matthew and handed him the flask. "Thank you."

Matthew shook the flask and repocketed it. He grinned. "I only keep it handy for such purposes."

Katie nodded understanding.

He tipped his hat. "Ma'am." The big man turned to go.

"Matthew, when we rode into town. . . "

When Katie spoke, the big man turned back, his face revealing surprise at a continued exchange.

Katie tilted her head toward the saloon. "There was a man on horseback that followed our wagon and then went into the saloon."

"Yes, ma'am."

"He's familiar to me, but I just can't place him. You wouldn't happen to know his name, would you?"

"Cliff Yosterman. He's new in town."

"I must be mistaken then. I don't know him." She put her hat back on and tied the ribbon on the side of her chin to show a nonchalance.

Matthew tipped his hat and said, "Ma'am." He turned to go.

Katie called out again, "Matthew."

He turned back again. "Yes, ma'am."

"You work every day at the mill, don't you?"

"Yes, ma'am, every day but Sunday."

"Do you recall Mr. Fletcher taking a day or a morning off in the last month or so?"

"No, ma'am. He's a good foreman. At the mill first thing every day."

"It's good to know we have such devoted employees." She paused. "Thank you, Matthew, you've been most helpful."

Brett emerged from the doctor's office and set the wide board and blanket into the back of the wagon. Katie came up behind him. "Please return to the mill with these men. I'm going over to Mrs. Turner's shop. I'll just have a cup of tea with her and settle myself a bit until you return."

He glanced at the clock near the newspaper office. "I can be back by five o'clock."

"That will be fine." Katie turned to go, eager to tell Meghan she had learned the name of Tricia's stalker.

* * *

Katie opened the dress shop door. It was a relief to step inside to the quiet.

Meghan was perched on a stool behind the counter that ran half the length of the room. Behind her were shelves with bolts of fabric in a variety of colors and textures. Below the shelves were wide drawers where Katie imagined Meghan kept all the other sewing paraphernalia. Meghan stood. "What a pleasant surprise to have you back in town." She held up two yellow ribbons. "Mrs. Dubois was in here earlier." Meghan scowled. "She pulled out half of my ribbon stock and then bought one strand for her daughter's hair."

A white-washed wagon wheel was suspended from the ceiling above the counter. Each spoke was draped with ribbons in a rainbow of colors. Meghan turned the wheel and threaded the two yellow ribbons on the spoke that held several others in shades of yellow.

Katie took off her hat and put it on the counter. "Humph, I'm sure Mrs. Dubois was trying to wheedle information from you on my investigation or maybe she just wanted a few tidbits to feed the village gossips."

"She didn't learn anything from me." Meghan paused. "Don't pay any attention to her."

"I don't. Or at least I try not to." Katie lowered her head. "It does hurt when old friends snub me, though. Caroline and Sally ignored me when I said hello the other day." She blew out her breath. "Oh, well! But I did learn a couple of interesting things today."

"What's that?"

"Whoever killed Stuart didn't take his boots. Do you know what happened to them."

"Well, I suppose he was buried with them. I didn't pay much attention. Hannah made all the preparations for burial and there was a blanket." She looked somberly at Katie.

"I see. Didn't anyone in the family think it odd that the bummers, who supposedly killed my brother, would leave behind his valuable boots?"

"Liam and your father both thought that suspicious. When asked, Marshal Gerber said he thought they must have been in a hurry to leave the area and left them behind."

"That man has slick answers for everything."

"So what else did you learn today?" Meghan asked.

"Tricia's tormentor is named Cliff Yosterman."

"How'd you find out?"

Katie gave a self-satisfied nod. "One of the men from the mill told me. I still need to find out more about him, but it's a start."

Meghan disappeared behind the curtain of the kitchenette-dressing room. She returned with a tray of tea things and set them on a small table. She sat down and poured a cup of tea for Katie. "How ever will you learn more about this Cliff Yosterman?"

Katie walked over to join her. "With help from Caleb Brown."

Meghan's eyebrows drew together in confusion.

"The newspaperman, he promised to help me. I gave him an interview earlier this afternoon. He mentioned again that he would help me find the murderer. I bet Yosterman spends a lot of time at the bar when he's not harassing Tricia. He seems the type, so I've asked Mr. Brown to learn more about him. Maybe he'll have a drink with him." Katie chuckled. "Can you imagine if I were to walk into the saloon and start up a conversation with Yosterman?"

Meghan's eyes and mouth widened in mock outrage. "Shocking." She poured a cup of tea for herself.

"Seriously, though, we need to figure out what's going on with Yosterman and Tricia. Mr. Brown may just be the man to do that. Honestly, the hair on the back of my neck goes up every time the man looks at me, and I've learned to trust my instincts. It occurred to me that there is a possibility that Yosterman was hired by someone to kill Stuart." She took a sip of her tea. "He surely fits the bill for a hired gun: surly, arrogant, and dangerous."

"But he only came to town recently."

"True, but he may have been hiding out somewhere."

"Quite possibly." Meghan tilted her head. "What was the commotion outside Liam's office?"

"That's what brought me into town. When I was at the mill, a log fell on a man's leg. Joseph is his name. He has a compound fracture."

"Oh, poor man," Meghan said. "But Liam's an excellent doctor. I'm sure he'll take good care of him. I'll stop by his office later to check on Joseph's progress."

Katie gave her a knowing smile. "I bet you will."

Megan blushed and reached for her teacup.

"Oh, and I am now taking the mill manager, Kevin Fletcher, off the suspect list."

"I never knew he was on your, what did you call it, suspect list?"

"I added his name when Papa said he was an ace shot. Think about it. Fletcher would have less oversight of the mill and the books if Stuart were out of the way. So, yes, he was a suspect."

"So what made you decide on his innocence?"

"A chat with Matthew, one of the mill men that helped bring Joseph in. I asked him about Fletcher's whereabouts in the last couple of weeks, checking to see if he was gone on any particular morning."

"You weren't specific on the date, were you?"

"No, I simply asked if he'd missed any work during the last couple of weeks. I'm sure Matthew thought I was asking for my father's sake, for business purposes."

"Good." She put her hand over her heart. "People do talk in this town. If Matthew thought you were checking on Fletcher, there are people who'd get riled up. Fletcher's well liked in this town."

Katie rolled her eyes. "You're as bad as your mother. I need to ask questions if I want to find Stuart's murderer. Believe me, hospitals also have small-minded people who take pleasure in saying unkind things about others. I've had more than my fair share of experience with that, so I can handle gossipers like Mrs. Dubois." Katie took the amethyst stone on her necklace between her fingers.

Meghan grinned. "I'm sure your fiddling with that necklace would have caused some talk at the hospital."

"Have you been talking to your mother?"

"No. Does she know something about the necklace that I don't?"

"Let's save that for another time, shall we?"

"So, I'm not the only one with secrets around here." Meghan lifted her cup and took a sip of tea.

"Hardly. Now getting back to Yosterman."

Meghan put down her teacup. "I am so worried about Tricia I can hardly concentrate on my work."

"We should tell the marshal about him."

Meghan's eyes grew wide. "No, we can't do that. I put a note on top of the muffins I gave to Tricia, asking if she wanted me to talk with the marshal about the man watching her house. She mouthed a very emphatic no, and the fear in her eyes at the suggestion made me even more scared for her." Meghan shook her head. "What are we going to do?"

"Caleb knew about Yosterman stalking Tricia, so I'm sure the marshal does." Katie frowned. "Well, maybe not, I hear tell, he's always got his head buried in those dime novels. Let's see what Mr. Brown learns."

Katie's face lit up. "I have an idea. Maybe you can ask around about Yosterman, pretending you have a friend that thinks he's handsome and you're asking on your friend's behalf." She shrugged. "He's not bad looking."

"No thanks. Most people would probably think I am really the one interested, and then the gossip would fly." Meghan raised a finger. "But. I do know just the person to ask for information. Sheila is the biggest flirt in Liberty. She may know something about him already."

Katie said, "Let me know what you learn. I've already set a trap for the murderer and I'm betting it will be Yosterman."

"A trap? What trap?"

"When I talked with Mr. Brown today, I told him about the emerald ring I found."

"What ring? Katie, what are you talking about?"

"I've been keeping this to myself, but I think it's time I used it. Right before Danior attacked me, I found an emerald ring in the stream. I'm guessing it belongs to the murderer. I told Mr. Brown about it because I'm using it as a trap." Katie sat back in her chair with her fingers tented. "When the ring's owner, possibly the murderer, reads about the found ring in the newspaper and then learns we will be conducting a thorough search of the valley on Saturday, he'll probably go to the valley in advance. And I'll be in the valley Friday morning waiting for him."

Meghan put her cup down and gripped the sides of the table. "That's too dangerous."

"I will be carrying a gun," Katie assured her. "I'm carrying it anytime I'm away from Six Maples." She patted her skirt pocket. "And besides Mr. Brown will be joining me on Friday morning. So stop your worrying."

Katie glanced at the lapel watch pinned to Meghan's dress. "I don't have much time, so let me tell you about Suzanne's letter."

Katie shared all that she had learned from the gypsy.

Meghan had no immediate suggestion for identifying the wealthy young man who would fit Suzanne's didicoy description. The few she did mention were quickly dismissed as having characteristics or history which disqualified them for one reason or another.

Meghan finished off her tea and held her cup in mid-air. "Unless you consider Victor Ross a possibility."

"Hmm." Katie tilted her head. "What makes you mention him?"

Meghan shook her head. "No, it couldn't be. Mr. Ross has been so good to those who lost loved ones in the war. He's even putting on that benefit ball."

"Tell me what made you think of Victor Ross just now. What made you consider him even for a moment?"

"I know you're kind of sweet on him, so I don't want to say anything against him."

"Sweet on him? No, I just want to get information from him. You are not going to hurt my feelings."

Meghan tilted her head. "I'm not entirely sure Mr. Ross isn't somehow connected with Tricia. I've watched her reaction when she sees him. I'm not sure if she's in love with him or fears him, but she watches his every move. Anyway, that bothered me. I even thought she might be jealous of you."

"That's a possibility if she's in love with him. He's giving me a lot of attention."

"Consider this too. Victor Ross has only been in Liberty for about ten years, and he's got plenty of money. He fits several characteristics mentioned in Suzanne's letter."

Katie shook her head. "Perhaps. But Cliff Yosterman makes me very suspicious. He's tall and lean."

"What has tall and lean got to do with it?"

Suzanne told me that before he died, Stuart told her the man on the ridge was tall and lean and was wearing a wide-brimmed hat."

"Well, so does Mr. Ross."

"Point taken. Very well, when I see Mr. Ross on Saturday, I'll try to learn more."

Meghan said, "Here's something else to think about. Suzanne described this gypsy as a half-breed."

"Didicoy is the term she used."

"Mr. Ross has the complexion of a gypsy, don't you think?" Meghan asked.

Katie pressed her lips together, thinking, then said, "He is dark complected,"

Meghan's eyes narrowed. "I think I'll make a trip out to his ranch and take care of that leather seat this evening. I promised that I would stitch it up before Saturday." She winked. "Perhaps I'll snoop a bit too."

"No. Promise me you won't snoop. It's too dangerous."

Meghan gave Katie a look that all but accused her of howling hypocrisy. Then she shrugged, perhaps remembering that she, unlike Katie, did not have a weapon. "All right, no snooping. How about I let you know if I see anything odd? Will that suit?"

"Please be careful."

Meghan got up and began tidying up the tea things. "Tell mother I'll pick up the boys tomorrow morning." She paused, holding the cups and saucers. "I have a funny feeling about Mr. Ross. Perhaps you should cancel your date. The newspaper will be out by Saturday. What if it's him? He's capable of killing. He served in the war."

"Only for ninety days." She paused. "If you can go sneaking around Mr. Ross's barn, I can't imagine why you have a problem with me going out to a public place with the man on Saturday night." Katie crossed her arms. "For some reason, he's interested in seeing me, and I need information from him, so I'm going. I'll have my gun near at hand."

"You can't bring a gun on Saturday night. None of your gowns have pockets."

Katie turned in her chair and lifted a black-beaded reticule off a nearby shelf. "Ah, but I can hide it in this."

"I'm not sure if that's a good idea. Your gun is bulky. What if he notices it?"

Katie stood. "I will be sure to keep it tucked out of sight. I need to learn more about him and what better way to wheedle information from him than over a nice dinner with a couple of glasses of wine?"

A rap on the door drew their attention. Brett poked his head in, behaving as if stepping inside would contaminate him in some way.

Katie laughed. "We don't bite."

Brett ignored the comment and took off his hat. "Miss Katie, I'll be in the wagon out front whenever you're ready to go."

"I'll be there in a minute."

Brett stepped back outside, and the door closed.

Katie put the reticule back on the shelf. "No snooping when you go out to the Ross ranch."

"Don't worry. I'll be fine."

Katie tapped her lips with a finger, then said, "Do you want to take my gun?"

"No. I'm only going to do the work that he's requested. I'm sure there's no danger in that."

Katie left the shop and hailed Brett, unaware of the danger the evening would bring to Meghan.

CHAPTER 14

MEGHAN GOES MISSING

Thursday, June 22, 1865

The smell of coffee led Katie to the kitchen earlier than usual. Pouring cups of coffee, for both of them, Hannah announced, "We need rain. Six o'clock in the morning and it's already hot and humid."

Katie sat and accepted a cup from Hannah.

The pounding hooves of a fast-paced horse caused Hannah to draw back the window curtains and look outside. "What's got Liam in such a state?"

Katie stood quickly, her chair nearly toppling backward as she scurried to the door. Both women were on the porch before Liam dismounted.

"Is Meghan here?"

Hannah shook her head. "No, she's at home. The boys are here."

"I can't find Meghan. I've searched for her all morning, but she's not in town, not in the shop. I can't find her anywhere." Liam dismounted and wrapped the reins loosely around a post.

Hannah said, "Maybe she's still sleeping and didn't hear you. Sometimes she works late."

Liam removed his hat and ran a hand through his hair. "I was coming back from the Stauffer place. I delivered a baby this morning. I left their house at about four. There was only a slice of moon this morning, but it was bright enough to see parts of Meghan's pony cart in a ditch." His eyes narrowed, and he shook his head as if re-living his confusion. "Daisy must have taken off in a frenzy considering the damage to the cart. One wheel had fallen off its axle. And I found pieces of her broken cart wedged between rocks."

Hannah put her palm to her mouth and wavered.

Katie put her arm around Hannah's shoulders to steady her.

Liam said, "Daisy came back to town with parts of the cart trailing behind her. Mort found her outside the livery stable." He took a breath. "Daisy's at Mort's now."

"No sign of Meghan? Her clothes? Blood?" Hannah asked.

"I searched all around the area where I found the cart and checked the ditches at the sides of the road leading into town. When I got to town, I stopped by her house and even the shop. I pounded on both doors and called for her, but she didn't answer. Mort heard me and came around to her shop door. He had just brought Daisy into the stable and alerted the marshal."

"The marshal knows?" Hannah asked.

"Yes, he said he'd get a search party." He paused. "Meghan and I had dinner last night. Afterward, she left for the Ross place about six-thirty. She intended to stitch the seam in his carriage seat."

They all turned at the sound of a fast horse in the distance. George Schneider came into view at the bend of the road and rode up the drive at a canter. Meghan's business neighbor reined in his horse in the yard. "Is she here?"

Liam shook his head.

"There's a search party meeting at that section of road where you came across Meghan's wrecked cart."

Hannah spoke up, "Maybe Meghan's at home and couldn't answer the door. Don't you have a key?"

Schneider's eyes grew wide. "Yes. I do. But I didn't want to take liberties. I tried her doors. They were locked."

"Take liberties!" Hannah said, hysteria creeping into her voice. "Use your keys to check on both the house and shop! We need to be sure she's missing."

"Yes, ma'am." Schneider turned his horse to leave.

Hannah's face blanched, but she regained control of herself. "What else can we do?"

Liam put on his hat. "I'll join the search."

Katie said, "I'll go too." And then she turned to Hannah. "If you're going to be all right here."

"I'll feel better if you're out there searching for Meghan."

"Very well." She looked at Liam. "I'll just be a minute."

Liam untied his horse's reins. "I'll see if Hank's got a fresh horse I can use." He put a hand on his horse's neck. "Been a long night for old Tim."

Once Katie had retrieved her gun and put her trousers under her skirt, she walked quickly to the barn, where she found Brett preparing to put a side-saddle on Mouse. "I'll need a Western saddle," she said.

Brett raised his eyebrows.

"I don't care what they think. I am not riding through hill and dale on a side-saddle."

Without a word, just a firm nod of approval, Hank put a Western saddle on Mouse, added a sheath, and inserted a rifle. "There's rabid coyotes and wolves this time of year," he remarked.

"Thanks, Hank." After Brett had given her shooting lessons, she had practiced using her new gun and that very rifle.

When they left the barn, Katie, Brett, and Liam found five workers from the mill on horseback in the yard. Word traveled fast. Fletcher had sent mill employees.

When they reached the road, Katie glanced back. Hannah and Meghan's boys watched from the yard. Hannah had a firm grip on Billy and Tommy. Billy was crying and Tommy looked ready to bolt.

* * *

Katie, Brett, and Liam found the marshal and his men gathered along the road. Parts of Meghan's cart were strewn over a twenty-foot span.

Katie swallowed, holding back her panic. "Any other signs of Meghan?"

The marshal tipped his hat. "Ma'am, this is men's work."

Katie glared at him. "So you say."

The marshal ignored her and turned to Liam. "Glad you're here, Doc. The more men we have lookin' for Mrs. Turner the faster we'll find her. Me and my men followed some tracks through the fields and ended up at the Ross ranch. Seems Mrs. Turner came out for a visit last night. Ross figured she came to stitch up his carriage seat. We can't be sure of the time because there was no one to vouch for her. Ross spent most of the evenin' in town playin' cards, and his housekeeper spent the night at her mother's, celebratin' a birthday or some such. Just the housekeeper's at the ranch now. Ross is out with a search party checkin' the woods and fields between here and town."

Marshal Gerber's horse took a step toward Mouse, nudging the horse's neck. Mouse stood her ground. Katie patted Mouse's neck in appreciation.

"Ross couldn't think of any other reason for Mrs. Turner's visit, so he checked the carriage in the barn. The seat's been stitched. She was there."

Liam said, "She had dinner with me and left about six-thirty." A few men raised their eyebrows at that. Liam picked up on the need to save Meghan's reputation. "I can ask my housekeeper for the exact time, as she was there the entire evening. I know Mrs. Turner had a task she wanted to finish last night. It must have been the carriage work."

Liam and Meghan's dinner last night would soon be fodder for town gossip, by Katie's reckoning.

The marshal said, "I'll go back into town and check on things. See if I can learn anything new."

Liam said, "George Schneider is going to see if Mrs. Turner's returned to her shop or house. He has keys for both."

"Good enough."

Katie said to Gerber, "You might check on Cliff Yosterman as well. Find out his whereabouts last night. His actions lately have been suspicious."

The marshal pointedly stared at Katie's legs straddling Mouse, smirked, and then turned to Liam. "George came to talk with me yesterday about Yosterman bothering Tricia McDowell. Says he's been a real nuisance. I planned to talk with him today."

Katie's lips narrowed and then she said, "I sure would appreciate your checking on Yosterman's whereabouts yesterday."

He tipped his hat. "I'll do that, ma'am, soon as we find Mrs. Turner."

Liam picked up his reins.

"Mrs. Turner could be anywhere. How many men are with Ross?" Liam asked.

"Two. Most of his men are with the cattle this time a year in the upper pastures."

Liam lifted his chin toward the men from the mill. "How about we have these fellas help your men out?"

"Yeah, the more the better." The marshal addressed his two town men and two of the mill men. "Head to town and ride out on both sides of the road some distance." He turned to the three remaining mill men. "Take your search down toward the ravine. Maybe Mrs. Turner took a wrong turn on foot." Addressing all the men, he said, "Space yourselves out a bit, maybe a few hundred feet apart, and call out to Meghan Turner often. Listen too. Give her a chance to call back. She may have been thrown from the cart and be lyin' unconscious somewhere in high grasses, so look sharp."

Some men acknowledged their assignment with a tip of the hats, and all parted as directed.

The marshal turned to Liam. "We'll meet back at my office in a few hours if you don't find her. Fire three shots if you do."

Katie moved Mouse closer to Liam. "Liam, you want to ride back to the Ross place and look around? We might notice something the others may have missed. I want Brett to come with us too. He's very observant." She glanced toward the marshal, who was listening. "You all right with that?"

He gave her a two-finger salute. "Let us know if you learn anything." He took a few steps away and then turned back. "Three shots, ya hear."

Katie turned her mount toward Ross's ranch. She needed to get away from the marshal quickly before she said something she'd regret and cause further problems between them. Liam and Brett followed.

Liam's horse caught up with hers. "Any ideas?" Liam asked.

"Let's follow the road and call out for Meghan till we get back to Ross's. It was early light when the marshal's men were searching. They could have missed something."

When they arrived at the Ross ranch, Liam and Brett searched the outside perimeter of the barn while Katie tied her horse to a nearby post and went inside. The barn smelled of clean horses and leather.

A fancy black carriage was parked in the corner of the barn. Katie walked over and circled it. The passenger door on the west side of the barn was beneath a large window giving ample light. A good place for Meghan to work on the seat last evening. The dirt floor beneath that carriage door had been newly swept. The hackles on the back of Katie's neck lifted. Something had happened here, and the tracks had been swept away.

Chapter 15

The Carriage Evidence

Thursday, June 22, 1865

A booming voice startled Katie. "Guten morgen. I'm Anna, Mr. Ross's housekeeper." The woman spoke with a strong German accent.

Katie came out from behind the carriage to greet her. Anna's bulky body matched her big volume.

Anna's brow furrowed when she spotted Katie, but she turned and directed her comments to Liam. "I saw you coming into the barn." She put a tray with three cups on a large barrel. "I brought you some coffee. I thought you might need a little refreshment by now, ja?"

Katie walked over and took a cup from the tray. "Thank you." She took a sip. "Did you hear any commotion out here last night?"

"No, I was visiting my mother. I only arrived back this morning in time to fix Mr. Ross and his men some breakfast."

"And what time was that?"

"Six o'clock. Mr. Ross starts his day early. The marshal's men came when Mr. Ross sat down to eat. He never had a chance to finish his breakfast."

"Could I ask you a favor?" Katie asked.

"Ja."

"Would you bring us three canteens of water? In our haste, we forgot water. We may be riding for a while, and it's going to be a hot day."

"Ja." With that, Anna left.

Katie put her coffee back on the tray and walked over to the carriage. "This spot under the carriage door is a bit suspicious."

Liam and Brett put down their cups and followed Katie.

She pointed at the dirt floor beneath the barn's window and in front of the carriage door. "Someone's swept the area here. That bothers me." She opened the door and climbed up.

She ran her hand over the seat seam and found the area that had been stitched. She ran her hand over it again. "Meghan was here. This is where the seam has been stitched. At least the marshal got that right."

Brett and Liam came around the back of the carriage and Liam opened the door opposite Katie's to get a better look inside.

A black fringe decorated the bottom edge of the seat. Katie kneeled on the carriage floor. She slid her hand through the fringe and pulled out a small basket. She held the basket up. "These are Meghan's things."

"Here are your canteens," Anna announced.

Liam and Brett quickly closed the carriage door. Katie slid the basket back where she'd found it under the seat and closed the door on her side too. She came around the back of the carriage and walked toward the housekeeper. Something about the woman made Katie uneasy.

Anna distributed the canteens. "You need a lot of water on hot days." The woman's eyes flashed, taking in the carriage and the rest of the barn. Then she pursed her lips and picked up the tray. "Anything else I can get for you?"

Anna's actions were wooden now, her manner nervous. Was she hiding something?

Liam glanced over at Katie, who had moved after the canteen distribution and was now standing behind Anna. Katie shook her head.

Liam said, "I think we're done here. We're going to circle the area on horseback. You see any problem with that?"

"No, I am sure Mr. Ross will not mind." She took a few steps toward the barn door and then turned. "I will work in the garden today and listen carefully for anything odd."

"Thank you," Katie said.

Anna left.

When Anna was out of earshot, Katie whispered, "Meghan would not leave her sewing things in the carriage. Something happened to Meghan here in this barn. And I don't trust Anna."

They came out of the barn and untied their horses. Brett walked his horse over to a path behind the barn. He bent down to examine it.

Katie followed him. When she reached Brett's side, she asked, "Did you find something?"

Brett pointed to the sides of the path. "See how that grass is flattened?"

"Yes," Katie said.

"Somebody's been through here within the past few hours."

Liam joined them. The bent grass on each side of the path was still green. "The damage is recent and wide. A wagon, I'd say."

Katie glanced at Brett. "Good work."

Liam said, "Let's follow this path up the hill. This will lead us to Ross's upper pastures. Stu and I often played up there."

Liam turned to Katie, "You need a leg up?"

"Nope." Mouse was only about fifteen hands high. She put her foot in the stirrup and settled into the saddle. "Lead on."

They stopped their horses at the first small clearing with a divide in the road. Liam turned his horse to the path on the right. "The wagon went this way."

"Both paths lead to the yard and barn," Brett said. "That one." He pointed to the path on the left, "goes to a small shack first, but it'll eventually lead to the same yard. Just take us a little longer. Old man Munson didn't like to stay with the hired hands when he was up here. Here tell, he liked to come up here and drink."

Katie turned to Brett. "Maybe you should ride back and let the others know about this."

"I want to stay with you."

"We may be heading for trouble. If something happened to you, I'd blame myself for taking you along."

"I can help and I ain't scared."

Liam said, "We need to get going, Katie."

"Very well." Katie narrowed her eyes. "If there's any trouble at all, I don't want any heroics out of you."

"Yes, ma'am," Brett said.

The path took a steep incline and then flattened out. Liam asked Brett, "Does Ross use Munson's barn or either of the cabins?"

"Mr. Ross spruced up the hired hands' shack when he bought the land. He's using the barn for pigs this summer."

"When did Ross buy this land?" Katie asked, thinking again that Ross could be Suzanne's didicoy.

"When old man Munson died," Liam answered, "probably about two or three years ago. He had heart trouble and died while the war was on. His son had moved out West, so he sold the land to Ross. I'm pretty sure Mr. Overmeyer took care of the transaction."

"As soon as we get a chance, I need to talk to you." She wanted to let Liam know what she had learned from Suzanne about the didicoy.

"Right. Let's keep quiet for now. Who knows what we'll find when we crest this hill."

* * *

The western pastures of Ross's holdings were over a mile from his main house. As they cleared the woods, Katie's growing appetite was squelched by pig stench. From the barn, the pigs squealed in cheerful greeting. Katie scanned the yard; her tension building as she looked for movement.

The site presented a pretty picture despite the smell. The small cabin and large barn were old but recently whitewashed. The cabin porch had fresh wood railings. The raw wood used for the horse trough and hitching post confirmed these were recent additions.

All three looked around warily, dismounted, and led their horses to the trough. Brett pulled the well pump handle several times, spilling fresh water into the trough. The horses drank greedily.

Katie wiped her brow. Sweat was running down her back. The day was hot, but her fear was also a factor. They refilled their canteens.

Brett said, "Them pigs are tended. Someone's stayin' up here." Brett walked over to the alternate path entrance. "There's horse tracks on this path and I figure it's not too long ago."

Liam said, "Let's not get ahead of ourselves. That may be for legitimate reasons." He pointed to the side of the barn that bordered the woods. "Let's tie the horses over there. It's well shaded and there's plenty of grass. I want to have a look around."

Katie and Brett followed Liam and secured their horses to low branches. Liam pulled his rifle from the sheath. "Just a precaution," he said.

Katie walked back to the edge of the yard to see if the horses were visible from the path. They couldn't be seen, which would give them some advantage if they needed to leave quickly. This place put her on high alert. She wasn't sure why.

She caught up with Liam as he walked to the backside of the barn. The back of the barn served as one side of the pigpen. Sturdy fencing on the other three sides completed the outdoor rectangular pen. A pig pushed through a leather flap to go into the barn. The pigs that remained outside had lost interest in their presence and had quieted. Several pigs lay resting in the shaded mud. Others drank at a trough within the outer pen.

Beyond the barn was an outhouse next to a wide path that ascended to the thick woods beyond. Katie took advantage of the outhouse as Brett and Liam followed the path uphill for a few yards.

When Brett and Liam returned, Liam said, "There are no wagon tracks to the upper pasture. Maybe the wagon's in the barn." They moved through the yard toward the barn entrance.

A cabin with a railed porch was set about fifty feet or so from the barn at a high point in the yard. Katie didn't notice any movement from the cabin.

Liam slid the barn door open only wide enough for them to slip inside.

A much smaller pigpen was inside the barn. A few large pigs put their snouts over the fencing, interested in their new guests.

Katie walked toward the friendly pigs. She heard rustlings behind her and turned. Brett stood next to a wagon parked in a dark corner of the barn.

Brett said, "I bet this is the wagon that left Ross's lower yard."

Liam ran his hand along the wheel, checking for dirt or grass. "You're probably right." He turned as he looked all around the barn. "The barn's clear. I'll check the cabin."

Brett followed Liam. "I'll go with you."

"No," Liam said, "You stay here with Miss Katie." Then his face softened, and he pointed to the barn window with a clear view of the cabin. "But keep an eye out for me, will you?"

"Yes, sir." Katie moved to the window and watched as Liam made his way from the barn up the small incline to the cabin.

Brett continued to scour the barn. "Miss Katie," Brett whispered, "there's a saddle here with the initials SR. I think this is Mr. Stuart's saddle."

"Oh, my God," Liam shouted from the cabin porch.

Katie turned back to the window. Brett ran over to Katie's side of the barn to see what distressed Liam.

Liam clutched the sides of the cabin window, staring through the glass. "It's Meghan."

Brett and Katie hurried from the barn.

Liam moved from the window to the door and tried to open it. "The door's locked."

Katie peered in the cabin window. The window ledge was only thigh-high from the porch floor, making it easy to view the cabin's interior. Meghan's legs were splayed on the floor with her back propped against the wall. She was unconscious. "With so much color in her face, she couldn't be dead. The heat in the cabin had to be stifling. She'd probably passed out."

Katie ran her hand along the top of the sash. "The window is nailed shut."

Liam was back at the window and paused. He turned the stock of his rifle and was poised to break the glass when Katie saw an undulating movement on Meghan's skirt and let out a small yelp of surprise. She put up her hand to stop his movement. Several rattlesnakes writhed within the folds of her skirt. Another slithered over Meghan's shoulder. "The glass breaking might waken Meghan and frighten the snakes to attack!"

Their shouts and movement had caused the snakes to become active. The snakes crawling over Meghan repulsed Katie. She felt nauseous. She put a hand to cover her mouth and ran to the back of the shack and vomited. Ashamed of her reaction, she promised herself to be stronger and help not hinder Meghan's rescue.

She stepped back up to the porch but kept her distance from the window. She didn't want to vomit again. Focused on Meghan, Brett and Liam hadn't even noticed her retching. When she returned to the porch, they were whispering ideas for Meghan's safe escape.

"We need to get her out of there real quiet-like," Brett said.

Liam took a knife from the sheath on his belt and pried the nails from the window sash.

"Meghan moved her hand," Liam said. "So she may be waking up. It's imperative to get her out before the rattlers startle her. I can open the windows and step inside. I'll move quietly."

"You'll get yourself bit." Brett whispered, "I have another idea. When we were in the barn, I heard squeakin'."

Katie's brow furrowed. "The pigs?"

"No. It was little squeaks, like mice."

"What's your point?" Liam asked.

"Maybe we could lure the snakes with the mice. Let me check." Brett walked quickly toward the barn and Katie followed.

Once inside the barn, Brett went directly to the wagon and crawled under it.

Katie bent down to watch him. "Now I hear the squeaking."

He crawled to the corner of the barn, grabbed a burlap bag, and spent some time rustling under the wagon. Once he had shimmied out from under the wagon, he lifted a burlap bag that seemed to move on its own. "I knew it," he whispered. "Whoever planted them rattlers had to keep 'em fed."

Katie screwed up her face in disgust. "You feed snakes mice?"

Brett ignored her question. He turned toward the barn door and put his index finger to his lips. "Shh, I think I hear riders."

CHAPTER 16

THE SNAKE MAN

Thursday, June 22, 1865

Katie peeked through the gap of the barn door. Two men seemed to appear and disappear among the trees as they rode their horses at a walk along the path through the woods.

Liam slipped into the barn just before the men entered the yard. Had the men detected Liam's movement? Katie checked the crack between the boards. The riders' focus was on the cabin. Mouse neighed, probably sensing their arrival. Katie cringed and peeked through the gap again. The men never changed their gait. Loud grunts from the twenty or so pigs must have drowned out the horse's whinny.

Katie's heartbeat quickened. If they confronted them with guns or shouts, it might rile the snakes. But what if these men were unaware of the situation and would help them rescue Meghan? She watched the men approach and dismissed that idea. The men were focused on the cabin. They knew Meghan was inside. Katie leaned her back against the wall and took a few deep breaths. What could she do?

The men talked as they crossed the yard. She heard the squeak of the pump and the water running. They were watering their horses at the trough. Then a man's heavy footsteps crossed the cabin porch.

Brett was crouched at the barn window that faced the cabin. Katie joined him there. Liam stood with his back against the wall next to the window. He readied his rifle to fire.

Katie put a hand on the rifle's barrel and whispered, "No. You'll startle the snakes!" She crouched to hide from the men as she looked out the barn window.

One of the men, a short fat man, stood at the cabin window. His lower pant legs were caked in mud or manure. He had rings of salt around the collar of his shirt and under his arms. "My, my, my, ain't that just the prettiest sight," he said. "No time at all and they'll work their magic." His voice was raspy, a heavy smoker's voice with a Southern accent.

The tall blond man's clothes were clean, and he was well-groomed. He walked up the porch stairs to the window. "The snakes are doing nothing," he said in a German accent. "Unlock the door and shoot her," he shouted.

Katie whispered, "We have to do something."

Liam readied his rifle.

The short man unlocked the door but didn't open it. He turned back to the German. "No, let's wait. My snakes will do their work, soon as she wakes." He put his hands up in a gesture to calm down. "Don't you worry yourself. Folks probably ain't even lookin' for her yet." He put his hands down and spit a stream of tobacco. "Say, just how much of that sleepin' potion did ya give her?"

The Southerner turned toward the barn.

Katie, Brett, and Liam lowered their heads below the window. Katie's heart fell. Did the men see them? Right now the two men could be making their way to the barn.

"I had to dose her twice." The German's voice carried as if he was still on the porch. "She was starting to wake when you left to get your snakes. You took too long. We must get rid of her soon."

"We will, we will. She just ain't stirred enough yet." Katie heard him spit another stream of tobacco. "She wakes up and screams. Them snakes'll get her. And it'll look like some kinda accident."

The Southerner spoke from the vicinity of the porch too. Relief flooded through Katie. Maybe they hadn't been seen.

The German spoke again, "We do not have much time. Ross's men will be back soon."

Katie tilted her head, thinking. So does this mean Ross doesn't know these two men are using his cabin? Maybe they're acting without Victor Ross's knowledge.

The Southerner said, "I'll open the window and get some air stirrin'. It's too hot in there. She needs to wake up."

Liam had his back against the wall as he listened. This exchange had him take another peek. He whispered, "The windows. They'll know someone removed the nails. Be ready."

"No," the German said, "I do not like the snakes, better to just shoot the woman."

"Yeah, and have everybody in town askin' questions? What if somebody knows she went to the Ross place? She probably tol' someone."

"All right. We wait for your snakes. But do not open the window. I want to have a cigar in peace. When I finish, we will decide."

Katie listened intently. The German's accent alerted Katie to her earlier feeling that Anna was somehow involved in this. They had the same heavy accents. Were the two related? Married? Katie listened as the men's footsteps crossed the wooden porch. Were they heading to the barn? Her eyes widened in fear. Then the men's footsteps stopped.

The Southerner said, "Betcha by the time you finish your smoke, my snakes will have had their fun. It'll look like an accident. Don't you worry none. I figure we'll just put her at the side of the road, and somebody'll come along and figure she got bit by some rattler. Ha, ha, ain't that a good plan?"

The strike of a match near the porch gave Katie a sense of their whereabouts.

After a moment, the German spoke, "The snakes, the plan is good. How did you come to know snakes?"

"I done some work out West. Back in sixty-one, during the Indian wars. Learned me how to harvest rattler venom from Black Horse, meanest son of a bitch you ever met. Used to keep venom in a tin container. He wore it tied to his side. I once seen him toss it in a man's eyes durin' a fight, painful way to die, painful."

Katie heard him spit again.

"They used it mostly on the tips of their arrows, though. Black Horse is the injun that learned me how to handle rattlers without gettin' bit. Venom fetches a real good price if you know the right buyers."

"Now we need another plan to get rid of that other woman, ja?"

"Did ya use up all the sleeping potion?"

"No, we have more."

"I got a plan. Once these rattlers take care of this one, we'll move the body to the woods tonight. All kinds of varmints in them woods. They'll take care of things. By mornin' the marshal may not even suspect a snake bite." He spit again. "That way we can do this again with that other gal."

Katie jumped when Brett tugged on her sleeve to get her attention. He signaled for them to follow to the wooded side of the barn. Brett pulled aside a few loose boards and held them up. Katie and Liam crawled through the gap. Katie came out about ten feet from the horses. Mouse whickered her concern about this unusual arrival, so Katie stood slowly and put her hand on the horse, gently massaging her neck and shushing her while Liam held the boards on the outside of the barn for Brett.

Katie scanned the woods and both sides of the barn. The pigs' grunts must have covered any sound they had made.

Brett whispered, "We can't fire guns 'cause it'll get them rattlers all riled. I think we need to distract the men by gettin' them to chase one of us and then the other two can come around from behind and knock 'em out. I think I can run the fastest."

Katie's lips tightened. She didn't like to risk Brett, but he could get the men's attention and then leave. She and Liam would take the major risk and knock out the men with the butts of their guns. Brett's idea could work.

She whispered, "Very well. Take your horse and go through the woods. The barn will block their view of you. Tie up the horse and then duck behind those trees and throw some of that corn. I saw a bag of corn cobs in a burlap bag. That'll get the pigs riled and get the men's attention. Once you've distracted them, go back to town for help."

"Yes, ma'am, I saw that feed next to the pen."

Liam held the boards while Brett stepped back through the loose slats. Katie said to Liam. "The men will probably check out the back of the barn to see why the pigs are squealing. Once they're near the pen, we can come around the barn, get behind them and knock them out with the butt of our rifles." She brought the rifle out of the sheath attached to Mouse's saddle.

"You think that will work?" Liam asked as he moved to further separate the loose boards Brett had pushed aside. Brett crawled out and pulled the bag of corn through the gap. He raised it triumphantly.

"I think so. And it sounds like she'll be waking soon," Katie said.

Liam said, "Risky, but I don't think we have any other choice. You able to run in that skirt?"

Katie handed her rifle to Liam and unbuttoned the waist of her skirt and let it drop. She put the skirt in the saddlebag.

Katie put her hand on the boy's shoulder and whispered, "You head for those woods and throw the corn cobs into the pigpen. Give us a signal when you see the men have reached the pen. After you've signaled, Liam and I will sneak up behind them and take them out while you ride into town and get the marshal."

"I can caw like a crow.".

"That'll work." Liam turned to Katie. "Do you think you can swing that rifle hard enough to knock a man down?"

"With pleasure." Katie put on a brave face to conceal her growing fear.

* * *

The pigs squealed with delight when Brett threw the corn cobs into the pen. "What in tarnation's goin' on?" the Southern man shouted. Their quick footsteps alerted her to their location near the pigpen.

Brett's crow signal barely rose above the din, but Katie was listening for it.

"You ready for this?" Liam whispered.

Katie tightened her lips and nodded.

They moved quickly to circle the barn, keeping close to the sides. They paused at the back corner where the pigs' outer fence met the barn. Katie's stomach churned. She was relieved there was nothing left to vomit.

Liam glanced around the barn's corner and then moved aside to let Katie see. The men were only ten feet away, their attention on the woods where Brett had been pitching the corn cobs. Suddenly Katie caught the flash of Brett running. He was now behind the outhouse. She moved so that she was behind the corner again. Her back against the barn.

The Southern man, or snake man as Katie had mentally re-named him, called out, "Hey, boy, what're you doin' out there?"

No answer came.

"Come out and look at me when I'm talkin' to you, boy, or I'll shoot. A bullet'll go right through that crapper wall."

The need to protect Brett shot through Katie with adrenalin and made her fearless. She glanced at Liam and then both ran toward the men's backs. With their focus on the outhouse and the noisy pigs, Meghan's captors didn't hear Katie and Liam until they were within striking distance.

The German turned first, and Liam cracked him on the side of the head with the butt of the rifle. The German man swayed, clutching his head with one hand but holding onto his gun with the other. The snake man's face registered surprise. The momentary pause was long enough for Katie to sweep the butt of her rifle in his direction. She hit him on the side of the head, and he fell, either unconscious or dead.

The German recovered his balance and reached to grab Katie, but Liam had slipped behind him and slammed the butt of the rifle into the center of the tall man's back.

Seeing Liam's intention, Katie stepped aside. The force of the blow knocked the German to the ground. The German's gun flew from his hand. Katie scrambled to retrieve it, but the momentum of her speed caused her to pitch forward, and she fell. She and the German were now both at ground level. She shifted so that she faced him and then squared herself on her haunches and stood. She now held his gun in her right hand and her rifle in the left. The German lay face down in the dirt.

She pointed the gun at his head. "Don't move."

His hand, like a lightning bolt, reached out to grab her ankle. Katie jumped back out of reach, and Liam's boot stomped down on the German's wrist to stop him and hold him in place. The German winced from the pain.

The snake man was beginning to stir. Liam lifted his chin toward him. "Keep that rifle on him. And use it if necessary."

Katie positioned herself in front of the snake man. Her hands shook from the adrenalin rush. While watching the snake man in her peripheral vision, she put the German's gun down and kicked it out of reach. She kept both hands on her rifle and pointed it at the snake man.

Liam called Brett, "We got 'em. Come on out."

Brett came out from behind the outhouse.

"Find some rope," Liam said.

Brett didn't answer and Katie glanced up to check on him. The snake man must have regained consciousness and been watching her. In the moment that Katie's attention was diverted to Brett's welfare, the snake man grabbed the gun barrel and pushed. The butt of the rifle smacked Katie in the chin. Her head snapped back, and the jolt of pain radiated. She lost her balance. To break her fall, she let go of the rifle.

The snake man scrambled for it.

Katie tried to prop herself up on her elbows but fell back again. She was dizzy and nauseous.

Liam moved to help Katie. The snake man gripped Katie's rifle by the barrel and swung the gun butt at Liam's legs. Liam dodged the rifle's arc, but the distraction allowed both of Meghan's captors to get on their feet.

Liam still had his rifle pointed at the German, but the snake man had now turned the rifle and pointed it at Katie. A loosened metal band on the butt of the rifle had split her chin. Blood trickled down her face and neck.

Meghan's captors now stood side by side. Liam waved his rifle menacingly at both men.

Katie lay on her back in the dirt. She wasn't as nauseous now but still dizzy when she lifted her head.

The snake man stood over her with the rifle barrel inches from her chest. His eyes shifted from Katie to Liam and then to the German. "Now we got ourselves a little standoff."

The snake man gave a brown-toothed sneer and spit tobacco close to Katie's face. She grimaced. He put the end of the barrel in the cut in Katie's chin. She winced from the pain and turned her head.

The snake man gave a mocking smile. "Yep, we got ourselves a real interestin' problem. Ya see, it don't matter to me if you shoot ol' Hahn." The snake man glanced at Liam and then returned his focus to Katie. "But I think it matters to you if I shoot her?" He moved the rifle, waving it now at Katie's chest.

Katie's mind raced. What could she do? Did she dare kick the rifle barrel and roll out of the way? If she did, would Liam be able to shoot both men? She was so caught up in her plan that she had forgotten all about Brett until she saw his movement behind the captors. She kept her eyes on the rifle pointed at her chest, but she could see Brett. He was about twenty feet behind the snake man walking in a crouched position. His knife was poised to strike.

Katie was sure Liam could see Brett too, but she didn't think the captors could. Both still had their backs to the woods.

Liam addressed the German, "You hear that? He's ready to sacrifice you so he can get away. Some friend, huh?"

Hahn glanced at the snake man.

Katie held her breath. Did Hahn see Brett with his peripheral vision? If he did, he didn't acknowledge it.

Hahn said to the snake man, "I wish I had some of that venom of yours, I would throw it in your eyes."

The fat man laughed, dribbling tobacco juice down his chin.

Brett was only a few feet away now. The snake man must have sensed Brett behind him because he turned, but Brett was too quick. When the snake man turned, Brett ran toward him in a tackle position and stuck the Bowie knife into the back of his thigh.

The snake man dropped the rifle and cradled his thigh as he absorbed the shock of the pain.

Katie scrambled to pick up the rifle, lifting her eyebrows with the hope of staving off the dizziness. She swayed but kept her balance. Liam kept his rifle aimed at Hahn.

Brett had put the knife in deep. As the man writhed in pain, Katie aimed the rifle at him. She kept her eyes wide and blinked, hoping the dizziness would pass.

Brett pulled a rope out of his pocket and bound the man's hands and feet. Although he posed little danger while he was in so much pain, Katie kept the rifle pointed at his head, keeping her distance. She wasn't taking any chances. After the snake man was secured, Brett tied up Hahn.

Liam pulled a handkerchief out of his pocket. "Let's gag them. We don't need them shouting and scaring those snakes."

Brett took the handkerchief from Liam and gagged Hahn. Then moved over to the snake man. Brett pulled off his own bandana and straddled the fat man. "You might want to get rid of that chew, mister, before I put this gag in your mouth."

With the side of his head on the ground, he let the chew dribble out onto the dirt. Brett tied the gag.

Dirt and sweat ran down the snake man's face from exertion and pain.

Liam said to Katie, "You steady enough? I need to put a tourniquet on his thigh and pull that knife out."

Katie said, "I'm all right. But forget him. We need to get Meghan."

"It'll only take a minute." Liam pulled the bandana off the snake man's neck and tied it tightly around the injured thigh, then pulled out the knife.

The snake man groaned in pain and curled over on his side. He'd passed out.

Liam swiped the knife across the leg of his pants and gave Brett the knife. "You probably saved our lives."

Brett put his knife back in the sheath he wore attached to his belt. "I'm gettin' them mice." As he walked toward the barn, Brett picked up the German's gun that Katie had kicked aside and put it between his belt and his back.

CHAPTER 17

MEGHAN'S RESCUE

Thursday, June 22, 1865

With Meghan's captors disabled, Katie and Liam ran to the cabin window. As they looked in, Meghan moved her arm from her lap.

Liam whispered, "She's waking. I'm going in." He opened the window and put his leg through in readiness. Turning to Katie, he said, "I'll grab Meghan. You get the door."

"No, don't." Brett came up on the porch and set the burlap bag of mice and a wooden box down next to the window. "We'll use the mice."

Liam moved his leg back through the window and stepped back onto the porch.

Katie whispered, "How are we going to get mice to stay at the opposite end of the room once we let them out of the bag?"

A breeze blew through the open window, causing both the rattlers and Meghan to stir.

Liam put his arms along the side of the window, readying himself to crawl through.

"Wait." Katie grabbed Liam's arm.

Brett lifted the box by its handle. "I think that Southern man uses it to corral 'em." He pointed to the little hatches that surrounded the lower portion of the trap and gave a gentle push to one of the doors. "See? With a little push on any of these hatches the snakes can get in, but they can't get out. I'll load it up with the mice and move it away from the window." He glanced around the porch. "I need something with a long handle to set the trap far from Miss Meghan."

Katie said, "I saw a pitchfork in the barn. I'll get it."

As she hurried to the barn, dizziness threatened. She slowed her pace and overheard Brett's explanation to Liam. "The top of the trap opens on these here two hinges when you release the latch. We just pour the mice into the trap. It's like pourin' sand from a bag into a box."

When Katie returned with the pitchfork, Brett put the trap filled with mice down on the floor of the cabin beneath the window. Using the pitchfork he slid it to the corner, away from Meghan. The mice squeaked, sensing danger and the snakes began to respond to the bait, slithering to the trap and gently nudging the doors to get inside. It seemed a familiar routine for them. Four snakes entered the cage.

Meghan moved again as a fifth snake moved near but not in the trap. Meghan lifted her hand, although she wasn't fully conscious.

Liam crawled through the window and ran to Meghan.

Brett used the pitchfork to bring the trap closer to the fifth snake.

Brett stood behind Katie. Her eyes darting first to Liam and then to the box holding the trapped snakes.

A sixth snake had concealed itself in the folds of Meghan's skirt. The snake rattled its warning. Liam bent down to pick up Meghan where she lay on the floor. The snake rattled again and struck Liam's upper arm. Liam grunted in response to the pain. The snake rattled and was poised to strike again. Liam lifted Meghan higher to protect her from the snake and backed away.

Katie froze, her hand on her mouth. Memories of a hole filled with writhing snakes rattling their tales came surging to her mind. She was suddenly paralyzed with terror.

Brett nudged her aside and was through the door before she could stop him. He shifted around Meghan and Liam and stomped on the rattler's neck with his heavy boot, and then took his Bowie knife out of the sheath and cut the snake's head off. He followed Liam as he carried Meghan to the door. One of the five remaining snakes had still not entered the trap. It lifted its body poised to strike and rattled from the corner.

The snake didn't move while Liam crossed the threshold and handed the semi-conscious Meghan to Brett.

Liam's arm was already swelling from the rattlesnake bite. He tore his sleeve off at the shoulder. The sleeve dangled from his wrist by the wrist button.

Katie closed the cabin door and shut the window. She stood for a moment, chastising herself for her helplessness. Why couldn't she have been braver? What if Brett hadn't pushed her aside to save Liam and Meghan? She'd frozen in fear when she was most needed.

She took a deep breath. Her head was throbbing, but the dizziness had stopped. She would make herself useful in other ways. She turned to Brett. "Meghan needs water. Let's put her in the shade of that big oak tree." Katie walked over to the base of the tree with her canteen. Brett positioned Meghan so that her head was cushioned in Katie's lap. Katie lifted Meghan's head and dribbled water on her lips. Some ran down Meghan's chin, but she began to stir and to lick her lips.

Liam collapsed into a sitting position and leaned against the same tree, cradling his left arm.

Katie's attention was now on Liam. "How bad is it? Take a look, Brett."

Brett squatted at Liam's side. "That rattler sunk his teeth in good, that's for sure."

Meghan's eyes opened. In a weak voice she asked, "Where am I?" She looked up at Katie. "You hurt your chin?"

Katie gently touched her finger to her chin then looked at it. "Yes, but it's stopped bleeding." When Katie bent her head to look at Meghan, her head throbbed. She lifted her face to keep her head level, which lessened the pain.

Liam said, "Brett, help me pull this sleeve off. My wrist is swelling."

Brett unbuttoned the torn sleeve at Liam's wrist and slipped it off.

"Get me my medical pouch. It's in my saddle bag." Liam said.

"Yes, sir." Brett headed to the wooded side of the barn, brought Liam's horse around to the cabin side and tied it to the post near the water trough. He slid Liam's saddle bag off the horse and set it down under the oak tree.

"Thank you," Liam mumbled. "I'll need water too."

Brett grabbed the bucket next to the well and filled it.

Meghan tried to sit up. Katie guided her to a sitting position using the large tree as a back rest. Meghan sat next to Liam and drank from the canteen.

"Clean this snake bite, will you, Katie? Use the soap in my bag."

"Of course." Seeing a bit of Meghan's white petticoat, Katie asked Meghan, "Mind if I tear off a strip of your petticoat to clean Liam's wound?"

Meghan nodded and lifted her skirt to reveal more of the white cotton of her petticoat and weakly began to pull on the hem.

"I'll do that," Katie said.

Brett handed her his knife and Katie was able to quickly remove a strip. With the soap and water, she gently cleaned Liam's wound.

Liam clenched his teeth but made no sound as Katie worked. She tore another strip off Meghan's petticoat and made a sling for Liam's arm to give it some support. His arm had swollen to the point where he could barely bend it at the elbow. Once the sling was set, she tore off another section of Meghan's petticoat and used soap and water to dab her own wound and remove the blood from her chin and neck.

Meghan was now fully awake. She spotted her captors tied in the yard. "Oh, those horrible men!" She became agitated and tried to stand.

"You're safe." Katie gently eased Meghan back. "You need to rest for a bit."

Liam took Meghan's hand with his good hand and pointed his chin toward the men tied in the yard. "Those men kidnapped you, rendered you unconscious and had every intention of murdering you." Liam was sweating and shaking, the rattler's poison taking its effect.

Brett gave him a drink from his canteen.

Liam took a sip and recovered himself for a moment. "Do you have any idea why they would do that?"

Her eyes widened. "You're hurt!"

"I'll be all right. The men, Meghan, why?"

She put her hand to her temple and let it fall. "Let me think. I was stitching the carriage seat. Those men talked about Tricia and snakes." She became agitated. "Is Tricia all right?"

Katie said, "Tricia's not here. She's quite safe back in town." Then Katie glanced at Liam's arm and frowned. His arm was hard and had turned a fiery red. Liam looked down at his own arm. "Katie, see to that man's wound using soap and water and then remove the tourniquet. We need to go."

Katie grudgingly obeyed. The snake man was alert now and Katie kept her head level, trying to quiet the dull pain of a headache. She ripped away the snake man's pant leg, bandaged the thigh with more strips of Meghan's petticoat, and removed the tourniquet. He grunted his displeasure through the gag. Brett watched Katie for a moment; he must have been satisfied that Katie was not in danger because he walked to the barn.

Katie finished dressing the snake man's leg wound and returned to tend to Meghan and Liam, giving both more water. Brett had hitched his horse to the small wagon they had found in the barn.

Katie walked over. "Good idea. Neither of them is fit to ride."

"The saddle. Remember SR is burned in it, Mr. Stuart's initials."

"Yes." Katie glanced at Meghan's captors. "I think we've found Stuart's murderers." The tall German would fit Suzanne's description.

Brett and Katie led Meghan and Liam to the wagon and settled them into the back. Meghan was still unsteady when she walked, and Liam was showing signs of delirium.

Katie put a hand on Brett's shoulder. "How about if you drive the wagon?"

"Yes, ma'am." Brett got in the wagon and pulled it closer to the oak tree, then got out and lifted Meghan to the wagon. With Katie's help and the overturned bucket as a step, she coaxed Liam in the wagon.

Once their patients were made comfortable, Katie donned her skirt again and rode Mouse with Liam's horse tethered to the horn on her saddle. She still had a fierce headache, but the dizziness had subsided. As they left the cabin, Brett fired three shots to let anyone in the area know that Meghan had been found. Katie winced in pain from the loud noise.

* * *

By the time they arrived at Six Maples it was nearly one o'clock. Hank took off for the marshal's office with a report that the kidnappers were trussed up and baking in the sun at the Ross pig barn with a cage full of rattlers in the cabin.

Liam's upper arm was swollen to twice its normal size. The skin threatened to split. Hannah quickly took charge, applying herbs to Liam's wound that cooled and soothed the infected area. With Hannah's help, Meghan tucked Liam in bed just as the afternoon rains came.

Hannah bustled into the kitchen with a headache powder and went to work with herbal compresses on Katie's cut. The herbs soon eased her pain. Hannah insisted she wear a bandage over her chin until tomorrow morning.

Hannah may not have had the training of a doctor, but she knew much about medicine. It would be advantageous to learn her methods as well as those found in conventional medical practice, Katie decided.

After all the medicinal chores were completed, Katie and Brett sat down to ham sandwiches. Both were hungry and talked little during the meal.

Hannah pushed a slice of strawberry rhubarb pie in front of Brett when he finished his sandwich. "Your mother's probably beside herself with worry," she said. "How about finishing your pie and letting her know firsthand about your day."

"Yes, ma'am," Brett said between mouthfuls. "I aim to do just that, but I sure could use another piece of that pie before I go."

Hannah mussed up his hair as she walked by, but she put another slice on his plate. There was an easy camaraderie between them. Brett had played a large part in saving Meghan's life. Katie knew Hannah would not forget that.

Shortly after Brett left, Hank returned from the village. He stood at the kitchen door. "Miss Katie, seems the marshal wants to see you, Doc, and Brett."

"He can't come here?" Katie blew out a long breath. The headache powder had eased the worst of her headache. "Well, Liam's in no shape to ride and Brett's gone. I'll go."

* * *

Katie returned from town around four o'clock. Brett and Hannah were sitting on the porch rocking chairs. Brett had been home to reassure his mother and then returned to Six Maples. At Katie's arrival, Meghan stepped outside and leaned on the kitchen door frame with her arms folded across her chest.

Katie tied her horse to the post and came up onto the porch. She rested her backside on the railing to address Hannah, Meghan, and Brett. "The snake man's name is Daryl Plumpton, and the German's Hans Schmidt. Hans is Anna Schmidt's brother. Anna had told the men about the cabin, so she's been arrested too as an accomplice. The marshal's still not sure why they kidnapped Meghan. I told him what we had overheard when we were hiding out in the barn." She directed her comment to Hannah. "I overheard Plumpton and Schmidt. They planned to murder 'some gal,' and I think they meant Tricia."

Katie glanced over to Meghan. "You just got in their way. What they have against Tricia, we don't know yet. Nobody's talking."

Katie then directed her attention to Brett. "When we brought Joseph to the doctor's office, were you there when Dr. West realized the chloroform stock was low?"

"No, ma'am."

"Well, it was Anna Schmidt who stole Liam's anesthesia. She offered to clean the office when Liam's housekeeper, Mrs. Davey suddenly took ill on Tuesday afternoon. Anna was probably responsible for Mrs. Davey's illness."

Meghan said, "Liam thought Mrs. Davey's had a mild case of food poisoning.

"Anna Schmidt and Mrs. Davey are friends." Katie smirked. "Well, they probably aren't any more. Anyway, Mrs. Davey and her children shared a picnic lunch provided by Anna on Tuesday when the Davey children went swimming. Anna made Mrs. Davey her favorite chicken sandwich. She made the children cheese sandwiches. Mrs. Davey's was too sick to clean the infirmary that evening, but Anna was right there volunteering to fill in for Mrs. Davey. Anyway, Anna Schmidt is very involved in whatever is going on." She paused. "I need to trust my instincts more. I had a bad feeling about her."

Meghan walked toward Katie and then stopped. "So that's what happened to the chloroform. Its disappearance had Liam puzzled."

Brett asked, "What's chloroform?"

"A drug that puts you out cold. That's what they used to make Meghan sleep."

Hannah stopped rocking and turned to Meghan. "It pains me to think you were in the hands of such evil men."

Meghan walked over and put her hand on her mother's shoulder. "I'm fine now."

Brett stood and gestured towards his chair. "Please sit down, Miss Meghan."

"Thank you." Meghan sat in the rocker.

Brett moved to lean on the porch railing next to Katie. "We may have found Stuart's saddle in Ross's pig barn. Tell 'em, Miss Katie."

"No, it was your discovery. You tell them."

He nodded and turned to Meghan and Hannah. "We found a saddle with SR burned in the cantle."

"Brett found it. If the saddle is Stuart's, my guess is that Plumpton and Schmidt killed Stuart for his horse and have some kind of connection to Yosterman."

"But why target Tricia?" Meghan's eyes narrowed.

Brett said, "Maybe the marshal will be able to find out. He's pretty good about gettin' information out of prisoners."

"Yeah, I bet," Katie said. "Well, the good news is the men responsible and their accomplice are locked up. Dr. Stephens is tending to Plumpton's wound."

Brett said, "He's the new doctor helpin' out Doc West. I met him the other day when Joseph broke his leg."

"Richard Stephens comes to us straight out of the Western Reserve Medical College." Meghan pursed her lips and then said, "Although I like him and Liam swears by him, what I don't like is that Liam's mother set it up. Dr. Stephens arrived about three weeks ago and is staying in Liam's spare room. If Bertha West has her way, Dr. Stephens will complete his practical training with Liam and then take over the Liberty practice. That way Liam can return to Cleveland and marry the daughter of one of her friends."

"So thoughtful of her," Hannah muttered.

Brett's face was a study in confusion.

Katie turned to him. "Now don't you repeat any of this about Dr. West and his mother, you hear? We're just gossiping."

Brett's eyes widened. "Yes, ma'am."

Katie swiveled her head to address Hannah and Meghan with a tinge of pain for her quick movement. "Here's a question," Katie said. "Did Stuart have his initials burned on the cantle of his saddle?"

Hannah shrugged her shoulders. "I'm not sure, but Hank will know."

Katie turned to Brett again. "I didn't want to say anything to the marshal about the saddle you found until I was sure it was Stuart's." Katie stood. "I'll be right back. I want to check with Hank." She untied Mouse and took the horse to the barn.

Ten minutes later, Katie returned to the porch. Hannah had brought out a pitcher of water and handed a glass to Katie.

"That was Stuart's saddle." Katie returned to her perch on the railing and clicked her glass with Brett's. "Good work."

She took a long drink of the water. "Well, we've all had a big day."

Brett finished the last of his water. "Is it all right if I don't come back until tomorrow afternoon? I got a lot of chores at home to catch up on."

"You don't need to worry about that. I'll let Hank know," Hannah said.

Brett tipped his hat. "Good afternoon, ladies."

A flash of lightening and the roll of thunder quickened Brett's walk across the yard.

"Oh, I hope Brett makes it home before the storm hits," Katie said.

The women picked up the tray and empty glasses and moved into the kitchen where the savory smell of stew greeted them.

Katie pushed the curtain aside and shut the window as the rain began to come down in heavy sheets. "I'm afraid Brett will get sopping wet."

"Oh, I'm sure he'll be fine," Hannah said. "He's a trooper."

"He certainly is," Katie let the gingham curtain fall and turned back to Hannah and Meghan. "So is Ross involved in this?"

Meghan's eyes narrowed. "You know I thought so, but after today, I'm not so sure."

Katie set the table as Hannah ladled the stew into bowls. Katie, Hannah, and Meghan sat down to supper.

Katie was quiet as she ate. She couldn't figure out why Stuart's saddle was in Ross's barn. Yosterman was not staying at the hotel; she had checked on that when she went to town to see the marshal. Maybe Yosterman was staying at the cabin unbeknownst to Ross? Was Yosterman in cahoots with Plumpton and Schmidt? What would these men have against Stuart and Tricia? Katie needed to find out more. Her date on Saturday night with Ross might give her a few answers.

Satisfied with that thought, Katie joined in the conversation, rehashing the morning's events as they ate, and then she was quiet again.

"You're far away." Hannah said as she picked up bowls, clearing the table.

"Just thinking." Katie got up and walked over to Hannah's desk. She picked up her notes and a pencil. "I want to add the facts we learned today."

Hannah put the dishes in the sink, washed her hands, and turned to Katie. "I'll leave you to your thinking and check on Philip."

"I hear Liam stirring." Meghan left to take a bowl of stew to him.

About fifteen minutes later, Hannah and Meghan returned to the kitchen. Katie was reviewing her notes with a cup of tea at hand.

"Oh, no, tea won't do," Hannah said. "This calls for a bit of celebration." Hannah opened a bottle of plum brandy and poured out three glasses. She handed glasses to Katie and Meghan. Hannah turned to Katie and raised her glass. "I am forever in your debt."

"You saved my life." Meghan's eyes welled up with held back tears. "But only a bit of brandy for me. I'm starting to feel like my old self and don't care to have my senses blunted." Meghan's eyes took on a faraway look.

"What is it?" Hannah said.

Meghan slapped her hand on the table. "I am so angry. That awful Plumpton man bragged about scaring Tricia with his snakes. That's what I overheard when I was in the carriage. If I hadn't let out a cry of surprise at their comments, I probably wouldn't have been found out."

"You're starting to remember," Hannah said.

"I was in the coach sewing the cushion, working so intently that I didn't hear the men come in the barn. The way I was situated. . ." Meghan hunched as if hiding. "I was hidden from their view, but I could hear their conversation." She sat up straight again. "I wasn't trying to hide. I simply wanted to wrap up the last of my work before I lost the light. One of them mentioned Tricia's name."

Meghan put her palm to her forehead and then lowered it to her cheek. "I don't know why they wanted Tricia's cooperation or why they wanted her to stay away from me." She dropped her hand. "Anyway, when I heard Tricia's name, I gasped. And then Schmidt came around and surprised me as I crouched in the carriage. I only had the door open on the barn window side as I worked." Meghan's whole body went rigid as if reliving the experience. "He put a rag over my mouth. It's the last thing I remember."

Katie leaned across the table. "There was chloroform on that rag. From what I overheard, they planned to kill Tricia the same way they tried to kill you. Douse you in chloroform, lock you in that shack, and when you awakened the snakes would kill you. Your death would be ruled an accident." She grimaced. "Plumpton sells snake venom for a living."

Hannah took a deep breath and put her hand over Meghan's.

Meghan face shifted to concern. "What about Tricia? What information is Tricia keeping secret? How scared she must be all alone in that house! We must do something."

Katie said, "You're right. The rain's stopped and we still have an hour or so of daylight. Are you able to ride into town with me to talk with Tricia?"

"I feel better now. What do you have in mind?"

"We can start by telling Tricia what happened today. Let's take the pony cart."

Hannah shook her head. "No. I will not let you two go alone with Cliff Yosterman still a threat." She sighed. "Hank can take you."

"You win on that count. Although with all that's happened and that thunderstorm, there's a good chance Cliff Yosterman won't be on guard duty tonight. If he's left his post, maybe Tricia will talk to us. We can let her know Schmidt and Plumpton are behind bars."

CHAPTER 18

TRICIA'S STORY

Thursday night, June 22, 1865

The rain had cooled the air, making it a comfortable ride into town for Hank, Katie, and Meghan. They left the wagon at the livery stable and walked the two blocks to Tricia's.

At Tricia's end of town, the houses lined the street on the left. On the right were thick woods where Yosterman had kept his watch. The setting sun sent long shadows. Katie scanned the woods for any movement, keeping her hand on the gun hidden in her skirt pocket. She saw no sign of Yosterman.

They reached Tricia's door. Hank pointed to the lilac bush at the corner of the house. "I'll just step over there out of sight until I'm sure you're safe. Signal me from that window above those bushes to let me know all is well."

"I can do that," Katie said.

"If I don't get your signal within five minutes, I'll come in with guns blazin'."

Katie laughed and then muffled the sound with her hand.

"I'm serious, Miss Katie. I need to know you're all right. When I know you're safe, I'll leave and wait for you on that bench in front of Schneider's. Take your time. I brought me a good cigar."

Hank moved to the side of the house and Meghan knocked.

Katie felt for her gun.

No answer. Meghan knocked again.

Through the unopened door, Tricia's muffled voice asked, "Who's there?"

"It's Meghan. Katie's here too. May we have a word?"

"Please go away. I can't see you right now."

"Tricia, we know about the men. It's safe to talk to us. Yosterman's not watching."

The bolt slid and the door opened halfway. Tricia was beautiful in a blue silk dressing gown that matched her eyes, although her eyes were bruised with exhaustion. She still had dark stitches in her lip, but the swelling had gone down. Tricia's attention was focused on the woods across the road.

Katie turned around and scanned the street. Yosterman was still nowhere in sight. The wind stirred the leaves on the trees and drops of the earlier rain were released. One or two made their way down the collar of her dress. Katie shivered. Tricia seemed unaware of their discomfort, being too focused on her own fear.

"You're sure that man is gone?" Tricia glanced across the street and then from left to right. "Yosterman, is that what you said his name was?"

"Yes, Cliff Yosterman," Meghan said.

Tricia stepped back inside the doorway. "Come in, but please hurry."

Meghan and Katie were led into Tricia's sitting room, which was stuffy after the fresh evening air. All the windows were closed.

"Please have a seat." Katie and Meghan sat on the couch and Tricia perched on the edge of the chair on the opposite side of a low table with books, a crystal cut pitcher and a glass. Tricia focused on Katie after she sat. "Oh, you've hurt your chin."

"Yes, but it's not serious."

Tricia studied Katie's face intently, then spoke quietly, "Would you like a cup of tea? I can put the kettle on."

"That would be nice." Katie was thirsty. She couldn't seem to get enough to drink after their long ride in today's heat.

Meghan put a hand on Katie's. "No, we haven't that kind of time. We just want to tell her what happened today."

"Mind if I pour myself a glass of water then?" Katie asked their hostess.

Tricia gestured towards the pitcher of water and Katie filled the glass.

After taking a few sips, she put the glass down and looked around. The house was richly furnished with comfortable chairs and thick carpets. Tricia had an entire wall of books, titles on etiquette and decorum, along with numerous novels. Katie asked, "Are you safe here? Is anyone in the house?"

"I'm safe here. It's that horrible man outside that I fear."

"We brought a friend with us, and he's waiting outside for a signal that we're safe."

Tricia put a hand to her mouth and scanned the room. "Oh, yes."

"I'm going to rap on the window to let him know that." Katie walked to the window and knocked. Then she called over to Tricia, "Do you mind if I open this window? It's a beautiful night with a pleasant breeze."

"Oh, no." Tricia sprang from her seat and scurried to the window. "I don't want to open any windows."

Katie turned, surprised by Tricia's vehement protest. "We'll leave the window closed." Katie guided Tricia back to her chair. She concluded by stating that both men had been arrested.

When they were seated, Meghan explained how Plumpton and Schmidt had kidnapped her, and Katie, Liam, and Brett's bravery in saving her.

Tricia's hands shook. She tried to conceal the fact by keeping them folded in her lap, but then she broke down in tears.

Meghan got up and put a hand on Tricia's shoulder. "We thought this would be good news."

"It is, but I've been scared for so long. It's relief, I'm feeling."

This was the first time Tricia's Irish brogue was revealed. The young woman took great care with her speech and mannerisms, lessons probably learned from the books on the shelf and her careful attention to others. Under stress, Tricia's façade had slipped.

Tricia's manner returned to poised and polished. "Those are horrible men. You're sure they're in jail? Did you see them behind bars?"

Katie said, "No, we haven't seen them behind bars, but we've been assured that they are."

Meghan returned to her seat next to Katie. "Do you understand what's going on? They must think you're a threat."

"The shorter man, Plumpton you said his name is?"

Meghan nodded.

Tricia said, "He has a barrel of rattlesnakes."

Katie said, "We overheard Plumpton talking about it."

Tricia stood and moved behind her chintz-flowered chair, gripping the back as she spoke. "I have been seeing Victor Ross for several months now. We had an argument on Friday. I wanted our relationship to be less secretive, but he was vehemently against the idea, saying it was too soon after my husband's accident and that for propriety's sake, we needed to continue meeting in secret. I didn't agree, which is why we quarreled."

She took a deep breath. "He grew so angry that he hit me." She focused on her hands. "I'm sorry that I lied to you and Dr. West about being attacked in the street, but I was so embarrassed."

"I understand," Meghan said.

"Thank you." Tricia sat back down in the chair. "On Monday, one of the boys that work in the livery stable brought over a note from Victor. He waited while I wrote my response. It was an invitation for dinner with Ross at his ranch that evening. Of course, I agreed. I was so happy. I thought Victor had had a change of heart. Meeting at his house rather than here would have been a start. In the note, Victor said he would have one of his men pick me up, but he didn't mention a time. I waited for several hours. It was nearly ten o'clock when a man finally arrived in a wagon. He never introduced himself, only said he was a good friend of

Victor's and would be happy to escort me to the Ross ranch for a late supper. He had a German accent."

"Schmidt," Katie and Meghan said in chorus.

"Oh, but there are so many from Germany who have settled in Liberty."

"I'm sure it's Schmidt," Katie said.

"I'll take your word on that. I thought that was rather late for a supper, but Victor had always met me here late in the evening." Tricia used her fingers to gently pat away the tears that had pooled under her eyes. "Do you remember how dark it was on Monday night? The clouds covered what little there was of the moon."

Meghan shrugged. "I suppose so."

"Well, as I left the house and turned to lock the door, I was overcome by the man. He bound my hands. When I cried out, he put a gag in my mouth, nearly ripping out my stitches. Since it was so late, no one was about to help me." Tricia swallowed. "Then he threw me over his shoulder and put me in the back of the wagon. That's when I saw the other man, Plumpton. He's a foul and dirty fellow. He helped Schmidt put a canvas over me. They said they would kill me if I tried to escape."

She shook her head as if trying to clear the memory. "They were so rough with me. I believed them. The trip in the back of that wagon was at least a half an hour's ride. When we finally stopped and they pulled the canvas away, I saw that we were not at Victor's ranch. We had pulled up next to a remote cabin. I was unfamiliar with the location. The whole place smelled of pigs."

"We know of it," Meghan said. "The old Croft place. That's where they held me as a prisoner too."

Tricia's face revealed her sympathy for Meghan. "They are terrible men. They took the gag out of my mouth and untied my hands. They led me into the cabin. Schmidt, who seemed to be the leader, told me that I was to quit working for you. I asked why I would do that when I like my job? Schmidt said never mind asking foolish questions. He told me that I was not to tell anyone of my arrangement with Mr. Ross. I knew then that they were working on Victor's orders because those are his words for us, our arrangement." A few tears spilled down her cheeks. She didn't bother to wipe them away this time. "And then I asked, who are you to make such a demand of me? Schmidt just walked up to me and slapped me across the face."

"I was stunned. He hit me so hard that I fell back. Plumpton was behind me." Tricia's eyes were swollen with tears, but she continued. "Plumpton grabbed me by the back of the neck and walked me over to a barrel in the corner of the cabin. It had wires tightly crisscrossed across the top forming a lid, so tightly crossed that the snakes could be seen but not escape. He pressed my face to the wire lid, and I could see that the barrel had snakes in it. Rattlesnakes."

"You poor dear."

Katie stood. Her agitation was making it too difficult to stay seated. Although she wanted to pace, Katie merely walked over to the bookshelf and stood. Tricia needed quiet and stillness if she was to continue with her story.

Tricia's hands shook. She folded her hands in her lap to quiet them. "The snakes began to rattle. I thought they were going to spring up and bite me through the mesh of wires. I pushed back on the barrel sides, fighting against Plumpton." She stood and walked behind her chair, holding the top of each of the chair wings just as she probably had when she gripped the sides of the snake barrel. "I managed to keep my face a few inches from the mesh, but Plumpton kept his full weight on me. He had riled the snakes with all his shouting and by bumping the barrel when he shoved my face into the mesh. It was horrible."

Tricia closed her eyes, probably reliving the horror of that night, Katie thought. Meghan rose to stand in support at Tricia's side.

Tricia opened her eyes and gave Meghan a weak smile. "I'm all right now. Let me finish."

Meghan took her hand for a moment and guided Tricia to sit next to her on the couch.

Tricia bent her head, looking at the floor as she spoke, "After holding me over the mesh, he lifted my head by my hair, so that I was now standing upright next to the barrel." She lifted her head, mimicking the experience. "I had wet myself because I was so scared. That disgusting man pointed to the puddle I had made, and he laughed. I was so ashamed, and he laughed." Tricia put her face in her hands and began to sob.

Meghan embraced Tricia. "Shh," Meghan cooed. "It's all over now. You're safe."

Katie seated herself on the chintz-covered chair, now that Tricia sat next to Meghan on the couch.

Tricia blew her nose. "I think I can finish my story now. Those horrid men took me home in the same way, gagged, tied, and hidden under a canvas in the back of the wagon. It was nearly two in the morning by the time I returned. I couldn't fall asleep for hours. When I awakened on Tuesday afternoon, I went to the window and saw that man on horseback."

"Yosterman," Katie said.

"I knew he was watching me and that those awful men would keep their promised threat."

"What threat?" Meghan asked.

"They told me that I wasn't allowed to leave the house except to tell you I was quitting my job. I was a prisoner here. They said if I talked, they would use the snakes to teach me a lesson, set them loose in my house. I was terrified. That's why I quit. I didn't know what else to do."

Katie's mouth tightened into a thin line and then she said, "Victor Ross is behind all of this? And to think that I was to have dinner with him."

Tricia glanced at Katie. "He wants to be rid of me so he can marry you."

"What?"

Tricia was more composed now. "Let me explain. On Friday evening when Victor and I had that argument, he had arrived here angry and irritable. He was itching to pick a fight with me. I wanted to see a formalization of our relationship, and I pressed him. These secret meetings had been bothering me. I felt dirty the way he treated me."

Katie said, "So, Victor wanted no one to know about his relationship with you while he was pursuing me. Damn him."

Tricia's mouth curved into a small smile. "My sentiments exactly."

Meghan asked, "But why? He never had an interest in Katie before."

Katie stood and paced, trying to rein in her anger against Victor Ross.

Tricia said, "He's after your money, Mrs. Harris. I've had a lot of time on my hands to think about this. Your family is wealthy. Everyone knows that. Your brother's dead and your father's dying." She made a small gasp. "I'm sorry! That was inconsiderate of me."

"It's all right. Go on."

"Well, everyone knows you'll be the one to inherit all the Reynolds' holdings. I'm sorry for being so blunt, but you must be warned. It is for that reason Victor is pursuing a marriage with you. I'm sure of it."

Katie took a deep breath. Victor's insistence on dinner, his courtesies, and the tension in his face when she told him of Philip's marriage to Hannah. Was the anger she had seen in his face due to greed, thinking he might be sharing her inheritance with Hannah. Tricia's story rang true in her mind.

"You're beautiful and wealthy." Tricia shrugged. "I know Victor. Your money is an enticement, but he also flatters himself on his so-called discriminating taste. You are all that he would desire in a woman, but Victor's greedy too. And it is money that matters to him most."

Meghan glanced at the clock on the mantle. "It's getting late. I think it would be best if Tricia packed a bag and spent the night at Six Maples. The snakes may be at bay, but Victor's still out there and will probably be angry with all his plans foiled."

Katie said, "I agree. I don't want you to bear the brunt of his anger. You need to stay at Six Maples at least for tonight."

"That's so kind of you. Let me change and pack a bag." Tricia took the stairs and then turned back. "I'll be ready in a few minutes."

Katie whispered to Meghan, "The lack of chloroform must have kept those scoundrels from killing Tricia when they took her to the cabin on Monday night. They didn't get their hands on Liam's anesthesia until Tuesday, so they had to frighten her and keep her from talking until they could use their snakes."

"I got in their way."

Katie put her hands up in exasperation as she paced. "How could I have been so stupid? He wants to marry me for my money." She paused. "Could he have had the foresight to kill Stuart to gain even more money?"

"He couldn't be that greedy." Meghan tilted her head. "Could he?"

"I believe he is! I am so angry I could spit." Katie blew out her breath. She needed to think logically. "Two can play the deceit game. Saturday night, I'll get some answers. I'll find out if he was in the valley that morning. I'll bring up Stuart's murder and ask him where he was when he heard the news." She blew out her breath. "If he's the murderer, we have to find a way to prove it."

"What about Stuart's saddle in the barn. That's proof."

"Yes, but Schmidt or Plumpton could have taken it too. It won't be convincing enough. Marshal Gerber is in awe of Ross. No saddle is going to convince him to investigate Victor Ross as Stuart's murderer." Her mouth twitched. "But that emerald ring trap might do the trick."

Their conversation was interrupted when Tricia descended the stairs. She had changed into a black skirt and blouse and carried a small bag. Tricia locked up, and the three women left for the livery stable.

Mr. Schneider was outside his store talking with Hank. Upon seeing Meghan, he bolted from his seat and gave her a hug. He cleared his throat and stepped back. He was probably a little embarrassed by his emotional reaction.

Schneider shook his finger at Meghan. "You have no idea how worried you had us, young lady."

"That's what I hear, and I do apologize for worrying you so."

"Oh, don't apologize." His tone softened. "You're like a daughter to me. I was worried that's all."

Katie said, "We need to get back to Six Maples soon."

Hank put his stub of a cigar in the sand bucket. "I'll get the wagon."

Meghan said, "I want to stop home and pick up a few things."

"Not by yourself, you won't." Mr. Schneider turned to Hank. "I'll escort Meghan. I've got my rifle." He glanced up at the new clock on his store front and pulled his watch out of his vest pocket and flipped open the case. "Good, both are keeping accurate time. We'll meet back here in ten minutes. I insist on following your wagon home. My horse is saddled and I'm ready to go."

With only a sliver of a moon and heavy cloud cover, they had to rely on their lanterns to guide them home. A slight breeze kept the mosquitoes away and the twenty-minute journey proved to be a pleasant one.

When the men left, Hannah poured the three women cups of tea, and the complete story of Victor's duplicity was told to Hannah. After an hour, the women were yawning and making good night remarks.

"This house is like a hotel this evening," Hannah said. Tricia followed Hannah to a guest room. She would be sleeping in the room next to Katie's.

Meghan left the kitchen to check on Liam. Hannah had reported that the swelling was already beginning to recede, and he was less feverish.

Katie sat alone for a few minutes in the kitchen. She was nearly convinced it was Victor Ross who'd murdered Stuart and the man behind all the other shenanigans. If all went as planned, Ross would be caught searching for any tell-tale evidence tomorrow morning. But would it be enough evidence for the marshal? Her grand plan didn't seem so grand anymore. Well, she certainly wouldn't marry him, so he'd at least lose on that account.

She finished her tea and set the cup in the sink. As she ascended the stairs, Katie could hear Meghan's and Liam's murmured voices, their quiet confidences, evidence of their relationship. She smiled with the pleasure of it.

Then her smile faded as she touched the amethyst stone on her necklace. Would she ever see Andrew again? Memories of working side by side with him intruded as she settled down to sleep. She longed to be with him. Tired as she was, sleep refused to come

CHAPTER 19

CALL TO ACTION

Friday, June 23, 1865

Katie bolted to a sitting position. She must have fallen asleep for a few hours. She had spent most of the night thinking about problems that might arise from her appeal in the morning's newspaper. Was the plan too dangerous?

Then there was Victor Ross's involvement to consider. Last night Katie had been convinced it was Ross who'd murdered Stuart, but in the light of morning she was beginning to have her doubts. He seemed genuinely concerned about the plight of war widows and orphans and was putting on the charity ball to help them. His actions had touched her heart. Maybe someone else was behind Plumpton and Schmidt's kidnapping of Meghan. Was Yosterman behind all this? Could she trust Tricia's story? She hardly knew the woman. But then Meghan believed her and Katie trusted Meghan's judgment.

The sun was up. She glanced at her bedside clock, half past five. *The Gazette* would be delivered in a couple of hours. Some townspeople might have even picked up the newspaper at Schneider's store yesterday. Her heart pounded with the danger and anticipation of the day. If her trap worked, she might learn who was the ring's owner and quite possibly Stuart's murderer. Was it going to be Victor?

Katie got up and opened her bedroom door. She stood outside of Tricia's door and listened. No movement. She bent over the staircase railing and listened for kitchen sounds. Hannah wasn't up yet either. Good. No arguments. She walked back into her room and quickly dressed, tucking the gun into the pocket of her skirt. She couldn't wait for Caleb Brown. What if the murderer began searching the valley at sun-up? Caleb wasn't going to meet her until seven-thirty. She'd go to the valley and leave a message with Hank for Caleb. He could meet her at the valley instead.

Katie stepped out onto her bedroom balcony. Her palms were sweating, and she ran them along the sides of her skirt to dry them. Even if it scared her, she could do this. She could confront her brother's murderer if it meant finding justice for Stuart.

Hank was already in the yard. She needed to move fast if she wanted to avoid an argument from Hannah. She took the balcony stairs and strode across the yard.

Hank was putting a lively mare in her stable. He turned to Katie. "Mornin', miss."

Katie tried to act nonchalantly. "Good morning. I'm in the mood for an invigorating ride this morning. Would you mind saddling Thunder?"

"Thunder's a lot of horse. You sure you don't want me to saddle up Mouse?"

"No, Thunder will do. I need to check something out in the valley with a horse that can get me there quickly."

Hank moved to Thunder's stall. "He'll do that. Would you like me to go with you?"

"No," Katie said quickly. Checking herself, she softened her response, "I appreciate your concern, but I'll be fine." She raised a brow. "Oh, and a regular saddle will do."

Hank led Thunder out of his stall.

"I'll meet you out in the yard." Katie's stomach churned. She needed to use the outhouse.

When Katie returned to the yard, Hank had lined up Thunder next to the horse-mounting steps. "Thank you," Katie said as she took the reins. Hank had attached a rifle to her saddle. "You think I need a rifle?" she asked.

"Bobcats still roamin' early in the mornin'." Hank held the horse until Katie was balanced in the saddle, and then he released Thunder.

She turned the horse to the valley path and called over her shoulder. "When the house begins to stir, please tell Hannah I've gone to the valley. And Caleb Brown that newspaper man will be here at seven-thirty. Would you tell him to meet me? He'll know the place."

"Yes, miss," he called back.

Katie left the yard at a trot. The big horse had speed and battle experience. She might need both today.

The steady drum of the horse's hooves had a soothing effect. When she reached the ridge, the murmur of two angry voices caused her to rein in Thunder. She pulled her Pepperbox from her pocket and rested it in the folds of her skirt. With one hand on the reins and the other on the gun, she emerged from the woods and approached the raised voices.

Suzanne and Victor Ross stood on the hillside. Both stopped talking as she approached.

The valley was quiet. Not even birdsong to break the tension. Katie called out, "Suzanne, when did you get back?"

"This morning." Suzanne lost her footing when she answered.

Victor grabbed her arm. Katie saw distress and fear in Suzanne's face.

Katie urged Thunder a few steps toward the right of the couple. She was within twenty feet of them and approaching them from a new angle. She gasped. Victor had a gun pointing at Suzanne's side.

Katie pulled up her gun and pointed it at Victor. "What's going on here?"

"This is nothing for you to be concerned about," Victor shouted. "I can manage this thief." Victor's face changed, twisting with disgust. "This gypsy came back to see if she left any evidence behind after killing your brother."

Suzanne's eyes were wide with indignation. "No, that's not true. I came back to pay my respects to Stuart. Victor found me here and has somehow reached this ridiculous conclusion."

Thunder, sensing danger, pranced and threw his head. She was a few steps closer. Her Pepperbox was only accurate for ten to fifteen feet. Victor stepped behind Suzanne, who now appeared small and vulnerable. It disgusted Katie that Victor could demean such a strong and proud woman. A few pebbles were dislodged as he made the shift. The pebbles skidded down the hill, which attracted Victor's attention for a moment. Katie took advantage of the diversion and brought Thunder forward. She was now only fifteen feet away.

Victor kept his eyes on Suzanne as he spoke to Katie. "Pay her respects, ha. This thieving gypsy or one of her clan murdered your brother for his horse and saddle." He glanced at Katie. "Put that gun away. I can handle her."

"I thought you blamed bummers. Now you think it was a gypsy that murdered Stuart?"

Victor spoke through clenched teeth. "That made sense until I found this thief searching through the brush. No doubt searching for anything that might tie her to the murder."

Suzanne said, "I was searching for the tarot cards I left with Stuart. Those cards were my mother's. They are dear to me. I should never have left them."

Victor smirked. "She probably wants to put a spell on us. I would be doing this town a service if I were to just get rid of her here and now." Victor cocked his gun.

Suzanne's face drained of all color, except for welts of red across her cheek.

"Put the gun down, Mr. Ross. If you think she's guilty, then we'll take her into town for a trial. There's no need for this."

"No, she's some kind of witch. She'll put a spell on her jailer and escape." He lifted his eyebrows. "Don't you want your brother's murderer brought to justice?"

"I do, but through the courts. Not like this."

Victor's voice became low and menacing as he spoke to Suzanne. "I'd be doing you a favor, killing you quickly rather than slowly with a noose around your neck."

Victor's features shifted. What Katie had once found handsome turned dangerous, slits for eyes and a cruel mouth. She was mesmerized for the moment at the transformation.

He grabbed a handful of Suzanne's hair, bringing her head back and her body closer to his. He spoke into Suzanne's ear, but loud enough for Katie to hear. "You ever see a hanging?" He yanked Suzanne's hair. "It's messy and painful. A hanged person dies slowly, choking as the rope closes tighter and tighter until they can no longer breathe. Is that how you'd rather die?"

Katie sensed a flash of movement near the stream. Was it an animal or Caleb Brown arriving early? Whatever it was, it had escaped Victor's notice. She moved Thunder a few steps closer, only ten feet from Suzanne.

"Stay where you are." Victor said to Katie. His voice still held the edge of anger. He softened his voice when he continued. "I don't want you hurt. Why don't you go on home? No reason for a lady like you to be involved in this."

Katie said, "Put the gun away. We can settle this through the courts." She detected another flash of movement in the brush below but didn't take her eyes off Victor.

Brett stepped out of the hillside brush about sixty feet below. He was holding a rifle and pointing it at Victor, "You heard the lady. Put your gun away."

Victor was trapped. His reaction was quick. He turned from Suzanne and fired his gun at Brett. Suzanne dove to the ground.

"No!" Katie yelled and shot Victor. She nearly lost her seat from the gun's recoil but grabbed the saddle horn. Thunder remained steady.

Brett was on the ground and rolling toward the nearby brush for cover. Katie steadied her hand, her gun aimed on Victor, waiting for him to move, to retaliate. He lay face down and still on the hillside.

"Brett, you all right?" Katie shouted.

"Yes, ma'am," he called out from the brush.

Suzanne got up and kicked the gun away from Victor's hand. Then she stepped over to pick it up.

"Suzanne, keep that gun aimed on him." Katie dismounted and let go of Thunder's reins.

Blood had pooled, forming small rivulets in the dirt and grass. He was bleeding, so still alive.

"Maybe we can help him," Katie said. She bent down next to Victor and turned him gently, keeping one hand on her gun. The slope of the hill made the move easy. She felt a pulse in his neck. It was weak.

Victor's eyes shot open.

Frightened, Katie yelped and pulled away from him.

Ross focused his eyes on Katie. "Your brother was there beside the boy, protecting him." He grimaced as he tried to swallow. "He's come back to haunt me. I rue the day I murdered him."

Tears rolled down Katie's cheeks. She cried not only for her brother but also for what she had just done. "What are you talking about? My brother was here?" She shook her head. Ross must have been delirious. Unless . . ." Tears welled up in her eyes, the result of her fear for Brett and thoughts of her brother's presence.

A few drops of blood dripped from the corner of Ross's mouth when he spoke, but he continued, "You're crying for me." He put his hand on Katie's cheek. Blood bubbled from his lips. His head rolled to the side and his hand dropped. His eyes were open but now lifeless.

Katie put her hand to her mouth, then said, "Oh my God, he's dead."

Suzanne took a step closer. "You're sure?"

Katie felt for a pulse at the side of his neck. "I've killed him." She stood and ran her hand across her face. "I didn't know what else to do. I didn't mean to kill him."

"Yes, I know. But he tried to kill your friend. Leave him. We must tend to the boy."

Katie made the sign of the cross and said a quick prayer. She put the gun back in her pocket as she continued to stare at Victor Ross's dead body.

"Look to the boy," Suzanne said.

Brett was clutching his arm.

"Brett, are you hurt?" she shouted.

"It's nothin'. The bullet just grazed me."

Katie blew out a sigh of relief. She turned back to Victor. "He's dead." She shook her head. "I can't believe I killed him." So many thoughts went through Katie's head. His last words were so tender. Had he regretted his actions in the end? Suzanne had relaxed her stance and stepped closer to Victor.

Katie said, "Did Victor murder Stuart?"

"Of course, he did. Did you not hear him say that he rued the day he murdered your brother? That your brother had returned moments ago to haunt him?"

"I'm sure he was hallucinating. What about me? Will I be tried for murdering Victor Ross? You and I heard his confession, but will the marshal believe us?"

Suzanne said, "He would have killed Brett and possibly the two of us. He was ruthless."Katie stood. "But I could tell he was sorry for what he had done. Would he have changed his ways?"

Suzanne put her hands on both of Katie's shoulders. "He took a shot at Brett and missed. You stopped him. He is, was, not a good man. Killing, frightening, and deceiving have served him well. These are the tools that have brought him his success. And now his downfall."

Katie bent down and gently touched Ross's arm. "Oh, how I wish things had turned out differently." Then she asked Suzanne, "Why did you come back?"

"We'll talk later."

Suzanne was right. They needed to see Brett first. Katie stood and the women took the steeper and quicker path to the stream.

Brett had taken off his shirt. As they reached the valley, Brett laid it on a nearby bush. He turned to Katie. "He's dead, ain't he?"

"I thought he would kill you."

"He aimed to do that right enough." Brett twisted his arm to get a better look at the bullet wound. Blood was dripping down his arm. "I reckon I'm not hurt all that much." He glanced at his shirt and shrugged. "Torn. Ma'll be able to fix it though. Didn't want to get it all bloody." Brett squinted in concentration. "You know, it was kind of strange. When Mr. Ross turned to shoot me, it felt like someone were standin' close by, right next to me." He turned his head to his left. "Mr. Ross musta seen somethin' there too. He changed his aim to my left. That's why he missed me." Brett shook his head. "It sure was a lucky thing, whatever it was that sidetracked him."

Katie blew out her breath. Maybe Victor Ross was right, and Stuart's ghost had come back to haunt him. Then she shook her head to dismiss the idea. "Well, whatever it was, I'm grateful for it." Katie took a step closer to Brett. "Let me see that arm." The bullet had taken a gouge out of his left arm. She took a handkerchief from her pocket and held it over the wound. "Hold this."

Brett held the cloth in place with his right hand.

Suzanne leaned over and tore a tier of cloth from her petticoat. It was a long tier, so she ripped off a portion. "We can use this to clean up the blood that's dripping down your arm."

She handed the longer piece to Katie, who tied the cotton strip over the handkerchief and around Brett's arm. Katie said, "We seem to be making a habit of using petticoats as bandages."

"Yes, ma'am."

Suzanne's brow furrowed.

"Remind me to tell you about Dr. West's snakebite," Katie said and then turned to Brett. "We'll have Miss Hannah take a look at that. Are you feeling light-headed?"

Brett shrugged. "Naw, I'm fine. That was some fancy shootin' for a lady."

"I have a good teacher." Katie took a deep breath to steady her nerves. "How about we clean off some of that that blood at the stream? We've got a bit of extra petticoat here."

Katie walked over to the stream and dipped the cloth in the water, then stood and washed the blood that had dripped down Brett's arm from the bullet wound. As she worked, she asked, "So, what brought you out here this morning?"

"Rabbits."

Katie tilted her head. "Rabbits?"

"Yes, ma'am. I woke up this morning with a hankerin' for rabbit stew. Ma said she'd make it if I could bring back a couple of rabbits. This valley's loaded with 'em."

"Doesn't look good for rabbit stew tonight, but maybe Miss Hannah can send you home with something almost as good." Katie rinsed off the petticoat strip, squeezing the water from it and laying it over a nearby rock to dry. She scanned the hillside. "Where's your horse?"

Brett gave a sharp whistle. A chestnut mare came out from the path in the woods near the stream bed, the same path that Caleb had used. The mare made its way across the water.

The horse stepped lively over to Brett's side. He put his good arm under the horse's neck and held her close. Brett's eyes shined with pride. "Ain't she smart?"

Katie picked Brett's shirt off the bush "She certainly is."

They ascended the hill using the path further from Victor's body.

Once they reached the ridge, Katie said, "Suzanne, can you stay with the body while we go into town to get the marshal?"

She picked up the gun. "Yes, I'll be fine here." Suzanne set the gun on a large rock and removed a brightly colored wrap from her shoulders. She walked over to Brett. "This will help hold that arm still." She secured the scarf around Brett's neck and gently guided his arm through the sling.

Katie examined Brett's arm. No blood had leaked through the bandage. "The bleeding has stopped." She turned to face him. "Would you mind bringing Thunder over?" The horse had wandered over to graze in the shade of a tree about fifty feet away. With Brett busy, she could have a private word with Suzanne before they left.

"Yes, ma'am." Brett dropped his horse's reins and walked toward Thunder.

Katie called after him. "Move slowly. We don't want that wound bleeding again." Katie took a few steps closer to Suzanne and whispered, "What happened here?"

"You received my letter?"

"Yes."

"Then you know all about Victor Ross's past. He had no concern for anyone other than himself."

"Ross is the didicoy you wrote about?"

"I'm nearly positive. I came back for my tarot cards and found Ross searching the bushes near the stream. I hid when I saw him, but my horse whinnied and gave me away. I ran. He beat my horse so that it ran the other way and then he chased me. With a head start, I almost got away from him. But I turned to see if he was still following. That is when I tripped and rolled to the spot where you found us. Victor kept asking me all kinds of questions. What I was doing here and the like. I told him that I was searching for my tarot cards, and then he accused me of putting a spell on him. He was crazed with anger."

"He admitted to the killing. Did you hear him say he rued the day he murdered my brother?"

"I told you that I heard him confess." Suzanne's tone showed her annoyance with the repetition.

"Would you be willing to tell that to the marshal?"

"I'm not sure if my word is good enough for the marshal, but I will tell him about Ross's confession. You saved my life."

The outline of a handprint swelled on Suzanne's cheek. "You've been hit, and your lip is swollen."

"I will be all right. Sometimes I did not answer Victor's questions quickly."

Katie shook her head. "You're tough."

"I just don't understand why Victor Ross was here," Suzanne said.

"I can solve that mystery. Ross was here to retrieve that emerald ring I told you about. I posted a note in the newspaper asking for volunteers to search the valley on Saturday for any evidence that could be found for Stuart's murder. Ross probably saw my post and thought he'd get a head start on the search party by finding his ring today, Friday."

"That makes sense. Now I ask the same question of you. What brought you to the valley so early and alone?"

"Caleb Brown, a local reporter wanted to help me trap the ring's owner. We were to meet at Six Maples at seven thirty, but I was restless and came without him."

"Risky, but I am glad you came." Suzanne's eyes narrowed. "I wonder if it was Stuart's ghost who distracted Victor when he aimed at Brett."

Katie chuckled. "Stuart as a ghost! You have a great imagination."

Suzanne smiled and then grimaced, touching her lip. "Perhaps you gorgio don't know everything. If I am here alone, he may talk to me. I have been hearing his voice in my dreams. He asks me to help you find his murderer. He is not at peace."

"Well, we've found his murderer." A shadow of pain crossed Katie's face. "My brother may now rest in peace."

Suzanne glanced toward Victor's body. "I think so." She turned back to Katie. "I would still like to find the tarot cards I used when I warned Stuart and put a spell on you. The cards, they were my mother's and dear to me."

"I can get the missing tarot cards." Brett led Thunder forward. Another horse followed. "I believe Brett's found your horse too."

Suzanne nodded. "Daphne would never go far." She turned back to Katie. "The cards, you have them?"

"Brett has the tarot cards."

CHAPTER 20

HOME AGAIN

Friday, June 23, 1865

Caleb Brown arrived at Six Maples at about the same time as Katie and Brett returned. Meghan and Caleb sat in the kitchen drinking coffee as Katie relayed a sketch of the morning's events. Caleb took notes, no doubt for a future article. He didn't chastise Katie for going to the valley alone. She liked that about him.

Hannah bustled about cleaning and putting some strong-smelling salve on Brett's wound. Dr. West came in and examined Brett's arm too. Pleased with Hannah's ministrations, he took the offered coffee.

When Katie had answered all their questions, she turned to Caleb. "Suzanne is guarding Ross's body in the valley. If you would ride out there and wait with her, I would consider it a great kindness. I am going to ride to town to tell the marshal about Victor's death. I don't want him to take out any of his bias against gypsies on Suzanne. With you there, he'll be more polite."

"Of course, I'm on my way." He put his pad and paper in his miss-shaped pockets and stood. "Thank you for the coffee, Mrs. Reynolds," he said as he donned his hat and headed for the door.

Ah, Katie thought, news of Hannah and her father's wedding had been circulated around town.

Meghan went with Katie to town and accompanied her to the marshal's office. Katie told Marshal Gerber about Victor Ross's death. The marshal's disdain for Katie was obvious as he left for the valley. He insisted Katie stay in his office with his deputy while he was gone. It was one step short of locking her in the only village cell along with Plumpton and Schmidt.

Volunteers stepped forward to help Gerber transport Ross to the undertaker, find Ross's horse, and escort Suzanne to the marshal's office.

When Gerber returned from the valley, he questioned Katie and Suzanne. Gerber was firm in his belief that Victor Ross, a man he held in high esteem, could not be guilty of any wrongdoing.

As Gerber was preparing to ride out to the Williamson ranch and interview Brett, Tricia arrived. She explained to the marshal what she thought was Victor's plan, killing Stuart and marrying Katie to control the holdings of the mill and Six Maples. Marshal Gerber listened to Tricia with rapt attention.

According to local gossip, the marshal was attracted to Tricia. Katie could now see that was true by his attentiveness and positive reaction to her story.

Tricia's description of the cruelty she endured at the hands of what she surmised to be Ross's men and their snakes angered the marshal. Learning the women kept Tricia safe last night, softened the marshal's manner towards Katie and Suzanne.

It was nearly noon when Katie and Suzanne were released and returned to Six Maples with Meghan. As the women entered the kitchen, the smell of chicken soup and fresh bread greeted them, whetting Katie's appetite.

Hannah took the coffee pot off the stove. "Coffee?" she asked.

"That would be wonderful." Katie took a seat at the table next to Suzanne.

Hannah poured four coffees, then pulled a stack of blue-checked napkins from a drawer and set them on the table. "Tell us all that happened and more details this time. I want to hear right from the start."

Katie nudged Suzanne. "Will you tell the story, or shall I?"

"You start and I'll fill in."

Hannah put up her hand in a stop gesture. "Wait, the first thing I need to know is, are you cleared of any charges?"

Katie grimaced and moved her hand in a so-so gesture. "Suzanne and I were told not to leave town without telling the marshal. Although I think we convinced him of my need to shoot Ross to save Brett's life and possibly Suzanne's. The marshal is on his way to Brett's right now to check out our story."

Suzanne turned to Hannah. "Is Brett recovered?"

"He's fine. I sent him home with a sling, just not quite so colorful as the one he had." Hannah got up and went to the desk in the corner of the kitchen. She walked back with the wrap Suzanne had used for Brett's arm and handed it to her.

"Thank you," Suzanne said as she put it around her shoulders. "I will now call this my lucky scarf."

Hannah chuckled. "Making a sling for Brett's arm was a good idea. He's less apt to use that injured arm, and it might help to keep his bandages clean." Then Hannah turned to Katie. "What drew you to the valley so early this morning?"

"I had put a notice in today's paper for a search party to meet here tomorrow. They were to meet here and be rewarded with a hearty breakfast made by you."

Hannah raised her eyebrows.

Katie winced and then continued. "Ross probably came out this morning to ensure there was nothing left in the valley that would tie him to Stuart's murder, namely his emerald ring. When I arrived at the valley, Ross was holding Suzanne at gunpoint."

"Humph, Meghan told me all about the ring." Hannah shook her head. "I don't know if you're brave or foolish to take such risks."

Suzanne said, "Fortunate for me that she did."

Hannah continued. "Shortly after you left to talk to the marshal, Tricia asked Hank to take her home."

"The marshal doesn't think much of me, and he doesn't trust Suzanne. I think having Tricia show up at the jail and her explanation of Ross's dubious behavior saved our hides." Katie lifted fingers as she made each point. "She told Gerber about her relationship with Ross, the snake scares, and her thoughts on Ross's motives to marry me."

She relaxed her hand and sat back in her chair. "Of course, the marshal knew about Cliff Yosterman and his lurking around Tricia. Yosterman is nowhere to be found this morning. He probably left town."

"Really," Meghan said. "I can't believe Tricia told the marshal about her affair with Victor Ross. The rumor mill has Marshal Gerber sweet on Tricia."

"I notice that." Katie winked. "I think Tricia's on to him and explained her relationship with Victor as a friendship, which made it more acceptable to the marshal and will save her reputation."

"You believe what you want, is that it?" Meghan said.

Hannah moved the butter to the center of the table. "Well, I'm certainly relieved that you've cleared all that up. How about a bowl of soup? You must be hungry."

Leave it to Hannah to be sure all are well fed even in a crisis. "Yes, to that soup."

Hannah ladled soup into their bowls and cut bread into thick slices.

They were silent for a few minutes while they ate and then Suzanne spoke quietly, "How long do you think I'll need to stay in Liberty while the marshal investigates?"

"The investigation should be over when Gerber gets confirmation of our story from Brett. That's what Deputy Jones told me," Katie said. "We went to school together, so Ed Jones was more forthcoming with information than Marshal Gerber, who seems to enjoy keeping us guessing."

I must return to my clan soon, but I would like to get my mother's tarot cards."

"Yes, of course. I can get them." Katie turned to Hannah. "Brett has them."

Hannah said, "I'll take you out to Brett Williamson's place."

"I know where he lives," Katie said.

"Yes, but your father asked me to thank the Williamson family in person."

"Very well. Let's leave after our meal."

Hannah asked Meghan. "Would you mind staying with Philip?"

"Of course I will." Meghan turned to Suzanne. "Isn't it rare for you to leave your clan? For a woman to travel alone?"

"Yes, I did have to sneak away. Roma men. If I had told them I wanted to go back for my mother's cards they would have stopped me, saying the trip was dangerous and frivolous, not understanding my grief for my mother and my need to have her cards. But there is another reason I came back. I was concerned for you. I learned more from Milo, my friend who ran cons with Victor Ross. I learned much more the other night when our clan met with his in Massillon.

"Oh, do tell," Meghan urged.

"Yes, I will get to that, but I am sure my people are concerned about me now, so my time here must be short."

Hannah asked, "Where are your people?"

Suzanne wrapped her hands around her coffee cup. "We are English travelers. Our clan came to America only about twenty years ago, so we still hold on to some of our old ways. When we were in England, we met in early July for a great horse fair near Cambridge, so now we meet in Cambridge, Ohio, which is many miles southeast of here. Massillon is a customary stop on our journey to Cambridge. We spend time and rest there because it is safe, and we can sell horses to the local gorgio." She smirked. "We are much more welcome in Massillon than in Liberty. I left Massillon yesterday morning before any of the men were up to stop me or insist on accompanying me. I rode all day. I set up camp last night with the intent of arriving at the pine valley sometime this afternoon, but I was restless."

Suzanne lifted her chin. "I am not accustomed to sleeping on the ground with only a campfire to warm me and night sounds that frighten me. I had a clear night, and the sliver of a moon was bright enough to make my way here." She sighed. "My poor horse, no sleep for her either."

Meghan said, "Daphne's in good hands with Hank. By now I'm sure she's been well-fed, groomed and resting."

"Thank you." Suzanne took another drink of her coffee. "I arrived at the pine valley at dawn this morning. I thought my cards might be somewhere near the stream where I left them tucked into Stuart's hands. When I didn't find them, I circled the valley and then climbed the ridge, thinking that perhaps the wind had blown them into the brush. Daphne followed me. I was near the ridge top and still searching when I heard a rider coming. I wasn't sure who it might be, so I took Daphne's reins and slipped into the woods. I watched Ross conduct his own search near the stream bed. He seemed to be searching for something."

"He was probably nervous because of the newspaper article." Feeling somewhat smug, Katie said, "I called for a search party, basically causing the murderer to search the valley for evidence before Saturday morning. I'm guessing the emerald ring I found in the stream belongs to Ross."

"Ah, the ring, yes." Suzanne's eyes widened. "When Milo and his clan met up with us in Massillon, Milo and I talked as we sat by the fire the night before last." She lifted an eyebrow. "Now we know the didicoy is Victor Ross, so I will use his name. When Ross stole the money from the wealthy businessman, he also took a very expensive ring from the mark's finger."

"I've read your letter to Hannah," Katie said.

"Oh, you must tell me," Meghan said.

Katie turned to Meghan. "I'll let you read Suzanne's letter. It explains why Ross hated the Irish. His hatred has been festering for a long time."

Suzanne said, "Ah, but there's more. I can tell the story Milo shared and then I'll rest, yes?"

"Katie said, "Go ahead, as long as you're not too tired."

"It won't take long. Victor felt the ring brought him good fortune. Murdering your brother was probably only the first step in his plan. Next he had to convince you to marry him so he could gain all the Reynolds' fortune. But Ross would need his lucky charm to see it through. He probably panicked when he realized he had lost the ring. Victor Ross may have been half Irish," Suzanne lifted an eyebrow, "but he had enough gypsy blood to make him superstitious."

Katie said, "Believe me, gypsies do not have anything on the Irish regarding superstition. We've got leprechauns, fairies, and banshees."

Suzanne chuckled. "Yes, I've heard of such things from my querents." Seeing several confused faces, Suzanne added, "My tarot card customers."

Katie said, "My trap worked."

It was at the stream bed that Ross must have taken Stuart's horse. Brett did not see any other horse prints in the clay. Ross must have come without a horse."

Katie said, "To go to the valley without a horse would be unusual for Ross or anyone else for that matter. How did

Ross know that Stuart would be coming through the valley that morning?"

"Good question," Meghan said.

Katie slapped the table. "Danior. I couldn't figure out what brought him to the valley that day he tried to attack me. After leaving Danior in the valley, I started to go home when I heard fast hoof beats and then saw the outline of a rider coming through the woods. I couldn't see his face, but he must have seen me because he turned abruptly. I wonder if it was someone coming to meet Danior. That rider was probably Victor Ross."

Katie asked Suzanne, "Did you have any knowledge that Stuart was coming to see you on his way home from the war?"

"Stuart had written to me weeks earlier. The time was approximate, of course, but he knows our clan's pattern of travel. A letter was waiting for me in Wordsworth. It was our custom to communicate by letter or telegraph and leave messages in the nearby towns or villages."

"Did anyone else in your clan know that Stuart would be visiting you soon?"

"I told no one." She tilted her head and seemed to be thinking. "Oh, but Danior might have known. That same afternoon after receiving Stuart's letter, I found Danior in my vargo. He said he was checking to see if all was well with me, claiming that I seemed upset about the letter I received." Suzanne's eyes narrowed. "Now that I think about it. He probably read Stuart's letter. It lay open on my table. Danior seemed flustered when I arrived at my vargo. He was awkward. He is in love with me, so I thought he was just nervous. It was a few days later that Victor Ross came to the camp. He bought two horses. He has bought horses from us before, so that was not unusual. Danior handled the sale. He and Danior must have talked, and Victor used Danior's information to plan Stuart's ambush."

Katie said, "I wonder if Danior was meeting Victor Ross at the valley that day to collect his blood money. Danior must have reported to Ross that Stuart was with you for the night and that he would be returning home through the valley the next morning."

Suzanne clenched her teeth so hard Katie could see her facial muscles tense. Suzanne said, "Oh, the man is disgusting and greedy." She raised a fist in the air. "Wait until I tell the elders. He will be banished!"

"And then the marshal can get his hands on Danior. You can be sure Gerber will send a posse for Danior once we share our information."

Suzanne put a hand to her forehead, clearly distressed. "Oh, my people will be hurt and suffer for this."

"Not if he's banished, Suzanne. When he leaves the clan, he'll be off on his own. Your people will not be held accountable."

"I must get back. I must tell the elders what I have learned about Danior."

"But we have no proof, only conjectures."

"That is something your marshal needs. Our clan, no. My word will be enough. Danior has been threatened with banishment before. He is trouble." She flipped her hand in the air. "The elders will use this as a reason to get rid of him once and for all."

"All right, but we must tell Marshal Gerber what we know."

"Do not tell him anything until I have gone. Will you do that for me, for my people?"

"I will wait for one day after you leave, so act quickly, provided you leave Danior behind without a horse. Danior is an accomplice in murdering my brother, Suzanne. If we can catch him, he will spend many years in prison for his greediness. He may even hang for it."

Hannah said, "So what's the rest of the story? What led up to Katie shooting Ross."

"Yes, the rest of the story," Suzanne said. "Victor searched near the stream for some time, too long a time for my impatient horse. Daphne decided to voice her disapproval of too long a time in hiding. Her whinny alerted Ross to our presence. My swollen face is a testament to what happened next."

"You poor dear, I have a salve that might help that." Hannah got up out of her chair and opened a cupboard and pulled out a small jar. "This will help the swelling." She scooped out a light green lotion. "May I?" she asked Susanne.

"Of course."

Hannah leaned toward Suzanne and put the salve on her upper lip. "Now, let that settle for a minute before you eat or drink anything."

"Tingles, doesn't it?" Katie asked.

"Yes, but it also eases the pain."

Katie put her fingertips under her chin. "Hannah used it on me. I'm healing already."

Suzanne asked Hannah. "What's in this?"

"Aloe vera and marigold, mainly."

Katie turned to Suzanne. The gypsy's eyes were shadowed with exhaustion. "I think I can tell the story from this point. How about you go up to my room and rest?"

"Although that sounds wonderful, there are a few things about Ross's background that will help you understand him and his motives. I did not share everything that I learned from Milo in my letter to you. Milo is the man who once road the rails with Victor. He knew Victor as a boy. Some of this you already know from my letter. I want Meghan to understand too, so forgive me if I repeat some information for clarification."

Katie said, "Only if you're up to it. I want you to rest before you return to your people."

"I doubt that my clan will ever return to Liberty again. I want you to know all that I learned from Milo."

Suzanne continued, "I spoke with Milo on Wednesday night and learned that the didicoy he spoke about so long ago was Victor Ross. I had not paid any attention to the name when first told the story." She shrugged. "If Milo had even mentioned his name." Suzanne turned her attention to Meghan since she hadn't read Suzanne's letter. "Victor Ross was the son of a poor family from Romania. His mother was a gypsy but not his father. When they came to America, they settled in New York and lived among the poor immigrant Irish. It was a hard life for a boy so different from the others."

Hannah raised her eyebrows. "The teasing and pranks are cruel and can make a child bitter."

Meghan was sitting next to her mother at the table. She put a hand over Hannah's and pursed her lips.

Suzanne said, "Victor ran away from the city when he was about twelve, taking on the life of a railroad tramp. He made his way to Pittsburgh by what Milo called hopping rails."

Suzanne focused on Katie, "Now, here's what I didn't know when I wrote to you. Victor traveled the rails and settled in with low-class gypsies, who took him in and taught him pickpocketing skills." She sighed. "I am sorry to say that some gypsy clans resort to stealing, rather than work." She pushed her chin out. "Not ours, though."

Katie said, "Of course not. You sell excellent horses."

Suzanne nodded. "Victor quickly learned their skills and how to use the herbs found in the countryside to advantage. Milo met Victor at a travelers' summer celebration. Both boys were about sixteen at the time and soon became fast friends. Milo admired Victor's pickpocketing skills and they set out on their own."

Hannah sliced a rhubarb-strawberry pie that had been cooling on the table.

Suzanne went on, "Victor had enough money saved to buy fine clothes and taught Milo how to mimic the ways of the wealthy. The two posed as young gentlemen going off to school by train and in doing so gained access to first-class compartments and wealthy marks. With the money they stole from passengers, they bought fine food, drink, and stayed in expensive hotels. They kept moving along different rail lines and were never caught. Life was good until they began to argue."

"What happened?" Meghan reached for a slice of pie and the fork.

"Milo saw the cold and calculating man that Victor had become. He took too much pleasure in hurting his marks, leaving them with nothing and far from home."

Meghan lifted her fork in the air. "That makes sense, doesn't it? Look at the way he treated Tricia. It was as if he wanted to crush her spirit."

"Yes," Suzanne said. "Katie told me about Tricia when we were in town but let me tell you the rest of the story, the theft that changed Victor's life."

Movement from the dining room caused Katie to turn. Liam gripped the dining room chairs with his good hand while he made his way to the doorway. "Is this story for women's ears only or can I sit in? I am having trouble hearing from the parlor."

The women laughed and Meghan jumped up and pulled out a chair at the kitchen table.

"Of course, you're welcome," Hannah said. And then glanced at Suzanne. "If that's all right with you."

Suzanne lifted her shoulder. "Join us."

Liam sat down next to Meghan and thanked Hannah as she placed a cup of coffee and a slice of pie in front of him.

Suzanne turned to Liam. "I am telling them about Victor Ross. The theft that would change his life."

Liam said, "Please go on."

Suzanne continued, "On one train run, Victor spotted an old man with a locked case handcuffed to his wrist. He struck up a conversation and shared a pot of tea with him. Being adept at all types of trickery, Victor had laced the old man's tea with a sleeping herb. Within the hour, the old man was sleeping soundly. Victor planned to steal the billfold in his mark's jacket pocket and to make off with it at the next stop."

Everyone stopped eating while Suzanne continued.

"The train had pulled into Cleveland to unload cargo. Problems with local laborers caused a delay. The conductor announced that the train would be halted for at least an hour. With that news, all the first-class passengers left the train except the sleeping man and Victor. A conductor came back, urging Victor to stretch his legs while the train had stopped. He told the conductor that he must compose a letter, but he would soon take his advice. Once the conductor left, Victor picked the lock on the sleeping man's case. The case contained a fortune. He took the money from the case and filled it with newspapers. He left the billfold in the man's pocket, so that the man would be unaware of any theft until he opened the case later."

Katie asked, "How did you learn all this? I mean how did Milo learn about Victor's duplicity? I thought they no longer traveled together."

"Oh, they met up a couple of years later at a fair for tinkers. Many gypsies were there. Victor donned the traditional gypsy clothes and planned to lay low until news of his great theft quieted." She arched an eyebrow. "Victor, full of bravado, bragged about his good fortune to his friend Milo."

Hannah said, "You know your father never liked that man. He has good instincts, yes?"

Katie put her hand to her mouth, hiding her chuckle from Hannah. Katie turned her head so that only Meghan could see her roll her eyes. Then she turned back to Hannah, her face a study in seriousness. "Yes, papa has good instincts." Hannah was forever singing Philip's praises, and the two women chuckled about it in private. Katie turned her attention back to Suzanne. "I still don't understand how Ross came to Liberty."

"I will tell you," Suzanne answered. "Victor stayed in Milo's camp for the night and the two of them sat by the fire drinking whiskey. Late in the evening when Victor was full of drink, he shared his plan. He was tired of a life on the run and now he had the money to realize his dream to become a real gentleman. He planned to find some small town where fine manners and dress would inspire awe and draw few questions." Suzanne took another sip of her coffee. "Liberty welcomed him without question."

Liam leaned back in his chair and pushed out a deep breath. "Well, except for Bertha West. My mother used to call him a pheasant in peacock feathers, said his manners and comments never rang true." Liam turned to Suzanne. "As these women know, my mother is a snob and quite adept at spotting someone trying to pose as a gentleman."

"I'm sure that's why he avoided her," Hannah said.

"Which always infuriated her."

Hannah leaned forward. "I remember Mr. Ross buying his ranch in the late fifties, but he never spent large amounts of money after that, only as much as any successful rancher might, so we didn't think much of his spending. There was the usual flurry of gossip when he came to Liberty. All the women in town commented on his good looks. He has a bit of a reputation as a ladies' man. Other than occasionally seeing him in town, though, I didn't really know the man. Philip had some dealings with him, but they were minimal."

"I ran across him when I was contract doctoring during the war," Liam said. "Sharpshooter." Liam tilted his head. "He served early in the war with Colonel Hiram Berdan's

First U.S. Sharpshooters." He adjusted his seat to let his injured arm rest on the table.

Meghan said, "Makes sense. Ross's stint as a sharpshooter gave him plenty of practice when he took aim at Stuart."

Katie eased back in her chair and took a deep breath. "I have to keep that in mind whenever I start feeling bad about shooting Ross."

Hannah shook her head. "You saved Suzanne's and Brett's lives. We're grateful to you for that."

Katie put her index finger in the air. "But. I would have preferred that he went to trial, so all his nasty background would come out." Her eyes narrowed. "And that he would squirm in his seat from embarrassment and spend the rest of his life in jail."

"Understandable," Liam said, "but I think his story would have ended with his neck in a noose, for premeditated murder."

"You're probably right," Katie said.

Suzanne's eyes were dull and listless.

Katie touched Suzanne's hand which was resting on the table. "Why not take a nice long nap in my room? It's quiet and there's probably a nice breeze blowing through the window."

"I will rest now."

When they reached Katie's bedroom, Suzanne sat down heavily on the bed. "This is certainly an improvement from last night." Suzanne pulled the pillow from the bed and put it on her lap. "I would like my mother's cards before I leave. Brett has them?"

"Yes, I'll ride out to his place while you sleep."

"Good, I need to be fresh. By this afternoon, Marshal Gerber will have confirmed our actions with Brett. Then he'll let us go?"

"I believe so."

"I do not want to disobey his orders to stay put until further notice." She shook her head. "He has such a way with words."

CHAPTER 21

TAROT CARDS

Friday afternoon, June 23, 1865

After Katie left Suzanne, Hannah met Katie in the hallway. "Would you mind bringing your father his dinner?" She handed Katie a tray with a bowl of chicken soup.

Katie took the tray and brought it to Philip's room and set it on his nightstand.

"Thank you," Philip said, "I'll let that cool for a bit."

Katie touched the star on her necklace and wrapped her fingers around the stone.

A shadow crossed her father's face. "What's the matter, darlin'?"

"I'm just a little tired from the day's events." She took his hand. "If only life were sometimes easier."

"Ross's shenanigans bring this discontent on?"

"That and all the trouble it's caused for me with the marshal."

"I wish I could make your problems and pain go away. I could when you were a wee lass."

She dropped his hand and once again felt for the stone on her necklace, a habit she was no longer even conscious of.

He glanced at her necklace. "You're thinking about Paul again, aren't you?"

Her father had misread her, thinking it was Paul she was longing for instead of Andrew. A pang of guilt shot through her. She didn't want to try to explain her feelings for a married man to her father. She'd probably never tell him about Andrew.

When she didn't answer, Philip continued. "Now, listen to me, darlin'. All men aren't going to die in battle or turn out to be greedy and hateful, like Ross. You're a young woman. Lots of possibilities are left in your life for a good and long-lasting marriage. Hold on to your memories, but don't dwell too much on the past. Promise me."

It was good advice regardless of who was in her thoughts. She took a deep breath. "I promise."

"But I've got something else bothering me." She shook her head. "I stood there and couldn't move when Meghan needed me to be strong to save her. I saw the snakes and did nothing to help Liam. I'm so disgusted with myself."

"How can that be? Liam tells me you acted bravely out at the Croft place when you were fending off those men."

"I did let that Plumpton fellow get the better of me."

He shook his head, then said, "You are way too hard on yourself."

"No, Papa, it's true. When Liam was rescuing Meghan from the snakes, I just stood there, blocking Liam's exit. What if Brett hadn't pushed me aside to save Liam from another snake bite? I was less than worthless. I was in the way!"

Philip sighed. "Do you not remember that summer when you were four years old?"

"What about it?"

"Maybe you were too young to remember the details, or you've chosen to forget the circumstances, but there's good reason for you to fear snakes, besides just common sense." Philip pushed himself up to sit up straighter.

He coughed with the exertion, took a sip of his tea, and then continued, "It was early summer. We finally had sunshine after several days of rain. Hannah was hanging clothes. She had you in her sights, but you were probably about fifty feet away. You were building some kind of fort or house made from nearby stones." Philip put his cup back on the nightstand. "Your brother was only about two. He was playing nearby. When you moved a few rocks, you discovered a pit full of rattlers. You cried out. Hannah came to your rescue, but for the few minutes before she arrived the sides of their pit gave way from all the rain, and you slipped, falling nearly halfway down into the snakes' lair. It was only by grabbing onto nearby roots that you stopped yourself."

"I have absolutely no recall of that." She tilted her head. "You would think I would remember."

"You had nightmares for months afterwards." Philip took Katie's hand. "You have every reason to fear snakes. They're fearsome creatures and you've got a bit of history to add to those fears."

Philip dropped her hand and reached over for his tea. He took a sip and set the cup back down again. "Sometimes we block memories, a built-in protection for frightening times. I'd probably chalk it up to that. You did a world of good out there today and I'm proud of you."

"Thank you, Papa."

"I'm going to rest now." He patted Katie's hand and closed his eyes while he continued talking. "I'll just rest for a minute while this soup cools."

Katie said, "Is there anything else you need?"

"No, I'm fine. You'll remember what I said about your future, won't you?"

In a monotone, Katie said, "Yes, life goes on, happiness is possible even after great grief."

He opened his eyes. "Be nice if you said it with some conviction."

"I'll take your words to heart, I promise."

He patted her hand and closed his eyes again.

Katie left Philip's bedside and walked back to the kitchen.

Hannah turned from the stove as she entered. "Philip all right?"

"He's resting while he waits for the soup to cool."

"Humph, a likely story."

The sound of a wagon pulling into the yard stopped their conversation. Hannah leaned over the sink to look out the window. "Hank's back. Meghan's in the parlor talking with Liam. I'll let them know we're leaving. Would you let Hank know we'll be using the wagon? I'll just be a minute. I want to peek in on Philip before we go."

"Very well," Katie said as she stepped through the doorway to catch Hank in the yard.

When Katie returned a few minutes later, Meghan was in the kitchen and Hannah bustled through the doorway, putting on her hat as she walked. "He'll be fine for the time being." She said to Meghan, "It wouldn't hurt to coax him into eating that soup. It's on the bedside table. We won't be but an hour or so." Hannah turned toward the cellar door.

"I've made some fried chicken for the Williamson family. It's cooling in the cellar spring. I made a pie too. Katie, why don't you come downstairs and help me?"

Katie shook her head, bewildered. "How do you have the time to do so much cooking?" She followed Hannah to the cellar.

Hannah said, "I could never do it without this spring and the shelving that your father built." She paused and turned to Katie at the wooden door. "He is so clever."

Hannah pulled up the latch on the cellar door which led to a cave and stepped onto a three-foot square landing with a railing. Philip had designed the access to the cave when he built the house. Igneous boulders from the east separate the cellar from the house foundation because the local limestone would be too unstable."

The cave was much cooler than the cellar. On the right was a short staircase that led to the stream. Philip had built shelving a few feet above the cave floor and a sturdy walkway for easy access.

Hannah selected baskets from off one shelf. Other shelves held other items, a bottle of milk, covered pots, and fruit.

Katie said, "It's so nice and cool down here. I could stay down here forever."

"The chill does get to you after a while even on the hottest day." Hannah handed Katie the handle of a basket with a blue and white napkin covering it.

Katie lifted a corner of the napkin, and the fragrant smell of fried chicken filled the room. "Mmm, this smells delicious."

"You take this basket," she said. "I'll carry the pie."

They returned to the kitchen, said their good-byes, and loaded the waiting wagon. Katie took the reins.

They were silent as they drove. Thoughts of Andrew were on Katie's mind.

"What's the matter." Hannah put her hand on Katie's knee. "Why so sad?"

Katie tried to keep her expression calm to conceal emotions. "I miss Andrew, that's all. With all that's been happening, I've put my feelings for him aside. Now they're coming back and it's so painful knowing we can never be together."

"You're just tired, child. His memory will fade."

Hannah put her arm around Katie's shoulder.

Katie called out, "Whoa," to the horse, turned to Hannah and hugged her. Katie's shoulders shook as she sobbed, releasing some of the stress of the day and the uncertainties ahead with her tears.

After a few minutes, Katie regained her composure. "I'm sorry for that. It's not like you don't have enough to deal with." Katie turned her face forward and shook the reins to start Captain walking again.

"No, it's all right to cry. Crying makes us feel fresher and strengthens us, don't you think?"

Katie glanced toward Hannah. "You're right." Switching her reins to one hand, she wiped the tears from her cheeks with her fingertips. "I do feel better."

"The road's forked ahead. Take the turn to the right. We'll see the Williamson's place in just a minute."

As they approached the house, they could see Brett on the front porch reading a book. He put down his book and walked to the yard as Katie brought the wagon to the front of the house.

"The marshal just left a little while ago," Brett said. "Asked me all about our morning. So I told him what happened. How Ross shot at me and how you saved my life." He pulled a small stool from under the wagon's bench. After he set it down, he raised his good hand to help Hannah from the wagon.

"Oh, and what did he say to that?" Katie asked.

"Not much, just wrote stuff down and mumbled a lot." He turned toward the house as Katie stepped down. "Ma, we got company again!" he shouted.

Mrs. Williamson came out in her apron. She pushed stray strands of blonde hair out of her face as she descended the stairs to the yard. "Good afternoon, ladies. You just missed seeing the marshal. He's been out here asking Brett all about the morning."

"Good afternoon. We were very grateful to Brett. He is quite the hero."

"What a day we've had," Mrs. Williamson said.

Katie put a hand on Brett's shoulder. "We've come to see how you're doing, young man? I hope you're taking good care of yourself and not overdoing it."

"Yeah, Ma's making me rest even though there's plenty of work I could be doing with one arm. Nothing wrong with my right arm, and that's the one I favor."

"No, you need to rest." Katie turned toward Hannah. "Doctor's orders, right?"

"Yes, ma'am," Hannah said, and then walked to the back of the wagon. "I have supper here for you and a note from

Mr. Reynolds." She walked back to the wagon and picked up the baskets. "Fried chicken and strawberry-rhubarb pie."

She handed one basket to Mrs. Williamson.

"Mmm, Brett's favorite. If there's one thing we Northerners have learned fightin' the Rebs is how to make chicken so flavorful. Thank you. Would you like a cup of coffee?"

"That would be nice," Hannah said.

"I'll be in soon," Katie said. "We hit a few ruts on the way over here. I'd like Brett to look at one of the wheels."

Mrs. Williamson nodded, and she and Hannah went inside.

Katie walked over to the back wheel of the wagon and shook it gently. "Do you think it's still solid?"

Brett squatted down on his haunches to examine the spokes and axle. He pulled at the spokes with his good arm. "Seems sound." He stood.

"That's a relief." She paused. "I also have a favor to ask."

"Yes, ma'am."

"It's the tarot cards, the cards that you and your brother found in the valley. I need them."

Brett made a puzzled face. "Why?" Then he caught himself. "Well, you can have 'em if you want. I mean they was just different is why I wanted to show 'em off and such."

"Oh, that would be all right under normal circumstances, but I have it on good report that Suzanne needs a complete deck for her fortune telling, so she needs those two lost cards."

Brett's eyes widened. "The gypsy uses them to tell fortunes?" Brett gave a short whistle. "Ain't that somethin'."

"Yes, the cards help her focus."

"If the cards are hers, she should have 'em back. I didn't know they was so valuable."

"I know that. Suzanne asked me to give you this silver dollar for their return."

Brett shook his head. "She don't have to pay me for the cards. I just found 'em and they belong to her, so I'll just give 'em back. She still at your place?"

"I think you're just a little too anxious to get out and take a ride. You need to rest. I'll return them to her."

Brett tucked his head. "Ma's got me sittin' around readin' books all day long."

"Now, Brett, you've only been resting for a few hours. You don't want that wound opening up, do you?"

He lowered his head as he gave the dirt underfoot a slight kick. "No, ma'am. Let me get them cards. I'll just be a minute."

When Brett returned, Katie took the proffered cards and handed Brett a silver dollar. The money had come from her, but Brett didn't need to know that.

"No, I can't take that. It ain't right."

"Consider it a finder's fee and buy something nice for your mother. She's going to be taking care of that bandage of yours for a week or so."

"Oh, all right." His face brightened. "I know my ma's been looking at some fabric for a new dress. I'll just surprise her next time I'm in town and buy it for her."

"That would be nice." Katie tucked the cards in her skirt pocket. "Let's just keep this exchange of the cards between us?"

"Sure, I'll let Joey know private like, soon as he gets home. Ma gets a little funny whenever there's talk of gypsies or anything else interestin', so that's fine by me."

"Let's go have that cup of coffee, shall we?"

In the midst of the coffee conversation, Hannah handed Mrs. Williamson a note. "This is from Mr. Reynolds."

She opened it. "A twenty-dollar bank note! I can't accept this!"

Hannah said, "Please read the letter before you decide. I think Mr. Reynold's is grateful and wants to show his appreciation."

Brett's mother read it aloud.

Dear Mrs. Williamson,

I thank you for raising such a brave son.

She glanced up at Brett and her mouth curved into a smile. Emotion choked her speech as she read the rest of the note.

His heroism has saved the lives of those very dear to me. Please accept this small token of my appreciation.

Sincerely,

Philip Reynolds

"This is so generous and not necessary."

"Please, he wants you to have it."

Brett's mother nodded. "Thank you." She stared down at the note, rereading it silently.

"Mama, it would be a treat to go out to dinner sometime at that café in town."

Katie just shook her head and winked at Brett, then turned to his mother. "One of Brett's classmates works at the cafe nearly every day but Sunday," Katie said.

Mrs. Williamson smiled and put her hand on Brett's good arm. "Dinner in town sounds lovely."

Brett blushed.

"Speaking of classmates, I have a favor to ask of you," Katie said.

"Be happy to oblige."

"I know that Brett has many chores and can't always make it to school. I was hoping I could tutor Brett and Joey two evenings a week."

Mrs. Williamson put a palm to her chest. "Oh, that would be wonderful. We could pay you of course with firewood or something else you might need."

"No, that won't be necessary. Brett does so much for us at Six Maples, just consider it a part of his pay. We'll start in the fall when school is back in session." Katie rose from her chair. "Well, we had better let you get to your supper."

Katie and Hannah said their good-byes and were on the road back to Six Maples.

"Do you have Suzanne's tarot cards?" Hannah asked.

Katie patted her pocket. It held the two tarot cards and her pistol. "Yes."

The wind picked up. Dark clouds had gathered. Katie yelled, "Yeah!" And slapped the reins. Captain quickened his pace. The woods were filled with shadows. The outline of a horse and rider blocked their path.

CHAPTER 22

YOSTERMAN MAKES HIS PLAY

Friday late afternoon, June 24, 1865

Katie brought the wagon to an abrupt stop in front of Cliff Yosterman. She ran a hand over her skirt, feeling for the outline of the gun deep in her pocket.

"Afternoon, ladies." He turned his face to the sky. "Rains likely, looks like you could use an escort home."

Katie needed to let Hannah know who this was. "We're just fine, Mr. Yosterman. Now how about stepping aside, so we can drive on."

"Oh, so the wealthy Mrs. Harris knows my name. No, ma'am, you're not fine. To my way of thinking, you owe me some money."

"How's that?"

He walked his horse over to Katie's side of the wagon. His size and proximity were intimidating. "Well, here's how I see it. You murdered Ross and the man owed me money, so by my reckoning that means you owe me that money."

Hannah said, "How much money are we talking about, young man?"

"I haven't had the pleasure of meeting you, but from town talk, I'm guessing you're Hannah, Reynold's whore."

Katie's eyes narrowed. "How dare you talk to her like that." With that Katie slapped the reins and the horse moved forward.

Yosterman grabbed Katie by her sleeve, tearing the shoulder seam. The action caused Katie to pull back and the horse stopped.

"I will have my money, lady."

Katie glanced at her torn seam and pursed her lips. She wouldn't have time to pull out her gun with Yosterman so close. Outrunning him was also out of the question. A wagon's speed against a horse and rider was no match.

Yosterman was still holding on to Katie's damaged sleeve when Hannah stood and brought the flick of the horse whip across Yosterman's face. His horse backed up and Yosterman brought his hand to his face. His backward movements allowed Katie just enough time to pull the gun out of her skirt pocket. She pointed it at Yosterman. "Get out of here before I use this."

Yosterman smirked. "What, two murders in one day? That's quite a feat even for Katie Harris."

He backed his horse out of the whip's range. "I'll leave. For now. But fifty dollars is what Ross owed me and fifty dollars is what I'll get. I'll give you a day to get that money together." He wiped away the blood that was running down his cheek. "Get that money, missy, and keep it handy. I'll be calling on you again." He turned his horse and left.

Katie signaled Captain to walk. "Oh, that man!"

"We can round up fifty dollars." Hannah said. "It's a large amount of money, but the family has at least that much in the safe."

"No. I'm not willing to give into a bully, are you?" She didn't pause for an answer. "I can't believe it. He expects us to pay him for stalking Tricia! What nerve that bastard has."

"Now, that's no way for a lady to carry on. We can talk to the marshal about it."

"The marshal? Do you realize how isolated we are out here?"

"There's always Hank or someone nearby," Hannah said.

"Hank's often out and about and the marshal can't be everywhere. Yosterman carries a gun and has access to snakes and cruel people." The sky darkened, and Katie flicked the reins. Captain picked up his pace to a trot.

"I thought those snake men were in jail."

"They're in jail, but where are their snakes? We don't know, do we? Yosterman might have them. I should have made sure the snakes were released."

The wind became more intense and blew the brim of Katie's hat in her face. She pushed it so that it hung down her back. "Yosterman's serious trouble, Hannah. I have a gun, but you and Philip don't."

Hannah put her hand on the top of her hat to keep it on her head. The sky darkened with the increasingly strong winds. "Oh, yes we do. I have a gun in the desk and Philip has one in his nightstand drawer. Just let that man try to get in the house. He may be big, but a gun makes us even."

Katie glanced toward Hannah. The older woman lifted an eyebrow as if ready for a challenge.

Katie said, "We need to get the marshal involved. Now that he knows about Tricia's history with Yosterman, I think he'll be more willing to help us."

The rains came, big fat drops. Six Maples was straight ahead. Katie flicked the reins and the horse picked up his pace.

As they reached the yard, Katie focused her attention on slowing the horse.

Hank must have been waiting for them. He had opened the barn doors before they entered the yard. He ran toward them and grabbed Captain's bridle and kept pace with him as the horse slowed. Despite the rain, he walked the horse and wagon into the barn.

"Thanks, Hank." Katie said as she jumped off the wagon. "The rain came on fast and furious." She walked to Captain's side. Hank released the horse and Katie soothed it with pleasant murmurs and gentle hands.

"I've got a couple of blankets here." Hank glanced over at a shelf near the cross bars. "You're welcome to use 'em when you're ready to make a run for the house."

"This will let up soon." Hannah had been looking out at the rain as she spoke. Then she turned to Hank. "Be on the lookout for a tall lanky man. He goes by the name Yosterman. I'd keep the gun handy. He says we owe him fifty dollars because Katie shot Ross and Ross owed him money."

"Hmph, the man's nothing but trouble," Hank said, "I come across him in town the other day. He tried to pick a fight with a friend of mine, a little fella, that wasn't doin' no harm." He shook his head. "Be more than happy to chase him off for trespassin'." He cast his eyes to the opening in the barn doors. "The rain's lettin' up. Better get goin' before it starts again."

"Thanks for your help," Katie said. She and Hannah ran to the house dodging a scattering of raindrops. Their feet were muddy, so they took their shoes off on the porch and walked into the kitchen in their stockings.

Meghan was drinking tea and paging through *Godey's Lady's Book*. She paused at their arrival. "Good news. The marshal was just here. You've been cleared. A case of self-defense is how he's reporting Victor Ross's death."

"That's a relief," Hannah said. "Does Suzanne know?"

"No, not yet. What happened to your beautiful blouse?" Meghan stood up and touched Katie's sleeve where it was torn, folding it to see how it could be fixed.

Katie glanced toward Hannah. "You want to fill her in?"

"We've had quite a ride home," Hannah said.

Katie proceeded upstairs and knocked on her bedroom door. She could hear Hannah telling Meghan about Yosterman. Liam, feeling well enough now, stirred from his corner of the parlor probably getting up to join the women in the kitchen.

"Come in," Suzanne finally said. She sounded groggy.

"I awakened you. I'm so sorry."

"I needed to get up." She glanced at the tear in Katie's blouse. "What happened to you?"

Katie turned her head to look at the rip in her shoulder seam. "Yosterman did that."

"How? I thought he left town."

"Evidently not. The marshal stopped by. We're cleared of all charges, so you're free to return to your people."

Katie put her hand in her skirt pocket. "And I've got your tarot cards. They're right here." She pulled out her gun and set it on the nightstand and then reached into her pocket and pulled out one tarot card.

She reached into her pocket again. "Where's the other card? I put them both in my pocket." She turned in a circle, searching the room. "Did it fall out?"

Suzanne stood up. "Where could you have lost the other?"

Katie sat on the bed and rubbed her face. "Yosterman threatened us as we returned home from the Williamson's. I pulled out my gun as we made our escape, and I must have pulled out the tarot card as well."

"You pulled a gun on Yosterman?"

"Yes, he grabbed me, then said that we must give him the fifty dollars that Ross owed him. He said we killed Ross, so we pay his debts."

Suzanne tilted her head. "What kind of logic is that?"

"None, I agree. He called Hannah some names. She got angry and snapped a riding crop in his face. When she did, I drew my gun on him. That's probably when I dropped the card."

Suzanne turned the card over in her hand. "This is my Justice card, so Yosterman has the Death card."

"No, I don't think he has it. The card would have fallen from my pocket. I'll check the wagon. If it's not there, I'll go back to the spot Yosterman confronted us. Don't worry. I'll find it."

Suzanne's eyebrows shot up. "Sounds too dangerous to go alone. I will go with you." Suzanne was in her chemise and drawers.

Katie said, "No, you're not dressed, and I want to get back there quickly. It may rain again." She picked out another blouse from the chifforobe and a dry pair of boots and put them on as she spoke. "I know the spot where Yosterman pulled his shenanigans. It's not far from here. If the card's not in the wagon, it's got to be there."

"You are going back for the Death card. What if Yosterman is still around?"

Katie picked up her gun from the nightstand and held it aloft. "I'm not going alone."

Suzanne lifted her hands in surrender. "You are a very stubborn woman."

"I'll be back soon with the card." She turned at the hall doorway. "On second thought, I'm going to use the back stairs. I don't want to hear any arguments from Hannah."

Katie stepped outside to the balcony and descended the stairs to the yard.

Hank was putting away the wagon. If he was surprised to see Katie again so soon, he didn't show it.

"I need to check the wagon. I dropped an important paper." Katie had no intention of taking the time for a detailed explanation.

She searched the wagon, especially in slots where boards met. Hank helped her search.

After a few minutes, Katie gave a heavy sigh and said, "Please saddle up Mouse. I need to go back to find it."

Hank moved to Mouse's stall and called back. "I'll go with you. With all the commotion today, I don't like the thought of you goin' anywhere by yourself."

She patted her pocket. "I've got my gun. I'll be fine."

"Yes, ma'am." Hank shook his head as he saddled her horse.

* * *

It was only a short ride to the clearing where she and Hannah had been confronted by Yosterman. Katie slid off Mouse and looped her reins around a small tree branch. The wind had died down after the heavy rain.

She walked along the muddy road to the spot where her wagon had stopped. The outline of the wagon's wheels and Yosterman's horse were blunted from the rain, but visible. Mentally she reviewed Yosterman's threat, her anger rising with the memory.

She walked several paces back and forth on both sides of the road, searching the ground carefully, thinking it might have fallen under a wheel or hoof. No luck. She picked up a stick and poked at the brush outlining the road. Nothing. She walked back to Mouse. Her body ached for rest after the fury of the week's events. Katie dropped the stick at the side of the road and absently massaged the side of the horse's neck. "Maybe it blew further into the brush," she told the horse.

She took a deep breath, hoping to summon a second wind. "I have to keep checking." She picked up her stick, pulled up the hem of her skirt, and stepped into knee-high brush. The wet leaves soon made her skirt heavy. Walking through the thick green foliage was maddening. What if she couldn't find the card?

Her exhaustion and the slippery leaves made her clumsy, and then she tripped on the root of a nearby tree. She grabbed a thorn bush to stop her fall. "Ow," she cried aloud. Katie leaned against a large tree and sank down to examine her bleeding hand and pull the thorns from her palm and fingers. Everything was working against her: lost cards, stupid men, and slippery trails.

She put her head in her hands and leaned her elbows on her knees. Exhaustion overwhelmed her. So much in her life seemed to work against her. Paul's death ending her dream of having a family. Making a fool of herself by loving a married man. Her ambition to become a doctor thwarted by her family's need to run the mill. So many hopes lost. Tears threatened. She lowered her head into the crook of her crossed arms and had a long cry.

People had said she couldn't solve her brother's murder, but she had. She'd find a way to become a doctor too. Katie lifted her head and brushed the tears from her cheek. When she tried to stand her wet skirt put her off balance, so she used the tree to steady herself as she stood. She would find Suzanne's card. It had to be here somewhere. As she circled the brush yet again, a flash of white caught her attention. Was it the card? She picked up her skirt and ran to the spot. There, nestled between the stalks of a large-leafed plant, was the Death card, damp, but legible.

She tucked the card in the top of her camisole for safekeeping, knowing her body heat would dry out the card. Heading toward the road, she kept her focus on her feet, determined not to fall. So intent on watching her footing, she nearly collided with the horse standing in the road. Muddy boots met her at eye level. She whispered with some vehemence, "Yosterman."

A familiar voice answered, "No, ma'am."

Relief wash over her.

Caleb Brown tipped his hat. "Is it Yosterman you're searching for back there?" He chuckled.

"No." She had little patience for jest right now.

"I saw your horse and then you. Everything all right?"

"Yes, of course." Had Caleb had seen her put the card into her camisole? She walked briskly over to Mouse, turned her back to Caleb, and loosened Mouse's reins from the tree branch. Her hands were shaking, making an easy task difficult. Thoughts of confronting Yosterman had frightened her more than she cared to admit.

"You thought I was Yosterman," he called out to her.

She turned back to him and moved Mouse to stand near a large rock. "It was a mistake. It's long story. What are you doing out here?" She grimaced. "Oh, that sounded so harsh."

"No harm done. I was interviewing Brett. I hoped to interview you too. I talked with Mrs. Turner. She said that you had gone to the Williamson's for a visit."

"Yes, Hannah and I wanted to make sure Brett was recovering."

Caleb nodded. "I took the path through the valley. That's probably how I missed you. Brett gave me the details about this morning's events, but it would be helpful if you would confirm his story."

Katie's heartbeat was now nearly back to normal. "Mind if we head back to Six Maples while I'm confirming?"

"Not at all."

Katie stepped up on the rock. Her water-soaked hem would make it difficult to mount even the fifteen-hand high horse.

Caleb blushed and offered, "Do you need any help?"

Katie turned her finger in a circle. "Turn around."

He did so, and Katie mounted Mouse. "You can turn back now, Mr. Brown." Katie lifted her skirt to show off a few inches of the pants beneath.

"Oh," he said, his mouth holding the O in place for a few seconds.

Their horses walked along the path at a leisurely pace. Caleb asked a few questions, clarifying details, and then brought up the subject of Yosterman.

"He threatened us," Katie explained. "Said we owed him fifty dollars."

"Why's that?"

"Here's his logic. Ross owed him the money and I killed Ross."

"Not surprising. Yosterman's wanted for extortion in Pittsburgh."

"Whoa," Katie called out. Mouse stopped. Caleb's horse did the same.

"How do you know that?" Katie asked.

"You did ask me to do some checking. I called in a couple of favors from a friend in Pittsburgh, telegraphed him." He shrugged. "I thought Yosterman had left town, so I didn't bother to tell the marshal about it. But I will now. Do you know where Yosterman's staying?"

"My first guess would be to check the hired hands' shack on Ross's upper property."

"I'll let the marshal know that."

"How did you know he was from Pittsburgh?"

"When he drinks, he talks about home."

"You are a godsend, Mr. Brown. Thank you."

He lifted his bowler hat. "My pleasure, ma'am. They turned their horses to the path that led to Six Maples. Caleb continued to review what he had learned from Brett and the people in town as they walked their horses.

When they had finished, Caleb said, "I'll stop by the marshal's office with this Yosterman information. Perhaps I can accompany him to Ross's cabin, might be a good story there. You're talking about that same hired hands' cabin where you, Brett Williamson, and the doctor found Mrs. Turner, right?"

"Yes, the old Munson place."

They arrived at Six Maples. Both stopped their horses in the yard.

"Already wrote that story about your heroics at Ross's pig barn. You and your adventures are fodder for several articles, Mrs. Harris. Thank you for that." He turned his horse. "You take care now."

"Goodbye, Mr. Brown."

He turned his horse back toward Katie and stopped. "Caleb, ma'am. Sure would like it if you'd call me Caleb." He lifted his hat and turned his horse toward the road.

CHAPTER 23

RICHARD STEPHENS RESIGNS

Saturday morning, June 25, 1865

It was midmorning and things were settling down. Tomas had arrived at Six Maples during the early morning with plans to escort Suzanne back to their camp. Sitting at the kitchen table, Tomas worked his mug of coffee in a circle as he talked. "I returned to Liberty early this morning, hoping to find you. It seems you and your friends here are the talk of the town." He took his eyes off his coffee and looked up. "I stopped in at Schneider's Dry Goods. Mr. Schneider told me all that had happened and directed me here. I was so worried about you, Suzanne."

Tomas took Suzanne's hand. Katie smiled when Suzanne didn't pull back.

Hannah refilled his coffee and put ham sandwiches and pie in front of him. "Hank fed and watered your horse. The horse is in the barn. I'm going to check on Philip."

Like Hannah, Katie thought the couple needed a few minutes alone. "I'm going to take my coffee out to the porch and enjoy this beautiful day."

Neither Tomas nor Suzanne acknowledged that Katie had spoken as she left the kitchen.

Katie sat on the front porch, noting the temperate day as a good omen for the long ride Suzanne and Tomas had ahead of them. She and Suzanne shared much with their lost loves, like so many women, who'd suffered the loss of a husband or an intended during the war. Suzanne had loved Stuart and grieved his loss, just as Katie grieved Paul.

Tomas and Suzanne came out on the porch. "We're going to saddle the horses," Suzanne said.

Katie watched as they walked to the barn. Would Suzanne make the same mistake she had, assuaging her grief by falling in love again too quickly? Suzanne's case was different, though. Tomas wasn't married.

She would have to move on with her life. Liam had told her that her father was on the mend. If so, she would have the time to pursue her medical education soon. Hoof beats caught her attention. She put a hand to her brow to block the bright sunshine as she looked out toward the road. Dr. Stephens was slowing his horse as he turned into the drive. She stood. Was there a medical emergency in town?

Dr. Stephens brought his horse to the post in front of the porch. "Morning, ma'am," Stephens said as he tied his horse. There was no urgency in his voice, so Katie's shoulders relaxed. "Is Dr. West well enough to have a visitor today?"

"Yes, he's right inside. I'll take you to him."

Katie led Stephens through the front door to Liam's make-shift room in the parlor. Even with the privacy divider, it was easy to hear the men's conversation from the kitchen. Hannah and Katie sat at the kitchen table and eavesdropped.

Stephens started with a genial greeting, "Dr. West, you're looking so much better. I'd say you'll be fit to work in no time."

"Yes, I plan on resting for a few more days back at home. I'll leave here today."

Hannah's eyes widened. "I didn't know that. Did you?" She whispered."

Katie shook her head.

"Good, good," Stephens said. "As soon as you're back on your feet, I'm going to be leaving. I'm giving my resignation."

"What? You haven't finished your training. You still have much to learn, at least another year of apprenticeship."

"I know, but I've secured a position to continue my training with Dr. Andrew Peyton in Cleveland."

Katie's eyes grew wide with this news.

Stephens continued. "He's a friend of your mother's and has been looking for an apprentice to his practice since the war's end. You are familiar with him."

"Oh, yes, I am. Good man, good doctor." There was a pause and then Liam continued. "I thought you were content here. I am surprised by your resignation."

"I can't seem to please Liberty's patients with my diagnoses or my remedies."

"Mrs. Dubois and her lot, you mean."

"They seem to have taken a dislike to me. Mrs. Dubois is a hypochondriac. I told her so and she's turned all her friends against me. She's a potent force in Liberty and is making my life miserable."

"Very well, then, Stephens, I think you'll make a fine doctor, but you must learn to hold your tongue when it comes to women like Mrs. Dubois. I'm afraid you may need to humor patients like her at times."

"Yes, I learned that lesson the hard way, but the damage is done."

Katie's face lit up. She could take Stephens' place as an apprentice.

Hannah must have recognized Katie's thoughts. She shook her head and pursed her lips.

Liam said, "I'm truly sorry these women have driven you from Liberty. This town's population is increasing, so having two doctors in Liberty would be sensible. I can't be everywhere. I had hoped to keep you on as my partner when you completed your apprenticeship."

"Thank you, sir, but I've communicated with Dr. Peyton by telegram. He and I have been in correspondence for several weeks." He paused. "I was going to give you my resignation the day Mrs. Turner was kidnapped. I'll stay on for as long as you need me. Under the circumstances, Dr. Peyton is willing to give me a month before reporting to his surgery. I have told him of your circumstances."

"I don't want to hold you back, Stephens. A week's time is all that's needed."

Hannah got up out of her chair and went back to the parlor. "Dr. West, I could not help but overhear your exchange. Now, I am no doctor, but I think Dr. Stephens should stay on for at least two more weeks."

Stephens said, "I agree. You ought to take it easy for a bit longer. I can stay for two weeks. I'll telegraph Peyton with my report date two weeks from today."

Katie, distracted with the possibility of an opening for an apprenticeship in Liam's office, stayed in the kitchen and listened to the conversation going on in the parlor.

"Hannah's probably right, but I don't wish to wear out my welcome here. I plan to go back to town later today."

"Now, Liam don't you fuss. You're always welcome here," Hannah said.

Katie got up from the table and made her way to the parlor. She peeked around the divider. "I couldn't help but hear your exchange, gentlemen." She said to Liam. "If you feel you're up to it, I'll give you a ride home later today."

Stephens said, "I'd be happy to come back with a wagon from town in an hour or so."

"No need. I have much to discuss with Dr. West and a ride into town might be the perfect opportunity to talk." Katie put a hand on the divider. "This needs to be returned to the surgery, but Hank can load this in the wagon."

"Very well, if you're sure it's no imposition."

"I assure you, sir, it is not."

CHAPTER 24

KATIE MAKES HER CASE

Saturday early afternoon, June 25, 1865

Katie had been going over mill business with her father. His cough was beginning to ease. Liam had announced Philip was on the mend, yet he must take it easy and only work a few hours each day. Katie promised to help with the business until he was well.

When Katie left Philip's room, she stopped by Liam's corner in the parlor. "Knock, knock," Katie said as she stood outside Liam's divider.

"I'm just doing a bit of packing. I'll be ready in a few minutes."

"Oh, no, Hannah won't have you going without a meal. I just wanted to a word before we ate."

Liam came around the divider running a hand through his hair. He glanced around the room, probably searching for Meghan. "What can I do for you?" he asked Katie.

Katie held Dr. Peyton's letter of recommendation. Holding the letter in one hand, she ran her other hand down her skirt. Her palms were moist. This moment was important for her. She would ask Liam to take her on as an apprentice doctor, no small feat for him or her. Would Andrew Peyton's recommendation be enough to persuade him? Liam knew Andrew. She sighed. Liam might be taking a risk to his credibility. Was she asking too much of him?

Liam may have noticed her nervousness. He extended his good arm toward the parlor's sofa. "Please, let's sit down for a moment." Katie perched on the edge of the sofa.

Liam sat down on the opposite chair and leaned forward.

She carefully unfolded her letter of recommendation and placed it on the table in front of the sofa. Her mouth felt so dry she wasn't sure she could speak. She cleared her throat and put her hands on her lap, hoping to allay the evidence of their slight tremor. Then she turned to Liam. "I loved nursing and want to do more for patients, especially women patients. Women should have a choice, to have a woman doctor, I mean. I would like a medical apprenticeship with you. I can't attend medical school because I'm a woman, but I want so much to become a doctor. I see the preceptor route as the only avenue available to me."

"So I've heard." He smiled. "Meghan told me."

"Oh." She silently thanked Meghan for making this a bit easier, but she had mentally rehearsed her practiced speech. She wouldn't be diverted from saying it. "I know there aren't many women physicians."

He tented his fingers between his knees. "True, true, but there are a handful of women who have entered the profession."

"I know. Dr. Peyton told me that."

"That's right you worked with him at the hospital in Camp Dennison."

Katie picked up the paper from the coffee table. "Dr. Peyton wrote a letter of recommendation for me." She handed the letter to Liam.

He took it and read it silently.

To Whom It May Concern:

It has been a pleasure working alongside Mrs. Katherine Harris during the past eighteen months. She has been nursing wounded soldiers, assisting doctors during surgeries, and successfully triaging wounded soldiers on the front lines of battle. Having no children, Mrs. Harris began nursing at Camp Dennison in October of 1863, a few months after her husband's death during the battle at Gettysburg.

Mrs. Harris is an intelligent and compassionate nurse. She would make a fine physician with a degree from a medical school or by serving as an apprentice with a physician.

Please contact me at my offices 1400 Erie St., Cleveland, Ohio, if you have any questions or would like more information regarding her qualifications.

Sincerely,
Andrew Peyton, M.D.

"That is high praise indeed from Dr. Peyton. He's not an easy man to please," Liam said. He handed the letter back to Katie.

"I was hoping now that Stephens has resigned, you'd take me on as an apprentice."

Liam sat back and blew out a breath. "I agree you are a brave woman. He chuckled. "I've seen you in action, tough enough to handle Meghan's kidnappers. But the women of Liberty can be a slow burn with their gossip."

"I think I can manage Mrs. Dubois and her crowd. They seem to have forgiven me for investigating my brother's murder."

"Oh, is that right?"

"Yes, Mrs. Dubois stopped me in town on Friday, acting as if she and her group had never snubbed me. She told me she always knew there was something off about Mr. Ross. She even said I had good instincts and that the marshal should be grateful for my help."

"I am shocked," Liam said.

"So was I."

"One advantage you have over Stephens is that you know the Dubois women and their crowd. You grew up with their ways. Poor man, he had no idea they could be so vindictive."

"I think Stephens will be a good fit for Andrew. The doctor was willing to take me on as an apprentice." She inwardly cringed. She shouldn't have used his first name. "I turned him down."

Liam must have picked up on her faux pas. He lifted an eyebrow, but Katie ignored it and continued. "I am not interested in living in a big city like Cleveland. I want to practice in a village like Liberty. I want to know my patients, know their problems and their joys. I want to practice here or some other nearby village."

"Let me think about it for a bit." He stood and put a hand on her shoulder. "I'll let you know.

* * *

Katie and Liam were silent as she drove the wagon into town. It gave her time to assess her alternatives if Liam didn't take her on as his apprentice. She could go to the Western Reserve College and find another preceptor. Becoming a doctor was too important to let go after just one disappointment. Perseverance. That's what had led to finding her brother's murderer, even in the face of society's impediments. She'd succeeded in finding Stuart's murderer and she would succeed in getting a medical education.

Nevertheless, she would be disappointed in Liam if he didn't accept her as an apprentice. He would be taking on a challenge, but she had much to offer. She had served well on the front lines of battle, in the surgery, and managing soldiers' convalescing. He knew what she had faced. And where Stephens had failed, she would succeed because she understood the quirks of the people in Liberty. For all these reasons she would make a good doctor. The only thing that could stop her was her sex. Damn society's restrictions!

They arrived at the office. Stephens came out of the office to unload the room divider from the wagon. Katie picked up Liam's black bag. Its weight felt good in her hands.

Once inside, she found a young boy holding the side of his face and quietly crying as he sat in the waiting room with his mother. Katie bent down to talk with the boy. "What's your name, son?" she asked.

"Tommy Gilmore."

"What's wrong, Tommy?"

"Got a sore tooth."

Mrs. Gilmore explained. "Doctor Stephens said he'd pull it out. Tommy's afraid it may hurt more than it does now. It's a baby molar."

"Dr. Stephens is a kind man and will do his best to make you better, Tommy," Katie said gently. "How about if I hold your hand while he pulls out your tooth? I've heard that holding someone's hand makes that person twice as brave. Have you heard that too?"

Tommy scrunched up his face. "I think so."

"Would you like me to hold your hand?"

Tommy nodded.

"Good, and I think Dr. West has peppermint sticks for such occasions. He usually gives them out when he's all done."

"Really?" Tommy asked.

Liam had come into the room and stood next to Katie. "They're in the hall cupboard," he said kindly.

Katie stood and went to the cupboard and brought back the candy. "Would you like to hold onto it while the doctor works. I can hold your other hand."

"Yes, please." Tommy's eyes were shiny with held back tears. "You'll stay with me. Promise."

"I promise," Katie said.

Katie held his hand while Stephens pulled the tooth. The gum was slightly infected and swollen. Stephens prepared mouthwash and gave the boy's mother directions for its use. The boy waved to Katie as his mother gathered her things. She watched them from the window and turned when Liam called her. She walked into his office. Her stomach churned. Had he made his decision?

The room was well-appointed with a large desk, bookshelf, a plush deep dark maroon carpet and subtle colors of deep maroon, black and dark beige striped draperies. "This is a beautiful office," she said.

He stood behind his desk and waved away her compliment. "My mother's doing."

Liam motioned for Katie to sit in a chair in front of his desk. "You were good with that boy." Liam said.

"Thank you." Katie sat down.

Liam sat down behind his desk. "I've decided to take you on as an apprentice physician."

Katie moved to the edge of the chair. "Oh, Liam, thank you!"

"When can you start?"

Her face brightened. "Well, tomorrow if you'd like."

"Tomorrow it is. I know Hannah and Philip can still use your help, so let's start the next couple of weeks with a morning shift, say eight until noon until things get settled. By then, I'm assuming Philip will be back on his feet."

"Do you really think so?"

"Yes, he's strong and head strong. I think his illness will be a pneumonia success story."

She put a hand on her chest. "I'm so relieved." She paused. "In so many ways."

Liam cradled his swollen arm as he spoke, "In a few months, I will ask that you attend lectures in Hudson. The Western Reserve College allows women to attend their lectures."

He stood, walked over to a large mahogany bookcase, and reached for a medical book with his good arm. "First I'll want you to study several books, starting with this one." He walked over to her chair and handed her the book.

Katie took the heavy volume and read the title aloud, *Gunn's New Family Physician.*

"It's an important book. I want you to read it cover to cover. Read it whenever you have the time and let me know if there's anything I can clarify as you read."

"I am so grateful for this opportunity. I promise to work hard and attend any lectures you think are necessary."

"I know you will."

She beamed. "I'm so happy. I can't wait to tell Meghan." She paused. "Papa and Hannah may not be as pleased."

Liam leaned his backside against the desk. "If there's one thing I've learned, it's this: we must think for ourselves and do what is right for us. Sometimes those decisions will disappoint and surprise our parents. I plan to marry Meghan if she'll have me, which will not please my mother, who'd have me married off to some society girl." He paused. "But she'll come around. Perhaps." He winked. "You have fine parents in Philip and Hannah. They will eventually accept your decision and support you. They're just old-fashioned in their ideas. And it's our mission to help them come around to what the future holds, right?"

She took a deep breath. "I'll leave worrying my parents for tomorrow and savor this as my secret for just a day." She hefted the book in her hand. "Right now, I want to get started on this. My first step in becoming a doctor."

He smiled. "You need courage and perseverance to fulfill that dream, but you've got plenty of both. You'll make a fine doctor, Katie Harris. I'm proud to call you my associate and friend."

When Katie stood, Liam came around his desk and they shook hands. Katie said, "I can't wait to get started. May I take this book home with me today?"

Liam chuckled then said, "Very well." He walked Katie to the door. "I'll see you first thing in the morning."

Katie smiled broadly. "You can count on it."

THE END

ABOUT THE AUTHOR

MAE McGRAW

In *Bitter Medicine,* Mae McGraw transports readers back in time to post Civil War America to follow the exploits of Katie Harris.

Mae McGraw is the pen name for Kim Wuescher, who lives in Medina, Ohio, with her husband, Rick. They have two adult children, Christian and Diane. Her first career was teaching AP and Senior English at a public high school, where she shared her love of literature with her students. More recently, American history has become her passion.

She enjoys traveling to Civil War sites around the country for pleasure and research, where she digs deep to learn about the times and the people in order to create a suspenseful novel of historical accuracy. When not writing or traveling, she takes time to play golf and read historical mysteries. If she's not in Ohio, you'll find her anywhere near the blue waters of Michigan with family and friends.

Kim Wuescher is president of the Northeast Ohio chapter of Sisters in Crime, an organization of mystery writers and readers. She is also a member of the Great Lakes Fiction Writers, Literary Cleveland, and the Medina County Historical Society, where she learned more about Medina's role during the Civil War. With its close access to Lake Erie and Canada, Medina was instrumental in the underground railroad; discovering this was the spark to learning more about the Civil War period. *Bitter Medicine* is the result, her debut novel and first in a series.

The Glass Guitar

By

Marshall Riggan

Walter Woodrow Pillow would have moved through life unremarked if he had not committed the most outrageous and traitorous act in American history. A young design engineer in a Texas bomber factory, he had become consumed with guilt and remorse for his role in designing the deadliest weapons system of the Vietnam era. So, one day, in 1965, he sabotaged the mighty bombers. Wally made tracks for the border, the FBI, the CIA and Interpol hot on his trail.The Glass Guitar is the story of Wally's efforts to elude government agents and along the way champion causes promoting peace, fairness, and justice in an imperfect world. He is joined by a number of kindred souls, including a beautiful prostitute known as "Angel of the Arroyos," an Italian movie director whose mother dated Mussolini, and a reformed explosives expert who penned the classic Ethics and the Firecracker. In its efforts to make right the wrongs of the world, this merry band of fugitive-reformers leaves a path of devastation across the social landscape. The story is a cautionary tale suggesting that there are often unexpected consequences for doing the right thing.

PENMORE PRESS
www.penmorepress.com

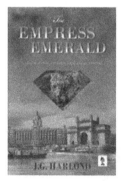

THE EMPRESS EMERALD

BY

J. G. HARLOND

Stolen: A child, a priceless jewel, and an identity

Abandoned as a child in a Bombay orphanage, Leo Kazan's life takes an unanticipated turn when he becomes the protégé of Sir Lionel Pinecoffin, the city's District Political Officer in Bombay. Under Pinecoffin's tutelage, the boy, adept at learning languages and theft, is trained as a spy and becomes immersed in international espionage, revolutionary politics, and diamond smuggling. In 1918, during a visit to London, he has a brief but memorable affair with a young English woman Davina Dymond in London before leaving for Russia.

Separated, their lives take different turns. As he matures Leo begins to question his family history, seeking to uncover the truth about his parents. A pregnant Davina is married off and exiled to Spain, where she gives birth to Leo's daughter. They are fated to meet again in Gibraltar in 1936, their love rekindled. But a new war plunges Europe into crisis, the Spanish Civil War tearing them apart, leaving, Leo and Davina in a fight to reclaim their lives and their love amid the violent storms of war.

PENMORE PRESS
www.penmorepress.com

Mistress Suffragette
by
Diana Forbes

A young woman without prospects at a ball in Gilded Age Newport, Rhode Island is a target for a certain kind of "suitor." At the Memorial Day Ball during the Panic of 1893, impoverished but feisty Penelope Stanton draws the unwanted advances of a villainous millionaire banker who preys on distressed women—the incorrigible Edgar Daggers. Over a series of encounters, he promises Penelope the financial security she craves, but at what cost? Skilled in the art of flirtation, Edgar is not without his charms, and Penelope is attracted to him against her better judgment. Initially, as Penelope grows into her own in the burgeoning early Women's Suffrage Movement, Edgar exerts pressure, promising to use his power and access to help her advance. But can he be trusted, or are his words part of an elaborate mind game played between him and his wife? During a glittering age where a woman's reputation is her most valuable possession, Penelope must decide whether to compromise her principles for love, lust, and the allure of an easier life.

PENMORE PRESS
www.penmorepress.com

MAE MCGRAW

Penmore Press
Challenging, Intriguing, Adventurous, Historical and Imaginative

www.penmorepress.com

www.ingramcontent.com/pod-product-compliance
Lightning Source LLC
Chambersburg PA
CBHW020243310125
21043CB00001B/3